The Mysterious Secret Guardians:

Final Chapter of the Mysterious Guardians

The Mysterious Secret Guardians:

Final Chapter of the Mysterious Guardians

Dorothy McCoy

SPEAKING VOLUMES, LLC
NAPLES, FLORIDA
2024

Final Chapter of the Mysterious Guardians

ISBN 979-8-89022-236-7

This volume is dedicated to my beloved mother who gave me my
greatest treasure—a love of books.
That treasure has enriched my entire life.
Thank you, mama.

Acknowledgments

My fabulous editor and fellow Guardian, Rita Kitenplon. She kicks Nazi butt!

My lovely publishers, Erica and Kurt Mueller, Speaking Volumes.

My enthusiastic supporters, Emmy, Bayleigh, Kaci, Cyndi, Ginny, Greg, Mick, and Margaret.

My beautiful readers are much loved.

And, finally, the Big Guy.

Prologue

Abigor, our green-eyed reformed demon, is hyperalert. He can read the high-ranking demon, Aaii, and knows he is playing with our Team like a nasty cat with helpless mice. Abigor observes the other demons closely. They are not well. The ancient Holy Symbols he carved into the ground outside the tunnel are working. The lower-ranking monsters are wilting and sluggish. The ravenous animal look is gone from their eyes. Abigor signals David to proceed with the frontal assault.

Following Abigor's lead, Big Soph leaps to the forefront and attacks without the slightest warning. All 120 pounds of pure canine beastliness is poetry in purposeful motion. She goes for the closest demon, the one with a red feather on his helmet. He is shocked and has no idea what she is besides an enormous, bad-tempered Great Dane. Big Soph knocks him to the ground and goes for his throat, tearing at it with savage teeth, and in his weakened condition, his demon powers are useless. He is terrified. He disappears, leaving the foul smell of sulfur behind. Sophie briefly sports a self-satisfied grin at her triumph, then tries to rid her sensitive nose of that hideous stench.

Meanwhile, hunky David Smythe, the former MI5 Deputy Director-General, turns his attention back to the demon Aaii. "We can continue this game if you wish. There are still a few of your bloody ruffians standing. Shall we continue or will you choose to be reasonable and lead us to the Doomsday Machine? You can then leave in peace and return to the netherworld. By the way, you look ridiculous in that outfit."

Aaii, dressed in his jousting metal clink-clink garb, is beginning to understand he is in quicksand and sinking fast. What is the power these beings bring to bear? Enraged, Aaii screeches the order to his costumed, 15th-century squire devils to attack. The game is afoot! Aaii clanks back to the shelter of his gold throne to watch.

The remaining demons attack: two cling to former demon Abigor, who immediately shoots them across the massive chamber. They land with a deafening bang, crash, and thud! He chases after them as if they are a fumbled football, and he needs a touchdown to win one for the Gipper.

Sir Winston is grinning from ear to ear. It has been a long time since he has had this much fun. A devil dressed in bright blue tights tackles Churchill. The Great Man gives him a smashing right to the nose and a deadly chop to the knee. Blue goes down with Sir Winston on top of him, knocking off his helmet and pummeling him about his evil head. Churchill claims the win without ever dropping his cigar. Blue disappears in a puff of smoke, not knowing who savaged him. The winner stands tall and makes a triumphant victory sign.

David grabs two monsters who are reconsidering their options at this point in the furious knockdown, drag-out clash. Knocking their heads together with fury, he keeps banging them like demon cymbals until they disappear from the battlefield: more sulfur and stench.

Aaii looks on in disbelief. His squires and pages should be terrifying these disrespectful invaders.

After being blindsided with an uppercut, retired and deceased MI5 agent Angus Snowden righteously kicks a tall, purple-plumed squire in his hindquarters and sends him sprawling. Because Abigor's Holy Symbols weakened the lesser demons' powers, they are suffering pain for the first time in their existence. Pain is a traumatic shock and a rude awakening for them and Aaii. War is an entertaining game if the combatants feel neither pain nor fear. Aaii's little dress-up game just got agonizingly real.

Aaii is enormously powerful and is not affected by the Holy symbols Admiral Stallings gave us. Abigor knew this, so he recruited the 96-year-old Father Antonio, a former adversary from Abigor's demon days. It's time for the magnificent second act!

David pops outside to summon Dr. Einstein, Father Antonio, and me. David and the others can pop from one location to another in seconds, not even a vapor trail in their wake. The Padre and I, as mortals, do not have this seriously advantageous ability. Refreshed by his rest, the Padre is eager to do his part in our righteous war. Axel, the bulked Neo-Nazi, tried to kill us earlier in the day, and that rumble sapped the energy from the elderly priest. Luckily, I, Raven "Bones" Wyndot, am accustomed to people shooting at me, choking me, and running me over with late-model Mercedes'. The three of us walk silently into the tunnel, along the path to Aaii and whatever fate awaits us.

As soon as we enter the inner chamber, Father Antonio grasps his silver cross with steady hands and begins the exorcism ritual. Dr. Einstein and Angus Snowden, our Dirty Harry doppelgänger, repeat the ancient words after him. Aaii feels the jolting spiritual surge from the exorcism throughout his depraved body. The Padre continues his relentless march forward without pause.

Father Antonio repeats the Holy words as he holds up his brilliant, radiant cross. Aaii lies crumpled on the floor, roaring in distress. His roars are punctuated by lightning bolts that shear through the chamber, crackling and sizzling. I duck down to escape Aaii's deadly electrical tantrum. Father Antonio is a pillar of righteous strength, utterly oblivious to the spectacular pyrotechnics. I watch, fascinated by the two powerful combatants and the electricity that hisses ominously in the air around me. My beloved David lays his hand on my shoulder and gently leads me away. The lighting fades as the angry screams wane in the still-charged atmosphere.

Stunned by what I have witnessed, I stumble along beside David and Abigor toward a gorgeous heavy tapestry hanging on the far wall of Aaii's chamber. Abigor, who, to my annoyance, speaks broken Shakespeare, points to the tapestry, "The door to the Dark World lies behind yond tapestry. Bones thee hast the compass, and I know the words to open yond door. We must find the fantastic device that may defuse the Doomsday Machine if it be there."

Before attempting to enter a world that terrifies me and has an unpredictable fate, I turn to David to embrace him and absorb some of his courage to stay the course. What? He is no longer standing beside me. Terror rises in me as I spin around, searching the chamber for him. David is gone! Dear God, what the hell just happened? Will this horror never end?

Desperate for reassurance, I run to Sir Winston, who has been quietly assessing our situation. "Where is David? I don't understand." Tears blur my vision, and my eyes silently plead with Sophie and Sir Winston: please, please help me. They look back at me with deep pity clearly written on their dear faces. Assaulted by their pity, I dropped to my knees.

Something whispers in my ear, "Thunder and lightning."

Chapter One

The Dark Castle

The dark, forbidding castle crouches atop Owl Mountain. From a distance, it is a giant menacing sphinx waiting to spring on unwary prey. Up close, it fades into the surrounding trees and rocks, retreating from the evil deep within the bowels of the earth. The fortress's weathered, partitioned windows press back into the structure, seeking shelter within the dingy gray moss-stained walls. The bleak castle is highlighted against a dark, moody sky with slivers of glinting knife-edged stars. The battered walls shiver in the sepulchral, haunted darkness. No one sees the reaction because it is hidden within the lifeless cells of stones and timbers. The scarred, massive oak doors that once repelled savage warriors now recoil in dread. The ancient building has seen many monsters in its long vigil atop the fog-shrouded mountain, and it has always defeated them through the slow passage of time. The morose structure is patient, yet no evil monsters have triggered this depth of dark apprehension. The ancient castle sees the godless creatures in the damp, sodden caverns deep beneath Owl Mountain. The venerable structure fears a grim fate.

Revelation's epic battle of good versus evil plays out in an endless loop in the blood-tainted caverns below.

Chapter Two

Wings of Fury

Father Antonio is still performing the exorcism ritual. He, Angus, and Dr. Einstein don't know David is missing. They concentrate their energies on the demon Aaii to send him into the fiery abyss. I pause to watch Father Antonio and Aaii before joining Abigor at the door to the Dark World, my own gaping chasm. The Padre suddenly stops chanting the prayer, pauses, and looks up. His luminous smile brightens the chamber. What is happening? Father Antonio slowly folds to the floor. Sir Winston, Red, Abigor, Angus, Big Soph, Dr. Einstein, and I run to help him. The Padre glances up at us and manages to whisper, "It is as it should be. Do not fear for me. This old priest is going home. Another is coming who is more powerful." Father Antonio is pitifully weak, yet he moves his eyes and gasps, "Look, look over there." Our beloved Padre points behind us, then stops speaking and closes his eyes. I thought my heart had utterly shattered when David vanished, yet now it breaks again for this good and decent man of God. The sharp shards cut into my chest where a heart once beat to find only the cold, stony crucible of excruciating grief.

When I glance up, everyone looks behind us where the Padre pointed. Dear God, what is that? I see an enormous being with long blond hair and extraordinarily piercing indigo eyes. I am losing my mind from grief. Yes, that must be it. I knew it would happen! He looks like the painting of Archangel Michael in the old Bible that vanished from our suite at the London Savoy. His cloak is purest shimmering white as if it were a living thing, and he has a vast wingspan of perhaps 15 feet, yes, wings, he has wings—a long sheathed sword swings from his gilded girdle.

The being pulls the sword from its sheath and swings it around his head, focusing his stunning gaze on the shivering, cowering Aaii. The demon appears to shrink before me. The terror in his gaze intensifies as he stares at the apparition above him. They have battled before, and Aaii and his wicked brethren lost. No doubt, the demon has an exceptionally long memory going back eons.

Sir Winston wraps me in his arms, trying to comfort me, and Sophie gives me a knee hug. Sir Winston searches my eyes. "Poor, dear Bones. You have had an immensely painful day. Remember, you are as strong as you need to be. Be at peace. We will all do our duty. Do not be fearful for he is an angel."

I continue to gape at the "angel" in astonishment. Red stands beside us, whispering in my ear, "Bones, I told you Archangel Michael would be here. Remember?" He told me a colossal, fantastical, uh, angel would be here? No. I would definitely remember that.

My attention remains riveted to the winged, uh, being. Sir Winston hugs me to him and soothes my aching heart. Sophie stands close beside me as she always will. We watch as, I will call him Michael (since I don't know what else to call him), terrifies Aaii. The angel hovers three feet above the floor, skewering the sniveling demon with his laser-like gaze. Aaii, the general of legions of lesser demons in Hell, freezes before Michael like a rabbit before a lion. He is unrecognizable as the once arrogant and terrifying devil now staring at Michael in horror. The demon Aaii disappears in the usual smoke and brimstone, and the winged angel vanishes without a word. The fantastic combatants are there one minute, and the following minute, both are gone. It is as if they were never among us, and we had a severe case of mass hallucination. I am perfectly happy with that explanation for now.

Everything is so strange. I must have fallen into the rabbit hole. I understand Alice when she said, "I almost wish I had not gone down that rabbit hole—and yet—and yet—it's rather curious, you know, this sort of life." This is my life, and I might as well embrace it.

We won. The demon who protected the weapon is gone, and we can continue our mission. Why don't we feel victorious? The price we paid for victory was exorbitant.

While I struggle to understand that angels are real and the proof was hovering above us in this very chamber, Angus gently lifts the faithful priest in his arms and transports him back to his beloved St. Albans Cathedral. Every member of our Team is wiping away tears and grieving our loss. In minutes, Angus returns to help search for the Doomsday Machine. Father Antonio believed in us and our Holy mission. We shall not let down our beloved Padre. Damn it, we won't! I am angry, furious with the cruel fate that took David and now Father Antonio away from me. My rage burns blistering hot, reinforcing my resolve and tempering the formidable tool I must become. I hover between rational acceptance and an all-consuming fury.

Sir Winston reminds us that we must find the Doomsday Machine as quickly as possible. We must move to Plan B if we cannot locate or neutralize it. I had hoped Plan B wouldn't be necessary, and Abigor and I would not have to enter the Dark World. Abigor is an angel, but he doesn't sport wings and an MGM movie presence like Michael. Abigor is just an ordinary redeemed angel and former demon. I, Bones, am mortal, a well-balanced (questionable?) psychotherapist. David says I am an intriguing Elizabeth Taylor with perpetually bewildered brown eyes. Remember, he is from the 1940s.

I didn't mention that her eyes were violet. Since we lost the Padre, I am now the only one on our Team who can die—not a desirable attribute.

Team History

To this day, it has been a long journey to the Demon Chamber. We came together because the Powers in Beyond proclaimed it would be so.

The others are from Beyond and were returned to life, well, not exactly life, more like an existence, to save the planet and humanity. Sir Winston and my beloved David died in 1965. Sir Winston passed in his bed. David was shot in the head by a rogue IT guy recruited by our Nazi enemies: Dr. Mengele, Hans Schmidt, and Franz Wolffe. Dr. Einstein preceded them to Beyond in 1955. Churchill died at his home at 28 Hyde Park Gate on January 24, 1965. He passed peacefully with his devoted wife Clemmie and children Randolph, Mary, and Sarah at his bedside. David Smythe was killed as he walked to his much-loved 1939 Rolls Royce Phantom on a chilling, snowy night. My love died alone on a dark, icy London street. That melancholy thought stabs me like a knife to my heart.

David and Sir Winston had been working on a highly classified case with long-term international implications. David, then Assistant Director-General of MI5, had been given an old journal with a strange, incomprehensible code written in a precise handwriting. David was alarmed because the name Mengele was printed in bold letters on the front. He knew the name immediately, the infamous Angel of Death from Auschwitz, and he was concerned about secrecy. He told no one except his old friend from WWII, Sir Winston Churchill. They finally deciphered a small section of the code, and it shocked and appalled them.

Dr. Mengele planned to clone three monsters from WWII: Adolf Hitler (born Adolf Schickelgruber), Paul Josef Goebbels, and Heinrich Luitpold Himmler. He could not accomplish this ambitious task until science evolved in biotechnology. Smythe and Churchill made a pact, their solemn vow as gentlemen to act when that time came. They didn't realize they would have been dead for over fifty years when science caught up with Mengele. They were brought back along with Dr. Albert Einstein, who had not made a pact. Beyond chose him, and that was that. I became part of the Team when I bought Churchill's book *Gathering Storms* from a rare book dealer in London, in which David had written the code. My dearest friend, Big Soph, who died in 2013, returned as much more than just a Harlequin Great Dane. She is an ancient entity of unfathomable power. I thought I picked her out at a Charleston Dane rescue. She actually chose me. It was all part of the plan hatched in Beyond.

Because he needed the book, Sir Winston arrived at my office in North Carolina asking for my help and brandy. I had only Diet Coke, and in my defense, he didn't have an appointment! We were off to a rocky start. Then, David Smythe walked through my door with tall, unruly dark hair, broad shoulders, and a WWII leather bomber jacket he filled out most wonderfully! Be still my thumping heart! I knew my life would never be the same. David is my fate, whatever that might look like in the permutations computed by the Powers in Beyond.

Since then, the five of us have been a team through many wild, deadly, life-threatening (mine) adventures chasing the ever-elusive Mengele and his henchmen. Later, we brought other invaluable Team members on board: Red Biggers, Angus Snowden, Abigor, and Father Antonio. Angus was alive when he joined us, though he is not now. Yet he remains active, a long story for later and well worth the patience.

We have followed Mengele's path through America, England, Austria, and France. Now, we are in Poland in dark tunnels beneath a castle because Mengele's Neo-Nazis and vile would-be dictators bargained with a demon to achieve their goals. The demon, Aaii, has a weapon left over from WWII that he plans to use. This Doomsday Machine can trigger earthquakes and volcanoes around the world, a catastrophe that would reduce the planet to fire and ash. All animals, including humans, would be reduced to residue if the weapon were activated. We must find it and ensure Aaii has not already calibrated it.

Our mission is complicated because Aaii can use magic. If he protected the Machine with magic, our task would become immeasurably more difficult, if not impossible.

Chapter Three

The Doomsday Machine

Sir Winston gathers us together to plan our next move.

Sir Winston makes the victory sign and says, "We won a tremendous victory over the Demon Aaii and his devils! We have earned the right to savor our win. Alas, we must move forward with haste. Thank you for your courage and determination, gentlemen and Bones. I am humbled to have the honor to work with you." He pauses, his mood and expression changing from victorious to grim. "Sadly, we lost two dear friends in the battle. I cannot adequately express how much these two courageous men meant to us and our effort." He defiantly glares in our direction. We bow our heads in shared sorrow and simmering fury.

Glowering deeply and holding his cigar between his teeth, Sir Winston directs us, "We must begin to search for that damnable machine immediately. I suggest we spread out and cover every inch of this appalling chamber until we find the horrid contraption. Do you have anything to add, Albert?"

Dr. Einstein is searching for his eponymous pipe, looking more chaotic than usual. He stops mid-search and adds, "Winston, I agree. We should begin instantly. Yes, we can disperse to cover as much space as possible in the least time. Aaii would have hidden its location well, so we must not trust anything to be as it appears." The excellent doctor glances around our little group to see if anyone else wants to comment. Red, Abigor, Sophie, Angus, and I shake our heads. What else is there to say? We feel a heavy void that only David and our Padre can fill.

We disperse and begin exploring the demon palace with its exquisite crystal chandeliers, gold throne, and treasured portraits of royalty. He probably stole everything during the War, like a latter-day evil Bill

Sikes. Suddenly, I wonder where Aaii's Fox "doorman" disappeared in all the chaos. Abigor had said Aaii used this unique little, uh, "being" as a servant, and indeed, this minion had greeted visitors at the entry to the chamber. He looked like a tall fox in a doorman's uniform.

Fox-doorman may not speak from what Abigor said, though he must have understood what his "employer" said to him.

I go looking for Abigor and find him examining the throne. I ask, "Abigor, we have not seen the doorman you mentioned. Do you think he might still be here? He could help us if we can communicate with him." Abigor jumps, realizing the logic of my query. "Of course! I had forgotten all about the poor creature. I saw him in the demon stream of consciousness, probably coming from Aaii. There is much confusion, and I do not always know which demon I sense in that stream. Come, we shalt look for him."

We find a narrow passage of the large chamber and follow it a short distance to a small rough-hewn wood door sitting slightly ajar. Abigor pushes it open, and we see a modest room with few furnishings. The poor little fox creature is sprawled on the floor. An arrow pierces his heart, and blood drips from the wound. He looks so tiny and vulnerable. A heavy, suffocating sorrow engulfs me. Who could have done such a cruel thing? Tears stream down my cheeks as I look at him.

Abigor is touched, too. He sees the tears in my eyes and says, "Bones, please let me share thy sadness. Thee hast been through much tragedy today." He puts his arm around my shoulders and pulls me toward him.

I desperately need comfort, but I cannot turn to Abigor. He has hinted at more interest in me than I could return. I grieve for and need David. I turn and stumble back to the main chamber with tears still pouring down my face. David, where are you?

Chapter Four

The Search

Slowly, I walk through the damp, gloomy passage to the Demon's chamber, brilliantly lit by its numerous crystal chandeliers. I move away from my laudable soft emotions because sentiment will compromise my ability to think logically and act decisively. Emotions are left further behind with each step I take toward what I must be: a fearless warrior. I can only be my best if I focus fiercely on my mission. I can't magically undo the injustices and cruelties of the past, but I can do everything within my power to prevent the monstrous eruptions that threaten our world. Big Soph once told me that as the only living member of the Team, I am its heart. Yes, she can communicate with me at times. Others on the Team feel deeply, and their emotions are intense at times, yet they are no longer a part of humanity. When they died, they became forever separate and apart from mortals. I am the battered gangplank between the two worlds.

I look behind me at Abigor and say through clenched teeth, "We have a crime scene to report. Let's find Sir Winston." He seemed shocked by my rapid transformation. He shakes his head and follows me.

I accepted my duty and the dangers a long time ago. No matter how shocking, violence is just another cumbersome hill for our Team to climb.

Abigor is close behind me, and we look around the room for Sir Winston. He is examining a portrait of a comely lady with fiery red hair and a dress accentuating her creamy décolleté. Churchill is sipping from his snifter and feeling around the outside of the beautiful gold frame for a switch to open a secret door to the machine. He looks up when we approach and greets us. "Bones and Abigor, where have you been? We should look closer at the bell-pull apparatus by the double doors." He peers at me for a few seconds and adds, "You seem angry, dear Bones. What has happened?" He takes my hand and pats it. Sophie strolls over to support me. She, of course, knows what happened. She always knows. Soph also understands I can take whatever the world throws at me, even if I have a good cry first. God bless her, she has trained me well.

Abigor steps forward and tells Sir Winston what we saw. He wants to save me from the pain of describing that painful, bloody scene. I passed the initial shock and moved directly into furious "hungering for revenge" Bones. Abigor doesn't understand me. David and I share a history. He knows me.

Abigor's eyes spark with righteous anger as he spits out, "Sir Winston, I think we should gather everyone together to inspect a crime scene, as Bones called it." Sir Winston scans the room and calls Angus, Red, and Dr. Einstein to join us.

They all gather, waiting for Sir Winston to explain why he interrupted the search. He begins, "Gentlemen, Abigor and Bones tell me we have a crime scene to investigate. Please follow them. I have not seen it either. Shall we go, gentlemen and Soph?"

Soph looks at me with blood-red lips and sharp white teeth bared in a deadly snarl. Danger. I nod in assent. The wickedness and depravity of this senseless killing infuriates Soph. If the killer were present, she would destroy him even if he were the Demon Aaii. Yes, I will admit that a smile is on my lips as I picture that scene.

We walk down the short passage to the horror that awaits us. Everyone is talking, wondering what further emotional assault is before us. We can't all fit into the tiny room and do not want to disturb the evidence, though no court in any land will adjudicate this case. Since

Angus and Red are the only trained law enforcement officers (intelligence agents, retired and dead), they go in first, followed by Sir Winston. The others follow when the first two leave.

Sir Winston is stunned by the carnage, and he, too, is visibly angry. He snaps, "Who, or perhaps more accurately, what is this, and who could commit this atrocity?" Abigor, standing at the door, tells the assembled group that this pitiful creature was Aaii's servant and doorman. He explained he had never seen the victim alive but saw him on the demon stream of consciousness. Obviously, the images came from the demon, Aaii.

Angus and Red ask Sir Winston to step outside while they examine the scene. Since I was a State Constable in South Carolina and worked in a Cold Case Squad, I asked if I could assist them. Angus looks briefly away from examining the body and says, "Certainly, Bones, I am sorry. I should have invited you to help." He points to a scuffed piece of furniture. "Please look through that old dresser. Since this crime will never have an official investigation, we won't have to worry about our fingerprints or disturbing fingerprints. I can't imagine going to the local Policja or Straz Miejskie I Gminne and telling them we found a fox doorman murdered with an arrow through the heart. Furthermore, we suspect a demon committed the crime. Bloody right!" Angus looks up and grins his Clint grin. Uh, dark police humor. We nod in agreement. The story sounds a bit insane. I don't know. On reflection, it sounds perfectly normal to me.

Red says to Angus and me, "There is very little to go on here. I am more interested in the reason for the murder. Why would Aaii want to kill his servant? I can think of only two reasons. The doorman knew something dangerous to Aaii, which begs whether he could communicate. After that, who would he tell? This tunnel does not seem to be on a popular bucket list stopover. Aaii planned to leave, and he did not want to leave the Fox here. Why would he be concerned about that? Obviously, the welfare of the Fox was not a concern." Red shakes his head in bewilderment and returns to his Sherlock Holmes thing.

I look through the dresser and find two red velvet uniforms and a couple of flattened black top hats. In the small top drawer, I see a silver brush and matching comb with the initials E.W. That is odd. These items look expensive—stolen, no doubt. Looking at the Fox's few meager belongings makes me incredibly sad for the little creature.

As I listen to Red's hypotheses, something occurs to me. "I know this sounds wild, but here goes. Where did the fox come from, and how did he get here? You will not find many of his, uh, descriptions looking for work on Indeed under the heading servant/doorman. What exactly is he, and what made him into a fox? We know from nursery rhymes that demons and witches can turn people into frogs and such." I look to Abigor, standing at the door, for an answer. He wrinkles his nose as he concentrates on my question.

Finally, he answers, "Bones, thou art correct, though I do not know about nursery rhymes. Demons have the power to turn humans into fantastic creatures, yet I know of very few instances when they have done so. It could have happened. I do not know how to determine if he was conjured. I shalt work on that for thee." Everyone starts to feel the rabbit hole thing again.

Suddenly, Dr. Einstein brightens up and pays close attention. He tells us, "We could, of course, check his DNA. That might give us useful information. No doubt, there is a lab in the vicinity where we could arrange testing utilizing the appropriate fictitious story. David was always very talented at liegen . . . excuse me, creating untruths."

My heart skips a beat when I hear David's name. Bones, just stop it! Dr. Einstein left Germany in 1932, never to return, yet sometimes he falls into German when excited. We may think we are badasses, but

Einstein stood up against the Nazis before leaving Germany. They raided his apartment twice and put a bounty of $5000 on his head. He split with his pacifist friends around that time. Dr. Einstein is a practical man. He cautioned us then and today, "Never do anything against conscience even if the state demands it." But he will fight if it is necessary for survival or honor.

Sir Winston had been listening and chomping on his cigar. He suggests, "You are correct, dear Albert. A laboratory may give us interesting data. Nonetheless, we must return to searching for the evil contraption at the moment. That is another explanation for the murder of this poor creature. Have you not considered the murder is simply a device to turn our attention away from our mission? Why investigate a murder when we cannot bring anyone to justice? We will give the deceased a Christian burial as soon as possible. Red, would you transport our little servant to St. Albans? Father Antonio will see to him. What say you?" Churchill looks around at each of us. Red leaves immediately and returns in seconds. We take a minute to show respect for the little fox.

Angus and Red are aggrieved to have to give up the hunt now that they have the scent. I can see it in their faces, for they are sleuthhounds who sense the prey around the next corner. I agree, but that is not why we are here and not why the Padre died. Poor Dr. Einstein can see the beautiful lab he envisioned disappearing into the mist. We agree with Sir Winston. Yes, we all despise injustice and cruelty, but we are too late to protect Fox.

We reluctantly leave the room, Abigor closes the door, and we return to our primary mission. I remember Sir Winston saying we should look closer at the fancy bell pull. I run to catch up with the former Prime Minister. He moves fast, which frustrated and amazed his younger colleagues, who had to keep up with the aging Prime Minister during the War.

I finally catch him and tap on his shoulder. "Sir, you said something about the bell pull before we left the chamber. What drew your attention to it?"

He stops to answer me. "Bones, we have covered every inch of this large chamber. If the switch that opens the door to the machine is here, the pull is the only thing we have not examined at least twice. Shall we go look?" The bell pull is slightly left of the double doors. Sir Winston, the perfect gentleman, asks me if I would like to do the honors. I certainly would! I stand at 5'11" with my red high heels and must stretch to reach the pull. Why install it this high and so far away from his idiotic gold throne? It would be inconvenient. Consequently, Sir Winston and I surmise it was used infrequently or not at all as a bell pull. Incongruent with frequent use, hence not a servant bell.

With a hearty "Yippee," I jerk on the bell pull. Immediately, we hear a loud ear-splitting rumbling as a stone wall moves to one side, and an opening into a passage appears. Impossible! There was not the slightest indication of a break in the solid rock wall that weighs many tons, and it just opened with a jerk on the bell pull. We have covered every single inch of that wall. No cracks. None.

The others watch in amazement and then run for the gaping mouth opening before us. We see a long passage lit with torches. How did Aaii do that? Oh, magic like the wall sliding trick. Excited, I recklessly dart forward until an iron hand clasps my wrist. Abigor is beside me. He calmly suggests, "Bones, do not go down yond passage. We do not knoweth what awaits us. Please pause until we test what may be a trap." At first, I was annoyed with him for stopping me. Then, I realized the wisdom of his words since I am mortal. Still, I hate to be treated differently, though that has become my maddening fate.

The others move slowly into the tunnel, paying close attention to any sign of danger. Angus is cautiously checking the stone floor for wire traps. Red examines the walls in minute detail. True, they cannot be harmed by anything in this world, but they don't want to trigger something that could cause a loud, nasty explosion, cover the Doomsday Machine in rock, or cause it to activate. Sir Winston marches courageously ahead as he has always done. He is a Sherman tank with a Cuban cigar and a laconic sneer. Abigor runs to get in front of the Great Man and plants himself like an emerald-eyed tree on Churchill's path. Naturally, the former Prime Minister, always fearless, is indignant and begins to puff up and balk. He does not take the implied word "stop" well.

Abigor puts his hand up, draws near, and confronts the Great Statesman. "Sir, wherefore are thee moving so fast? Aaii, the malevolent Demon, may have rigged this passage to kill intruders or . . ." Abigor pauses here for effect, then continues, "To activate the weapon. Please take thy time." Again, Abigor's warning of caution was logical. Churchill also reluctantly accepted the wisdom of listening to our angel. He gruffly chews the end off his cigar and spits it on the stone floor, but he cooperates. Abigor 01. Sir Winston 00. Game.

I watch from the relative safety of the main chamber. I hear Red tell Angus, "The walls appear to be nothing more than damp, foul-smelling rock. Yet, I just saw a solid stone wall open as if by magic. I believe nothing is as it seems to be here. Bloody creepy, if you know what I mean. What do you think?" Angus looks up at Red, rubbing his eyes and coughing, and chokes out, "Foul smelling is bloody right, mate. So far, I have detected nothing of interest, yet we may have missed something, as you said." Both men look at Sir Winston for direction. Churchill is never without an answer. He sips his brandy, looks around the tunnel, and then nods at Dr. Einstein, who frowns and brushes his wild eyebrows, hoping, futilely, to tame them. He coughs. Big Soph does the same and vigorously shakes her magnificent head. The pungent odor is overwhelming and growing more so by the minute.

Dr. Einstein is deep in thought. He finally says, "I have smelled this particular odor before, but I cannot place where I first smelled it." He vigorously rubs his temples to stimulate his memory. We must recall that he has memories going back decades. He was born in March of 1879, so he is searching through 141 years of memory files. Finally, the genius snaps his fingers and smiles. The smile dies abruptly.

I am still at a distance in the Demon's chamber. I hear a voice say softly, "My darling, hold your breath and run outside into the open air. Do not return until I tell you it is safe." I reel as if I have been shot! That was David's voice! I pivot to look for him, and no one is there. Did I imagine it? Then I hear his voice again, only louder, "Move." I move! I run down the long main tunnel to the woodlands outside. I take a deep breath, my heart pounds furiously against my chest, and I feel goosebumps on my arms. Slowly, I breathe normally, and my heart resumes a steady rhythm. I feel relieved to see our gargantuan rental Hummer still parked outside, faithfully waiting for a driver who may never return. David drove here following the map Sir Winston found in the military archives.

My thoughts go back to the voice in the Chamber. I am confident it was David calling me! I did not imagine it! Where is he? How did David know I was in danger? Was I in danger? I want to stomp my feet in frustration but resist the impulse. Still, I am happy to know that wherever David is, he still loves me.

Inside the tunnel, Dr. Einstein jerks his head around and stares at the chamber entrance to see if Bones is still standing there. Relieved, he wipes his forehead and relaxes when he sees she is not there. The genius explains to the guys and Sophie, "We are reacting to Phosgene gas, which causes coughing and choking. I remember it from the research Fritz Haber did in 1917. Phosgene was created as a toxic agent. Therefore, it does not exist in nature. Indeed, it cannot harm us since we are long past being harmed by anything. I theorize we reacted to it to warn us that Bones must get out. I was relieved that she left the chamber."

Abigor, listening with great interest, assures Dr. Einstein, "Bones is safe outside. We need not fear for her safety."

Einstein nods sagely and continues, "Notice you are no longer choking or coughing because it would serve no purpose now. Since Bones is safely out of what is, in effect, a gas chamber, we return to normal. There is no antidote for this dreadful devil's brew. Phosgene is a gas used in bioterrorism, and it causes a buildup of fluid in the lungs, quickly leading to death. At first, one notices a pleasant smell of green corn, yet the smell is stronger and decidedly unpleasant in higher concentrations. Haber's wife, a chemist, was so horrified by what her husband had done that she killed herself with his gun. He has the dubious distinction of being known as the Father of Chemical Warfare." Einstein shook his head to show his scorn for perverted patriotism and those innocents who died.

Abigor had walked deep into the tunnel. He returned and cheerfully told the group, "I hath removed the odious poison. The air is perfectly safe for humans now. There is naught more danger than a walk in a mid-summer rose garden."

Sir Winston is deeply troubled by what happened. He looks each one of them in the eye and spits out, "Are we saying the horridly wicked Aaii rigged the tunnel to kill anyone who entered without his permission? Abigor said the passage might be armed. I thought about an explosion and carefully watched for wiring, perhaps a tripwire."

Sophie had been by his side as they explored the immediate area. She disappears.

He knows she had gone to be with Bones. He speaks to Angus, "Check on Bones. I know she is unharmed. I feel it, but she needs solace. The poison gas has been another ghastly shock. She would have been poisoned here in this passage had she entered. We owe Abigor our sincere gratitude for checking her impulsivity." The Great Man bows to Abigor. He doesn't mention his own impulsivity, which the wise angel also checked. Then Churchill returns to his task for Angus, saying, "Bones has had too many appalling blows lately. She is facing down the tribulations that beset her as a Guardian. Stand with her, Angus." Angus nods, smiles, and disappears, always the perfect, stalwart Scotsman.

Abigor glances down so they will not witness his disappointment. He confesses to himself that he has loving feelings for Bones. The former demon sighs. Sadly, she loves David. To his shame, he momentarily hoped David would never return. He sighs again. Life was easier as a demon.

Sir Winston is observing. The brilliant former Prime Minister sees more than Abigor realizes and is sympathetic. Three of the most beautiful women of his time rejected his ardent marriage proposals. These lovely ladies included the famous actress Ethel Barrymore, Muriel Wilson, a high society debutante, and even his adoring wife Clementine, who refused his proposal more than once. Later, Clemmie relented. Until Churchill died, she lived for her beloved "Pig," and she was his ever-constant "Cat." Yes, Winston understands and feels sad for the newly returned Angel.

I am sitting with Big Soph in the Hummer, breathing and trying to move on from the most recent catastrophe. Didn't the sages say that practice is supposed to make perfect? I should be perfect anytime now.

Suddenly, Angus pops up beside me, jarring me from my Zen attempt at peaceful breathing. I jump and let out a little yelp.

Angus moves closer and apologizes, "I am so sorry, dear Bones. I should have popped up a little farther from you. I wanted to check on you as quickly as possible. Sir Winston sent me to stand with you, as he put it. So, now that I have alarmed you, how are you, my dear?"

He looks so sheepish that I must laugh. I hug the excellent gentleman and ask, "Angus, may I talk to you about something that frightens and confuses me?" He laughs and says, "There is only one thing that frightens you, Bones? You're bloody tough! Tell Uncle Angus all about it, and we will figure it out together." His broad smile makes me feel better immediately. After all, God Bless him. He is the man who stopped a bullet for me on another mission.

I sit down on the ground by the Hummer, run my fingers through my hair, and blurt out, "Angus, I smelled an odd odor when I was waiting in the chamber, as Abigor suggested." I absently pat Soph's head as I try to figure out what just happened and how to explain it to the practical Scotsman. "Immediately after I noticed the odor, I heard a voice ordering me to get outside and not come back until it was safe. Angus, I know this sounds crazy, but I am positive it was David. I didn't see him but would recognize his husky voice anywhere."

Angus is silent as he concentrates and shoves his hands down in his pants pockets. He gently asks, "Dear Bones, let's look at this logically. Isn't it possible you smelled something, as you said, and your brain reacted and commanded you to act?" He searches my eyes, hoping to see that I question my original interpretation and accept his rational explanation.

I would hate to disappoint Angus, but I will go to my grave believing the voice I heard was David warning me of danger. He continues to protect me as he always has. I reply, "You are probably right, my good

Uncle Angus. What are the guys doing now? Have they identified the gas?"

Though he still frowns, he looks much relieved. He tilts his head as he watches me closely. He may be dead, but they don't come any sharper than Angus Snowden. His cop intuition is fine-tuned and hard to fool. As we walk back toward the tunnel, he loops me into the deadly gas situation. "Dr. Einstein recognized the gas. He had smelled it when he was a young man. He knew the madman who created it for Germany in the First World War. The doctor said the toxic substance was Phosgene gas. It causes coughing, choking, and a fatal fluid buildup in the lungs. Rapidly, the fluid overwhelms the lungs and leads to certain death. We were greatly relieved to see that you left. Abigor told us he knew you were safe outside. He removed the gas, so it is safe for you to breathe now. We did not find a rigged explosive, but that disastrous possibility is still on the table. We continue searching for the door to the Doomsday Machine, which is cunningly hidden. Bones, I shall be bloody honest with you. I fear our time is running out, and we must move pretty damn quickly." I stop in my tracks and look at him; from the grim set of his jaw, I grasp he is deadly serious. A chill runs down my spine. Sophie and I started running for the chamber and the Team.

A massive shadow watches them from the mouth of the tunnel. Bones and Angus are blissfully unaware of his presence. He sees them running and immediately knows what has happened. He will stay close.

Chapter Five

The Choice

Angus, Big Soph, and I come to a screeching halt in the chamber, almost knocking over Dr. Einstein, who is in the midst of an animated conversation with Sir Winston. He points his cane at the scientist, punctuating his words with little jabbing motions. Dr. Einstein points his glasses back while swirling circles in the air.

Sir Winston shouts, "This is no time for ease and comfort, Albert. It is a time to dare and endure!" His jaw is tight and juts out at the physicist. He is in no mood to hear a dissenting voice. His chest is straining against his vest as he puffs up to his full, rotund, manly stature. The genius, not to be out-puffed, yells back, "We cannot find the hidden door! What are we supposed to do, Winston? I know time is ticking hell-for-leather; I feel the ticks of the clock pounding in my head. We must sit down and discuss a way to find that damnable Machine!" Angus, Soph, Red, and I are looking back and forth between them as if watching a match at Wimbledon. Suddenly, more drama arrives in the person of a giant.

Druid storms into the room like a rogue steam engine billowing smoke. All of us are staring at the apparition that is Druid, waiting for his usual angry tirade. He surprises us by sitting slowly down on Aaii's throne and simply eyeing us to increase our anxiety. We wait. What else can we do? Finally, he says quietly and deliberately as if scolding toddlers fighting over a candy bar, "I will not lose my temper and scream. I have said all of this before. The mortal for whom you are responsible was almost killed by poison gas. David saved her, or she would now be in Beyond." Dr. Einstein, Red, and I are shocked. What is Druid saying? David isn't here. But I think Sir Winston knows where he is.

I am thrilled to be assured it was David's voice. I knew it! Angus bows to me as an apology. I get it. Angus was trying to protect me from disappointment. Besides, there is that whole saving my life thing.

Druid is not finished yet. "What are you waiting for, an engraved invitation from Queen Elizabeth II? We all agreed that the deadly weapon must be destroyed. What have you done to achieve that end?" His voice gets louder with each word he throws at the Team. David isn't here to throw words back, as was their boisterous pattern. Sir Winston, annoyed, answers the giant, "We would be gratified to hear your thoughts on that subject, Druid. We have been vigorously searching for the room where the machine is hidden. We found the passage but not the room. The passage appears to be solid stone without the least indication that a door exists." Sir Winston scowls and shoves his lit cigar into his pocket. A circling trail of smoke now floats up from his vest.

Red knows Druid better than the rest of us. Druid sent Red to us to help him earn his way into Beyond. Red ticked off some of the Powers in Beyond when he was in Sir Winston's Special Operations Executive by overachieving in dispatching German psychopaths. SOE members were top-secret fighters who conducted espionage, sabotage, and surveillance in occupied Europe. They were specially trained, courageous men and women who fought from the shadows. The legendary prime minister ordered them to "set Europe ablaze. Red joined MI5 after the war." Druid usually shouts thunderous commandments at us, but he conversed somewhat sedately with our newest member. Red walks to the throne and says, "Druid, we have done everything to locate the weapon. We have not given up, but we are out of ideas. Then, we were interrupted by a crime. We found the body of the Fox who served as Aaii's doorman. A bloody savage murdered him. Are you here to help us, mate?" Red, standing close to the throne, looks directly and boldly at Druid, not the least bit intimidated by the immense blond man in the faded black suit. Going toe-to-toe with Druid is not for the faint of heart. I have seen people cross the street to escape Druid's path. A few elderly women crossed themselves as they hurried away.

Druid lowers his voice to a growl. "Yes, I am here to help, and since you apparently cannot do it, I shall find the weapon for you. Aaii sealed the door with magic. Let me assure you that I know about the killing of the little doorman, and it will not go unavenged." He slams his fist on the throne, and the entire chamber shakes as if hit by an earthquake, registering a solid seven on the Richter scale. It's possible the whole mountain range vibrated with the tremendous blow.

Druid stalks toward the passage, stops, and studies the damp stone wall on the left after walking a few yards. We were behind him and stopped en masse to watch the miracle. Churchill, the only leader in Europe not daunted by the bully Hitler is undoubtedly not in the least intimidated by the behemoth. He asks, "Druid, how will you open the solid wall, and how do you know the location of the door?" Churchill skewers Druid with his glare as he waits for an answer. For now, Druid is not responding to the Great Man's question.

We are gathered close to Druid in curiosity and excitement. It is a good thing most of us don't need to breathe. Suddenly, a disturbing thought hits me. This little adventure could be dangerous! Well, the usual. We are curious to know if the vile creep Aaii booby-trapped the door. He tampered with the passage. Why not the door? On second thought, I am confident Druid would know in his unfathomable way if there was danger. He would get me out of harm's way.

The giant runs his impossibly large hand along the wall, feeling around a two-foot square area. He stops, removes a peculiar silver ring from his pants pocket, and touches the wall. We hear the same loud rumble we heard in the chamber when we opened the door to the passage. About 8 feet of the wall magically disappears, and we can see into a rough-hewn stone room. Bone-chilling air spills into the passage, enveloping us in an icy embrace. Dr. Einstein takes Druid by the hand, thanking him profusely for helping us. Red happily pops the chap with the black suit and bowler on the back and survives. As excited as a puppy, Sir Winston slowly enters the room, mindful of Abigor's earlier caution before the poison gas starts pouring into the tunnel. Abigor stands back and motions me into the room with a little bow.

I know it is safe now. Angus runs over to a large steel machine with knobs, levers, and gauges sitting in the middle of the room. He muses more to himself than to us, "I wish David were here. We spent much time studying the blueprints of this monster together." (Yes, I admit it, I jump at the sound of David's name.) "There were no instructions that explained these various gadgets." Angus examines a screen about 12 inches by 10 inches covered in green glass. It is entirely blank. Two white knobs sit to the left of the screen, with a large chrome lever on the right. Angus describes what he and David saw. "I remember this screen from the diagram, and it showed numbers that look like hours and minutes in military time or a countdown. We theorized that the numbers represent the time left before the weapon would activate when it is engaged. With any luck, we won't find out if our theory was correct."

Churchill and Dr. Einstein hover over the unique weapon, fascinated by its alien appearance. They would not have been overly surprised to learn that little green men had designed it on Mars. Sir Winston addresses the excellent doctor, "Albert, have you ever seen anything like this in your many experiences with weapons?"

With shaking hands, Albert pulls his glasses out of his vest pocket and adjusts them on his nose. "Winston, I know you have extensive experience with all manner of war devices, much more than I do. This steel abomination is like nothing I have ever seen in my long life. Did you notice it is as shiny as if it were constructed just minutes before we entered the room? There's no dust or discoloration; very peculiar, that."

Sophie sniffs the machine and touches her nose to it. Suddenly, her lips pull back from her savage teeth, and she begins to snarl. Sir Winston looks intently at the lever and knobs, trying to intuit their purpose. He nods and says to Albert, "Yes, my dear friend, I have seen countless weapons of war, more than I would like to remember, and this machine is utterly foreign to me. I agree with Angus about the screen. I saw the diagram, too. Yes, I am puzzled by its pristine condition as well. I do not have an answer to explain that after eighty years." They continue to discuss the weapon as I watch Sophie. Something is incredibly wrong.

A black object swoops down from the corner of my eye. I spin around and see an apparition resembling a skeleton in flowing, heavy black robes. I duck down and emit a loud, earsplitting screech reverberating in the small chamber. Everyone sees the phantom now and reacts. Sir Winston, Angus, and Red attack with carefully calculated shots at the intruder. They are all armed, but they can't just go guns blazing in a stone room, risking a ricochet that could hit me. Sir Winston uses his stick to strike at it as it zooms over our heads. In complete 'creature- from-Hell' mode, Sophie's red eyes are blazing as she leaps high into the air to snare the monstrous intruder with extraordinary swiftness and agility. Abigor looks at the entity with great interest but no sign of fear or panic. He guides me out of the room into the tunnel to avoid stray bullets or attack monsters. Sophie calms down and joins us outside the room. Abigor looks into her eyes and seems to have a shared understanding. They nod and return to the weapons room as Abigor shouts to the others, "Gentlemen, this is a scare tactic, and it is no more alive than yond machine. Aaii sent it to frighten us. It cannot harm us, and more importantly, it has no power to harm Bones." As soon as Abigor reveals the truth, the bogus monster turns to smoke and fades away.

What is that sound? We all turn and stare at the machine. It has begun to rumble and vibrate into life. A bright glow now lights the screen. Oh Hell! We rush to look at the display, and it reads 72:00. Angus looks at the screen and reaches for the knobs and lever, but Sir Winston stays his hand. "We don't know what the gadgets were designed to do. We cannot just jump in recklessly and begin to manipulate everything."

He looks to Dr. Einstein for support, but our genius is frozen, staring at the screen. Finally, he gasps, "It is certainly possible, and perhaps probable, that this vile monster will activate in 72 hours. I have no data to make assumptions about our course of action. Obviously, we can pull the lever and turn the knobs, which may deactivate the machine, or it could precipitate an immediate catastrophic reaction."

Red, Angus, and I are shocked. We don't know what to do. Sophie is on high alert. Her ears are up, and she stands like a statue from an Egyptian burial chamber; the comparison is unnerving under the circumstances.

Abigor stands beside me, silent and still. If Soph is a statue, he is the enigmatic Sphinx. Inexplicably, I notice his chest rising and falling slightly. No, I can't explain it. By the way, in case no one has noticed, there are very few things I can explain. His intense eyes are riveted on the screen, and it is as if Abigor is trying to absorb something through osmosis. He moves toward the machine, turns to Sir Winston, and whispers, "I dost know what is happening. Since a demon hast dominion over the device, I have a unique insight, having once been one of the vile creatures." Abigor visibly shutters as he utters those last words.

Steadying himself, he says, "I believe I can read the otherworldly controls. The numbers on the screen represent how long we have to disable or destroy the Machine. It is protected by an evil force field created by Aaii. If we start hammering away or turning knobs, it will detonate. As Dr. Einstein theorized, it will cause tectonic plates in the earth's lithosphere to move violently asunder, leading to earthquakes and powerful volcanic eruptions around the globe. These violent eruptions shalt continue until the planet is reduced to flames, smoke, poison gasses, and high temperatures. Later, as smoke blocks the sun, the freezing temperatures replace the Hellish heat. The elimination of all animal and vegetative life will be complete. I assure you it will happen as I have described."

Collectively, as if by common consent, we are aghast after hearing Abigor's interpretation of humanity's fate. Red wipes his face with his brawny, rough hand. His ordinarily ruddy complexion turns ashen. Angus stares at Abigor, grimacing and rubbing his chin as he considers the outrageous prognostication.

Sir Winston, by contrast, is an unruffled and unfailingly craggy, immovable boulder, ready to crush any foe. He probes Abigor further. "How do you know this? Yes, I understand this was Albert's theory after his research in Austria. Yet, you seem to be adamant that this nightmare will happen. I would appreciate some facts."

Abigor looks into Churchill's eyes solemnly. "I wish I were uncertain. I am not. I hath seen the future through Aaii's eyes. Total destruction will follow the devil machine's activation, whether by time running out or inadvertently triggering it."

Indeed, we now know what we are facing and the limitations imposed on us, and we need a plan. We go into warrior mode. We will do everything within our power to avoid the destruction of our planet. Nothing, no matter how dangerous or challenging, is off the table.

Sir Winston chomps hard on his unoffending cigar and glares at us. "We shall go forward together. The road upwards is stony. There are dark and dangerous valleys upon our journey through which we must fight our way. But it is sure and certain that if we persevere—and we shall persevere—we shall come through these dark and dangerous valleys into sunlight broader and more genial and longer lasting than mankind has ever known. We have no choice, gentlemen and Bones."

The Greatest Statesman of any century inspires us as he had the millions of people who preceded us. We would happily follow him into the mouth of Hell and thank Heaven for the opportunity to do so. Churchill says, "Let us sit down and make a plan. The main chamber may be better suited for that. Our time is short. Thus, we must plan carefully and move quickly." We all nod in agreement and move steadfastly toward the Demon's Chamber with resolute purpose and steadfast boldness.

When we sit down, Sir Winston perches on the gold throne, and Dr. Einstein takes the floor to speak. "We must plan to stop the contraption from activating. Abigor is the, uh, man most likely to have insight into how we might accomplish that. We cannot destroy or recalibrate it as long as the force field is in place. Remember, as we discuss our best options in response to this crisis, the true sign of intelligence is not knowledge but imagination. We must seek the unimaginable and be ready to go forward with only our steadfast faith and tenacity to guide us. Abigor, will you tell us about your educated beliefs on removing the force field."

Abigor sits in a gilded side chair, pats my hand, stands, and bows to Einstein before speaking. "Friends, I have pondered yond evil trickery. Never have I removed a force field or seen such done. I have studied the occult in many lands and over numerous centuries. I learned much from ancient Mesopotamian legends. The holy men used various powerful incantations to ward away spirits and their evil works. One incantation may dispel the evil force field. Remember I said—may. However, only a righteous person could utter the incantation to activate its power. I will speak the incantation for you now.

'Agony of mankind, disease of mankind, suffering of mankind,
wickedness do not enter the house I enter,
do not come near the house I come near,
do not use the evil eye around the house I enter,
wherever thou be, thou art removed.
Thy wickedness art removed forevermore.'

"To my knowledge, this is the only incantation that can free the machine of its evil force field. Again, it must be uttered by a righteous man. He looks around at each of us, searching for some sign that we understand his meaning before continuing, "One must meet the criteria for righteousness to speak this ancient incantation handed down from the most ancient holy men. It hast the power to reverse a conjuration no matter how mighty the conjurer hast been. The requirements for a righteous man are:

"One who has a pure heart.
One who has sacrificed for others.
One who is loved unconditionally.
One who is utterly fearless."

"The Powers in Beyond are the judges who decide who meets the criteria. If they are mistaken, the incantation will not remove the spell. We must find such a man at once. We can begin with the men assembled here. They would not consider me because I am not a man. I am an angel. Shall we discuss the others?"

Sir Winston jumps in to begin the process of selection. "Gentlemen, who amongst us meet the criteria? We must choose him and apply to the Powers in Beyond immediately. Abigor has removed himself from consideration. What about Albert?" The former Prime Minister looks to Abigor for his opinion.

After consideration, Abigor replies, "Our most challenging problem, gentlemen, is that all of you have been dead for so long, no one is left to love you unconditionally. That would apply to Red, Sir Winston, and Dr. Einstein. Angus has been dead only a short while, but his wife preceded him, and there is no one else." Abigor looks to Angus for confirmation. Angus nods. Abigor continues, "Sophie and Bones are not men, so they would not qualify. The ancient Mesopotamians did not favor diversity or inclusion." Abigor frowns his disapproval of these ancient holy men and their narrow-minded ways and bows to Sophie and me.

Something strikes me like an arrow to the heart, David! David meets the criteria because I love him unconditionally and eternally. I shout to the others, "David meets the criteria. He meets every requirement. He is utterly fearless, has a pure heart, and sacrifices for others, and I love him unconditionally. David can say the incantation!"

Chapter Six

The Righteous Man

I am excited to have an answer to our predicament. "David meets all their requirements. He can speak the incantation and, I pray, give us access to the weapon!" Yes, I must admit we have a slight problem since we don't know how to reach David. Truthfully, I suspect Sir Winston knows more than he is saying, so I stare directly at him. Sophie lays her furry head in my lap and stares at the Great Man, too. Churchill ignores us and looks at Red, who is obviously becoming more impatient by the minute.

Red jumps up to speak. He is frustrated by the delays, and his brows are lowered and almost meet over his nose. Controlling his voice to keep from yelling as he would like, he snaps, "Gentlemen, I am a simple man of action, and I see a catastrophic Black Swan swimming towards us, and we must act. It is staring us down. We discuss magical force fields, Mesopotamian holy men, children's chants, and who is pure of heart. What the Hell are we doing?" By the time Red mentioned holy men, his volume had risen considerably. I feel sorry for the poor man. He is not accustomed to flat-out daft realities. We are quite used to daft realities and generally comfortable with the bizarre and outrageous. Red will get used to it if the planet doesn't explode.

Dr. Einstein smooths his mustache, pushes his glasses down, gazes at Red, and answers, "Red, I understand your point and evident frustration. We share your desire to tackle the weapon immediately. Abigor told us the weapon is protected, and if we start engaging with it, we can cause it to activate now rather than in 72 hours. We cannot afford to take that chance. Our most pressing goal at the moment is to remove the force field. None of us, other than Abigor, has any knowledge of a productive course of action. Essentially, we have two objectives: avoid premature activation and remove the protective field. If we do nothing, we can avoid the former as we brainstorm the latter. Since we have no other plan, we shall discuss identifying a righteous man according to the ancient criteria. We would all like to hear it if you have another suggestion."

Red is tangled in a trap of irrefutable logic thrown out by our genius. Angus, too, looks uncertain and frustrated. They are men of action accustomed to rational processes and scenarios. Our situation strains their belief systems to the breaking point. I get it. I think of Hamlet's words, 'There are more things in heaven and earth, Horatio, than are dreamt of in your philosophy.' Of course, both men are ghosts; we have an ancient Great Dane entity, and Abigor is an angel. Freakish is all around them. I have learned to just roll with the crazy or be consumed by disbelief.

Sir Winston, who has been listening carefully, coughs and takes the proverbial bull by the horns. "Shall we discuss the criteria set by the holy men and who might meet their exacting requirements? We must move forward with the information we have as quickly as possible. Bones and Abigor make excellent points. I believe we all would meet the limitations except the last one, who is loved unconditionally. Albert, Red, Angus, and I lost our loved ones to death many years ago. Abigor, I don't think we could argue against David sacrificing for others for his service during the war and his career, which required great sacrifice. We have seen David's courage under fire. The only other requirement is a pure heart, but I cannot define that term, Abigor. Could you explain it to us?" The Great Man rubs his chin in concentration.

Abigor rises from his seat to answer Sir Winston. He nods and says, "Thou art quite right, sir. It is an archaic term not commonly used in recent centuries. Without malice, treachery, or evil, I would define a pure heart as honest, sincere, and guileless. Before you ask, one can be a ferocious warrior and have a pure heart if one is just and uses only the force necessary to save oneself or an innocent. Thou art his friends and know David much better than I do. Does this description fit him?"

I wave my hand in the air and speak up first. "I have no doubts that David has a pure heart. He could not be more honest or sincere. What you see is what you get, other than a few creative interpretations to help us accomplish the missions set out for us by the Powers in Beyond. Sometimes, the truth does not serve us well." I nod to Angus, leaning toward me, sitting on the edge of his chair, eyes flashing with emotion.

Angus is an old-school Scotsman who speaks plainly and with apparent sincerity. He stands straight and tall, proclaiming, "I have known David Smythe for many years. First, as the Deputy Director-General of MI5 and later as a member of this Team working on a cold case in which I was a witness. I have always respected him as an honourable man. I would bet my reputation as a gentleman on David's veracity." He slaps his chair for emphasis and salutes me.

Sir Winston now retakes the floor and absently pats Sophie. He pulls his pocket watch out and puts it back. Time has taken on a new, urgent meaning. There is quite a telling story about that pocket watch given to him by his disapproving and distant father, Lord Randolph Churchill. We might discuss that when this emergency has passed. Hang in there. He finally gives up on the time and addresses us. "We have agreed that David Smythe is righteous, and that is precisely what we need right now. Yes, I know where we can find David. I think Bones suspected I was carrying a secret. It is a long story, and I feel quite strongly about it. The Powers in Beyond told me David had stomped all over the Prime Directive or words to that effect. As you know, David shot and killed the thug Axel as he was strangling Bones. She was gasping for air and could not break free from the brute. There is no doubt

Bones would have died if David had not heard her screams and interceded with a well-placed bullet to Axel's head."

"The coward attacked Bones and Father Antonio when he caught them alone. The Powers charged that David could have tackled Axel rather than shot him. David countered that Bones could have been dead by then, and he could not take that chance. Albert has told me it takes 10 seconds to strangle someone unconscious. Death is caused by compressing the airway. David had to choose whether to shoot and make that decision very quickly. I argued that charging David with a Prime Directive violation was unfair under these circumstances. They will hold an informal hearing, allowing us to argue for the defense." Churchill is angry, and I'm unsure if the smoke around him comes from the cigar he had finally lit. I am shocked by the Powers' abject arrogance. Yet, I feel tremendous relief. At least I know that David is safe for the moment. We are not powerless with this new information. We must have David counter the spell. Sir Winston said he is leaving for Beyond immediately to push the Powers to release David until we complete our mission. We have no time to play a Judge Judy courtroom drama.

Chapter Seven

Alpha and Omega

Sir Winston pops into what appears to be a magnificent, gloriously ornate, and imposing palace. It reminds Churchill of the Sistine Chapel in the Apostolic Palace in Vatican City. The chapel is a high-reformation art, and the ceiling was painted by the pre-eminent master artist Michelangelo at the request of Pope Julius II in the 15th century. The six arched windows on either side of the chapel are exquisite examples of stained-glass artistry, and the painted vaulted ceiling staggers the brain with incredibly brilliant stimuli. Sir Winston guesses this palace was the model for Michelangelo's extraordinary ceiling at the Vatican. Shockingly, he has overheard bits and pieces of conversation hinting that Michelangelo may have been an immortal. Naturally, Churchill has never shared this confidential information with anyone below. He is an honorable man who can keep secrets close to his vest. Michelangelo, an angel? That would explain a lot.

All furnishings in this room are purest white and glow as if each piece were lit from within by its personal sun. He counted 12 identical tall, majestically carved straight chairs and two large round tables. On the top of one of the tables, "The Four Apostles" by Durer is reproduced in its full creative brilliance. The other table features El Greco's "St. Paul." It, too, is a magnificent representation. Naturally, he is familiar with both stunning works. Churchill's brain is whirling with wonderment overload. Were El Greco and Albrecht Durer immortals too? He shakes his head. He will save that mystery for another day.

There are no lights, torches, or lamps. Nothing substantial illuminates the room. The purest light is simply there. The gleaming multi-colored mosaic floor tiles recreate various critical stories from the

Bible. The depiction in front of Churchill is Jonah and the dyspeptic whale. To Sir Winston's right, Noah and his multitude of animals wait to board the impossibly gargantuan ark.

To the Great Man's left stands Joseph in his coat of many colors, surrounded by his covetous brothers. Sir Winston turns, and courageous Daniel is in the lion's den behind him. The depictions appear abnormally natural, as if Sir Winston were looking at a reenactment of events rather than the artist's imagination reproduced in tiles. Visually overstimulated, he focuses on the problem at hand. He must convince the Powers to return David to the Team. He muses about a soothing cigar. No, Churchill cannot eat, smoke, or drink, but he likes to pretend.

Suddenly, Sir Winston jumps back. Out of the corner of his eye, he thinks he sees Daniel's serene lion move. He berates himself for childish fantasies and dismisses the illusion. Churchill shakes his head, sits in one of the glowing chairs, and composes himself to await the Powers that be.

Two "men" walk into the room. They look so similar that they may be twins. Both men are statuesque and elegant, with silky white hair hanging to their shoulders, and their eyes are the brilliant azure blue of the Caribbean Sea, yet with fathomless depth. They wear flowing white robes tied at their waists with golden ropes, and simple, weathered leather sandals adorn their feet. Churchill cannot tear his eyes away from their pure, unspoiled perfection. He has met with them many times before but never loses his sense of awe when in their presence.

Sir Winston stands, bows slightly toward them, and says, "Greetings, Alpha and Omega. I am grateful to see you again. Thank you for this meeting. As you know, I am here to talk with you about our esteemed team member, David Smythe. I pray we can come to an agreement on his release so that he can return to us as soon as possible."

Churchill continues to stand as he respectfully addresses Alpha and Omega.

Alpha points to the chair in which Churchill had been sitting and answers in a melodious voice, "Winston, our dear friend, how thankful we are to see thee looking so well, especially since you died in, when was it, Omega?"

Omega smiles and answers, "Of course, we remember, dear Alpha. January 24, 1965, was a terribly sorrowful day for the world. There was much weeping at Winston's passing."

Alpha agrees and continues, "Sadly, it has been a long time since you graced us with a visit. We have been watching over thee and thy Team. We are pleased with your wondrous work. You are aware of our concerns about David Smythe's transgression. We are greatly concerned that he may have broken the Prime Directive. That is the line one cannot recross." Alpha and Omega are silent and impossibly quiescent as they wait for Churchill to speak.

Sitting back down, Sir Winston puts his hands on his legs, straightens up, and suggests, "I have discussed this unfortunate incident with my colleagues. Dr. Einstein, as always, was quite helpful in describing the medical aspects of the confrontation. Albert explained that when Axel, a powerfully built man, was choking Bones, she could have been unconscious in 10 seconds and dead in 3 minutes. Axel could easily have crushed Bones' larynx, causing asphyxia, and compressed her carotid artery, resulting in cerebral ischemia. Albert assured us that is an agonizing way to die. We are quite certain that Axel was choking her because we have her statement and Father Antonio's supporting statement. David had to make a fatal decision in seconds. Also, the cowardly jackal, Axel, assaulted Father Antonio, which unequivocally contributed to the good Padre's death. By the way, please give my best regards to him." Alpha and Omega meet Churchill's eyes, and they listen attentively. Their serene and composed expressions never change, and their eyes do not blink, nor does even a single lash stir.

Sir Winston continues with his argument for the defense. "David is an essential member of our Team and the only one who meets the criteria for a righteous man. Abigor has told us that only a righteous man can save us. We must have David back without delay to read the ancient incantation given to us by Abigor. Those holy words chanted by a righteous man may banish the magic force protecting the Doomsday Machine. No doubt you are aware of this. Without him, it will activate in less than 72 hours, leading to the planet's destruction in the following earthquake apocalypse. Our time to act is growing short. I cannot adequately express the urgency we feel." Sir Winston pulls his monogrammed linen handkerchief from his coat pocket, wiping his forehead as he stares at the two extraordinary beings boldly. He knows they are aware of Abigor's knowledge and counsel. They also know we have no other option on the table or any other piece of furniture.

They glide a few feet away and whisper to each other. Churchill watches them converse, admiring their well-modulated voices, lack of pretension, and almost humble bearings. Finally, they nod in unison. They walk back to him, and Alpha says, at least Sir Winston thinks it is Alpha, "We have conferred about thy words and thy character which no man can besmirch. We shall allow you to take David Smythe back with you for 48 hours—unless there is an emergency. Please wait, dear Winston. David will join you in a few minutes. We have a meeting with John F. Kennedy and his Team, for which we are tardy. Thus, we must leave you now with profound regret." They turn, walk into a mist that was not there seconds before, and disappear. They leave a haunting celestial fragrance of orange blossoms in their wake.

Alpha and Omega have no sooner gone than David walks into the room. David is understandably angry about his detention, but this is not the appropriate place to allow his anger to express itself in an unholy explosion. Churchill feels the heat emanating from David's rage and observes the red splotches on that chiseled face. Sir Winston cautions David, "Please keep your righteous rage in check. Otherwise, we will never leave this place; it is, after all, eternity. We simply do not have that much time currently. We have a planet to save. And I know a black-haired lovely who anxiously awaits your return to her." Sir Winston beams when he says the last words. He touches David's arm, and they pop back to the Demon Chamber post haste. They can shake hands and slap backs another time.

Chapter Eight

The Homecoming

David and the persuasive Sir Winston are in the chandelier-lit chamber in seconds. They can breathe easy now, knowing they are back with their team and can resume their mission. I have been huddled with Dr. Einstein, Red, Angus, and Abigor, discussing our next logical move while waiting for the return of our illustrious leader and the dashing David. I look up and see David standing just feet from me, and he is smiling, that crooked smile that always drives me crazy! I squeal and run into his open arms. He lifts me and twirls me around until I am dizzy. We are both laughing, holding on to each other as if one of us might, without warning, disappear. The nightmare has finally ended. Well, this one has. However, that damned machine is still a threat we must overcome.

Sir Winston was young and in love once or twice, and he understood. However, we have the whole 'planet-about-to-burst-into-flames' thing hanging over our collective heads. Unmistakably, our Team feels the warmth of our love and vicariously enjoys our happiness. But there will be little time for joy. Our obvious delight at being together again gives us a much-needed boost.

As the Team celebrates its reconstitution, however short-lived it may be, Abigor stands at the periphery. A strange and alien pain overwhelms him. To be sure, he wishes only the best for Bones and David, but he cannot help but wish Bones was in his arms, looking at him with the same adoration emanating from those beautiful chestnut eyes. To be held in such regard by one so ingenuous and genuine in spirit must be what gives humans the strength and resolve to conquer all evils and monstrosities that threaten that exquisite sense of completeness and peace.

Sir Winston calls us together for a meeting, reasserting his control of the throne by mutual silent consent. Candidly, the gold monstrosity is horribly uncomfortable. While staring at an old royal portrait, Dr. Einstein says, "Once you can accept the universe as matter expanding into nothing that is something, wearing stripes with plaid comes easy." Dr. E looks around our group for an indication that we grasp the message. Not today. Abigor and Red look utterly confounded. The rest of us are accustomed to Dr. Einstein and smile warmly at him. We are sure there is a genius message in there somewhere.

Sir Winston blinks, pauses a moment, and adds, "Yes, quite right, Albert. We must decide how we are going to approach the weapon. According to the criteria set by the Mesopotamians, we have concluded that David is a righteous man, and the incantation may neutralize the spell. There is no way to confirm we are correct other than by trial with no error. Are we in agreement, gentlemen, Bones, and dear Sophie?" None of us are comfortable with that stark reality, but what choice do we have other than to try? We hope the weapon will not blow up in our faces just out of sheer malice.

Abigor stands and faces us, his clinched fist hints that he is troubled. "We art placing our faith in a centuries-old ritual from a foreign land. I wish it were not so, yet we have nothing but a trip into the Dark World if this fails. None of us feel optimistic about that journey into yond unknown. However, we may have no choice if the incantation does not work, or we cannot disable the weapon. I, for one, am willing to take that mysterious journey. As we know, both Bones and I will have to enter that world simultaneously. She shalt bring the compass, and I shalt bring the magic words that open the evil door." David is looking dark himself. If his jaw tightens anymore, I fear his teeth will break. He is worried for my safety.

Red is confused, and he wants to know more, just in case. "I am not familiar with the Dark World journey, but it doesn't sound bloody pleasant. Could you explain this to me? We seem to have two possible choices to stop the weapon, and I would like to compare them. Neither choice seems to have any guarantees." We are looking at each other, trying to decide who will answer Red's question. Angus said he would like to know more about that journey, too.

David steps up to the plate, responding to Red. "I wish I had a comprehensive answer for you and us. Admiral Stallings told us that a contraption called the Fantastic Machine might stop the Doomsday Machine if it is indeed in the Dark World. He did not tell us how this would happen. He believes Bones and Abigor would have to go in together and come out together. Naturally, he cannot be certain any of this is true. Their time in the dark should be as brief as they can make it. I take it that the journey is risky, and they must be cautious. If we turn to that option, we must learn more about this Fantastic Machine and how it works. We don't know if it is friend or foe, or who put it there, or if it exists. Going in blind would be foolhardy, and I don't plan to send Bones on a reckless death-defying mission." This description sounds very iffy to me, and Red rolls his eyes. He doesn't seem to take the idea very seriously.

Sitting with his arm around me, David turns to Sir Winston and addresses him directly. "Winston, do you think there might be information on the Fantastic Machine in the Archives where you and Dr. Einstein found the blueprints on the weapon?" A thought hit me before Churchill could answer, so I plunged in, "Sir Winston, I am troubled that Admiral Stallings knows more about the Dark World and the machine than he has told us, like what exactly does it do and how reliable is our information? I am not convinced that he has been completely forthcoming. He mentioned the Dark World the first time I visited him at the Old Royal Naval College."

Sir Winston looked around our group while he considered our questions. Rubbing his chin, he answers, "I will take those questions one at a time. Ladies first, Bones, the Admiral's brain is a belfry full of bats, and I mean that most respectfully. He is impossible to read. As we all know, Stallings shares information in little bits, like someone leaving a breadcrumb trail. All this is to say, indeed, he may very well know more than he has shared with us thus far." The Great Man turns his attention to David. Delighted to have David back on board, he smiles warmly and slaps him on the back and says, "David, there certainly is a possibility that information on the other machine may be in the Military Archives."

Dr. Einstein adjusts his glasses and looks through his vest pockets, apparently looking for something, but he doesn't seem to remember what. He gives up the fruitless search and looks up to address us. "I see a clear plan ahead. We must immediately proceed with our first plan, asking David to recite the incantation. If that removes the spell, we shall attempt to turn it off, recalibrate it, or destroy it. If the chant does not work, I suggest sending Bones and Abigor to question Admiral Stallings. You and I, Winston, can return to the Military Archives and look for information on the Fantastic Machine. If it exists, there should be documentation somewhere, and we must find it. What do you think?" Sophie stares at the genius and slowly nods her approval. We all agree with Big Soph. Why wouldn't we?

Abigor, who has been unusually quiet up to this point, says to David, "We must have the sanction of the Powers that thee art a righteous man. Only the Powers could make that determination. They ordained that thee should return for this ceremony, which I interpret as approval.

I must caution thee and thou, that does not guarantee the incantation shalt be successful. I shalt go over the incantation with thee. Every single word must be spoken exactly as written, or the words will fail, and there wilt be no second chance. Do you understand this as I have explained it, David?" David waves his hand to show his understanding. Abigor continues, "I have written it down for you." I am growing more troubled with Abigor's every word. I need an aspirin.

Abigor pulls out a sheet of paper that looks like old, yellowed parchment and reads the words for David:

"Agony of mankind, disease of mankind, suffering of mankind,
wickedness do not enter the house I enter,
do not come near the house I come near,
do not use the evil eye around the house I enter,
wherever thou be, thou art removed.
Thy wickedness art removed forevermore."

David and Abigor go over the chant, clearly enunciating each word. We are curious to know if the ancient Holy Men are obsessed with pronouncing words correctly. Finally, it is zero hour for David to read the incantation. Our collective anxiety is approaching dangerous hypertension, figuratively speaking. I can't seem to catch my breath. All of us, led by Abigor, bow our heads and pray that these holy words will reach the right ears and be powerful enough to break the spell and allow us access to the Doomsday Machine. David's forehead breaks out in a sweat, and he uses his hand to wipe it away. I get it. My heart is pounding, and I feel dizzy. Only Dr. Einstein looks cucumber cool. His hands are rock steady, something to do with E=MC2, no doubt. Sir Winston stands tall but shifts from one foot to the other as he sniffs his brandy. Seriously, I may take up drinking. This is a perfect time.

My beloved David is now a rock of determination, ready to take the most dangerous challenge. He pauses and slowly chants:

"Agony of mankind, disease of mankind, suffering of mankind,
wickedness do not enter the house I enter,
do not come near the house I come near,
do not use the evil eye around the house I enter,
wherever thou be, thou art removed.
Thou wickedness art removed forevermore."

I finally started breathing again. David was fantastic, like a phoenix rising from the ashes of our cataclysmal mission. We are smiling and shaking hands. Red and Angus are almost dancing in delight.

Abigor is worried as his brows arch, and he grimaces as if in pain. I wonder why my mood blackens in response. What does he know we do not? Sir Winston is watching Abigor closely, too. The great leader has learned to read men intuitively and accurately. He leans forward, seated on the throne, and speaks to David. "My boy, excellent reading! Thank you for handling that sensitive task as the genuine, unstoppable British gentleman you are!" Sparkling eyes now turn toward the troubled angel. "Abigor, please share your thoughts with us. What do we do to test the efficacy of our Mesopotamian effort? You are our expert on spells and incantations." Dr. Einstein has also picked up the danger ahead and peers at Abigor through his lopsided glasses. Naturally, as an immortal, the genius does not need glasses. He clings to them as a token of his mortal life.

Abigor rubs his delicate, long hands together, sighs, and answers, "We knew when we began yond task, it would be either successful or not. An old Indian proverb says, 'You do not stumble over a mountain, but you do over a stone.' We have defeated the mountain many times and are now at the vicious stone. There is only one way to determine if the incantation works, which is the answer to Sir Winston's question. We approach and try to touch the Machine. One of three things will happen: the Machine will be open to us, it will destroy the world, or it will do nothing. Our entire plan depends on the Machine's response. If we touch the Machine, it may be triggered and respond most unpleasantly, or the hours may simply keep ticking down. We merely opened a door and must think this out before walking inside." Abigor sits and waits for the others to discuss our options. I thought continuing would be easier than this. On reflection, I had no reason for my leap to optimism.

Dr. Einstein addresses us, and his mood is sober as he lays out the options. "It is simple, my dear friends. We either test the success of our Mesopotamian technique or we do not. If we do not, nothing changes, and we have gone to much trouble for naught. As Abigor said so well, we do not know what will happen if we endeavor to test our experiment. We walked too far along that path to turn back now. Naturally, Bones should go outside in case the blasted hunk of junk blows us up." David jerks his head up on high alert when he hears those words and holds me tighter. Dr. Einstein points his glasses at Sir Winston.

Sir Winston had gone to extravagant lengths to procure this opportunity for us. He shakes his head and quips, "Even the brave are scared by a lion three times: first by its tracks, again by its roar, and one last time face to face. We are now facing the terrifying lion. We must move onward with courage and accept the consequences. Otherwise, we are merely waiting for the 72 hours to tick away. That is not an acceptable choice." Churchill asks Angus if he will look at the Machine and tell us how many hours are left. Angus runs out of the chamber to the weapons storage room. He immediately returns and gives Sir Winston the requested information. "We now have 65 hours before execution." Red jumps in, as is his habit, spitting out through clenched teeth, "I am ready to test the success of the chant. Our options are bloody few, and our time is fleeting." Angus's face sports a fearsome grin, and he vigorously nods his assent. Nothing deters Angus, a stalwart retired and dead MI5 agent.

Sophie looks at us solemnly and growls a deep guttural noise, showing deadly canine teeth. We take that for a hell yes. Soph doesn't waste words.

David leads me out of the tunnel to the lovely woodland brilliantly lit by a bright, warming sun, and we sit in the Hummer. He puts his strong arms around me and crushes me to him. We may be saying goodbye, and we know it. My heart sinks. I just got him back, and we are in danger again. He will survive, the planet may not, and my fate is chained to the clay and granite planet. I am emotionally exhausted by so many painful goodbyes. David must leave me alone to work with the guys on the force field. I feel rebellious. I want to be there because this is not my first rodeo. I have almost been killed numerous times. I can accept consequences, whatever those consequences happen to be.

I have not been this peaceful since before David was grabbed up by Beyond and torn away from me. I may walk back in and see what is happening. Evidently, there was no catastrophic explosion. The mountain is still standing. I crawl out of the military-looking vehicle and walk back toward the tunnel.

Someone dressed in dark clothing hides in the dense, heavy shrubs and flowering plants behind the massive Hummer. The big man is breathing quietly. He has been waiting for Bones to come out alone. His broad, gruesome smile makes his handsome face repulsive and threatening when he sees Bones.

I hear a sharp snap, and something slams my right shoulder, and I feel an intense sharp pain. I throw myself to the ground, roll, and look back toward the Hummer. A tall, bulked man is sauntering toward me, smiling confidently as he moves closer. I have never seen a more wicked, depraved smile. Wait, I know him! That is Weber. He worked with Axel in the Neo-Nazi Group in London. I saw him at the lab the night Dr. Mengele went to his eternal reward. Hell! Weber is deadly dangerous. He and the newly deceased Axel tried to kill Angus and nearly succeeded. I must play this well, or I will not survive to see David again, and he will be ticked!

He smiles broadly, leering, and says, "Well, hello, pretty lady. We meet again. I see why David and the others keep you around. You are a sexy little thing. I like those red high heels. I am here to find my mate Axel, sweetie. I know he came here and never returned to our local base. I am sure you will help me." His mocking tone suddenly changes to a deadly, menacing growl. "Tell me where Axel is—now! If you don't, I will enjoy putting a bullet in your head!" He snarls like a wild animal as he says, "bullet in your head." He is buzzed by intimidating me, and I guess he is on a drug of some sort. Since he is bulked, I would venture he is using anabolic steroids, which can cause mood swings and aggression. Great! I am face to face with a psychopath on anabolic steroids.

He gushes, "I know you want to get to know me better. Women are always chasing after me. So, I want to find Axel. Your shoulder will be fine. Don't worry about it. We can make a bargain, sweetie. You tell me about Axel, and I will be really nice to you." Guess again, moron, I am furious and accelerating toward viciousness, but I keep my expression neutral. He mustn't see me as a threat. My gun is at my back and under my sweater. I can't reach it. He could shoot me before I can twist around. Damn!

I doubt he will just kill me, or he couldn't learn anything about Axel's fate. I suppose I could tell him that Axel is in Hell with Mengele.

Nah, not yet. OK, Big Boy, I plan to help you join their party. That is a promise! He rushes toward me and roughly grabs me, hurting my wounded shoulder. The pain is excruciating! I will not yell and give him the satisfaction of knowing he hurt me. He shoves me toward the tunnel, and I almost trip in my high heels. I must be patient and wait for an opportunity to grab my gun.

He looks into the tunnel and starts screaming like a little girl. I am startled by his bizarre behavior. I had been looking at Weber. Now, I whirl toward the tunnel. OH My God! I fall to the ground when I see what terrifies the wimp. It is Father Antonio, and he is hovering above the tunnel floor. He sternly commands Weber, "Leave this place immediately and do not return! Leave at once! How dare you try to harm this girl! The Gates of Hell are opening for you, Sinner! Be gone in the name of our Lord Jesus Christ!" I can't believe this surreal scene.

The Padre is waving his arms above his head, holding his magnificent blazing silver cross. He is marvelous to behold in his flowing black robes. I can picture him blowing a trumpet on Judgement Day. Weber finally stops screaming and stumbles toward the woods, waving his gun and scaring a brown bear away. He doesn't realize he can't outrun divine judgment. I turn back toward my beloved Padre. He looks at me with the light of Heaven shining in his eyes and whispers, "My beloved child, that monster will trouble you no more. Be at peace, my child. Do not be fearful, for we shall meet again soon. I shall hold you in my arms and soothe you." He disappears into the blackness of the tunnel!

I scream to him, "Please come back, Father Antonio! Please, I miss you terribly. I have your favorite Earl Grey tea!" I curl up in a ball and cry until my tear ducts dry up. The pain in my shoulder is getting worse, and it is bleeding more freely. I feel feverish and light-headed. Vaguely, I wonder how badly I am hurt, but as I float in and out of consciousness, I don't really care. I am distraught for David. The wound is bleeding more, probably an artery. A puddle of blood ominously soaks into the dirt. Merciful oblivion comes to embrace me, and I gratefully surrender.

Minutes later, an enormous man in a dusty black suit and a bowler hat strides up to Bones and doubles over in pain. His grief is unbearable. Druid is furious with the Team for not protecting her, as he has warned them many times. He screams in frustration, despair, and bitter self-condemnation. The giant knows he should have saved her.

Druid reserves his white-hot rage for Weber and the London Neo-Nazis from which Weber and Axel came. He has not forgotten that the NGA Committee members Annette Simmons-Wright, Juan Diez, Emerson North, and Julian Chan financed the group. He shakes an enormous fist toward heaven and vows," I am coming! I was in your meetings, a dark shadow, watching and hearing your wicked plans. Your judgment is coming. Vile villains, hear me! You cannot hide!" His head hangs low, his shoulders slump forward, and he shakes violently. The Giant treads onward on leaden feet, one wretchedly weary step at a time.

Alpha and Omega look down from the Celestial Palace, see Druid, and weep. They are saddened that Weber, the thug Neo-Nazi, killed the Churchill Team's only mortal. Bones had died again, even after Archangel Michael had made it his primary goal to protect her. Beyond was on her side, yet the Evil One had won this battle. He cannot win the final war, and he knows it.

Chapter Nine

The Plan

The Team returns to the Weapons Room after much back-and-forth-spirited arguing. They decide to let Red gently approach the machine since David had completed the ancient incantation. The question to be answered? Did the incantation work? Was the spell removed? Red is anxious to try anything rather than wait for eternity or many hours. Frustrated by the delay, Red stumbles when he leans over the weapon to examine it. As he falls, he slams down the chrome lever. To everyone's horror, the machine roars to life with loud clatters and deafening rumbles. David and Angus run over to help Red, who is lying on the floor, hitting the unyielding stones with his fists in furious self-condemnation. They gasp when they see the display screen now reads 36 hours. At least it didn't destroy the world. Yet.

The troubled Team looks to Churchill for direction since their situation has worsened substantially. Red is furious with himself for being clumsy, but it was an accident, and nothing can change that. Yes, they are losing the game, and the clock on the scoreboard is running out. David demands a rational path forward. A spirit of chaos and insanity permeates the environment. He scolds the assembled crew, "Agreed, we are in a place of darkness with little to show us the way. This confusion cannot continue, and we know there is a path. We must find it damn quickly! I am ready to act before things go any further asunder. I shall ask Sir Winston to lead us in creating a feasible course of action."

Sir Winston stands. "I will not offer useless platitudes. We are in an incredibly dark place, as David says. Because it is dark, we do not know precisely where we are or what threats confront us. Let's look at what we know: the weapon is fully activated and makes various ominous noises. The countdown was inexplicably cut in half, and it appears that it will activate as per its settings and with terrific force in 36 hours. Evidently, Aaii rigged it to cut the hours to destruction if it was engaged after activation. Aaii's phantom activated it. We assume the destruction will begin with the domino effect of earthquakes and volcanic eruptions in 36 hours. We shall accept Dr. Einstein's theories as fact for now." He nods to Dr. Einstein.

Red is inconsolable as he covers his face with his hands. Angus slaps him on the back to help him remember there is work to be done, mate. It works.

Winston presses, "We do not have the necessary information to disengage the weapon if that is even possible. We must act! Albert and I will return to the Military Archives for more information on this maddening weapon or on its fabled brother. As per our previous conversation, Abigor and Bones will return to London to seek out Admiral Stallings for whatever information he may have to share about either contraption. I wish we could also confer with Druid . . ."

As soon as the words were out of his mouth, Druid burst into the room shouting and gesturing wildly. The guys, stunned by the energy of his assault, just stared at him in amazement. They have seen him furious before, but this is an entirely new level of ferocity, a human tsunami. Druid shouts at them, "About what have I repeatedly cautioned you? What did I command you? Protect the humans! Where is Bones? Do you not know?" He wipes his face with his huge hand to catch the tears before they puddle on the floor. The Team reads the excruciating pain in his face and runs for the tunnel in one massive wave of panic.

Sophie is the first to get to Bones. She begins licking Bones' face and howling in the most pitiful, heartbreaking way. Her howls grow louder and more profound in despair. Within seconds, David drops to his knees beside Bones. He turns her around on her back and gently places her head in his lap. His screams reverberate through the tunnel until rocks fall away from the roof of the passage like great tears. Abigor is in such extreme agony that he cannot respond but stands frozen in a purgatory of emotions. He desperately wants to be the one holding her. He gazes at the woman he loves and tries to avoid exploding into violence—demon violence. He feels the Demon in him rising to the surface, and the evil being is furious! If the person who harmed her were here, he would tear the savage apart even if eternal Hell opened before him.

Sir Winston and Dr. Einstein watch the scene, unsure what to do. Is it too late to do anything? The two brilliant men cannot accept the helplessness and the despair that follows and fight fiercely against it. Red and Angus sit motionless on the ground near David. Rough men are used to danger and ready to fight, but how and with whom? Dr. Einstein breaks out of his inertia and runs to Bones. He puts his hand on her heart, listens intently to her chest, and touches her carotid artery, hoping for a flutter of movement. He sits back on his heels, looks sorrowfully at the waiting men, and gravely shakes his head.

Sophie knows at once and does not need to watch the doctor. She had been focused on solving end-of-the-world issues and momentarily lost track of Bones. She will never forgive herself. David looks at Soph and pleads, "Can't you bring her back again? You did before." It shatters the big Dane to see this rock-solid man begging for the hope she could not give him. Sir Winston firmly lays his hand on David's shoulder. "David my boy, you remember, Sophie cannot bring Bones back again. Sophie warned us about that and urged Bones to be cautious." Sir Winston is choking back tears as he tries to soothe David.

Druid sits beside Dr. Einstein, staring straight ahead in a daze, his emotions depleted by his recent personal nuclear blast. He is exhausted. He shakes his great blonde head, and his brilliant eyes stare at David. "I know the coward who did this, and he will not linger on this earth. I shall settle the debt, David. Please do not doubt that. Righteous anger will be satisfied." He slams the ground in renewed rage.

Druid turns toward Sir Winston, who is now fruitlessly trying to wipe the tears from his face while shaking with fury. Druid addresses the Great Man, "I heard you say you are going to the Military Archives. I shall help you as I did last time, and you shall find what you seek. I can say no more. I am pushing my limits."

David shouts at Druid, "I must go with you! Who did this? I must take my revenge, or I shall never rest. Don't you understand? She was everything to me!" In abject agony, he hangs his head, "I should have saved her. I loved her so . . ." Druid shakes his head sadly, puts his bowler back on, and silently disappears. David yells at Druid. His only answer is the sound of a distant owl echoing David's anguish.

Sir Winston turns to Abigor. "Is there nothing we can do, Abigor? Do you know anything at all? We are desperate. Albert and I must leave soon for the Archives. You will be visiting the Admiral alone unless we can do something to bring Bones back. She was precious to us." He stops momentarily to compose himself before continuing, "Think! Is there anything?"

Abigor tears himself out of his lethargy, "I must consider thine question, so please give me a minute, Sir Winston." After what seems an eternity, he snaps his fingers and says partially to himself, "A long shot. Yes, we must go at once to see Alpha and Omega. They have the power if they wilt only use it." Then to Sir Winston, "Come, we must go! David, we are leaving to consult the Powers."

They were simply gone without another word.

They popped into the magnificent room Sir Winston had so recently visited. The sheer otherworldly beauty is always a shock to one's senses, no matter how many times one sees it. He and Abigor sit down in white chairs to wait for their hosts. Soon, Alpha enters the room in the ether from which he left last time.

They know it is Alpha because he says, "Such a treat to see Winston and Abigor together, especially since I just saw Winston a mere short while ago. Yes, this is a lovely treat. I wish Omega could have joined us. Abigor, how are you doing in your new life as a warrior against evil on Sir Winston's Team?"

Abigor bows slightly and says, "I am pleased to be able to assist the team on our mission to protect the earth. I thank thee for giving me this opportunity."

Alpha turns to Churchill, "Well, Winston, what can we do to help you today? Sadly, Omega had scheduled a meeting with Agatha Christie and her Team. They have been battling vicious thugs with too much power and too little compassion. I am sorry, gentlemen, but I believe a tragic event affected your team. I am sure there has been a death. Bones is such an unfortunate young woman. I believe this is the third time she has died. There was that sad event with the black car, and what was the other death? Oh yes, the garrote. How could I forget? Never mind, just tragic, and how may I help you?" Alpha reaches out his hand and gently pats the former demon's shoulder. He knows, as does Churchill, that Abigor's heart is broken. Still, he must stay strong to help Bones.

Sir Winston takes a deep breath he didn't need and explains, "You are correct, Alpha. Bones was attacked and killed by a Neo-Nazi, We-ber Weber. He shot Bones and left her to bleed to death while we were working to disengage the Doomsday Machine. We blame ourselves for not protecting her. Guilt is a tremendous burden for us to bear. We ask that you allow Sophie, devastated by this loss, to bring Bones back to life. We need Bones on our team. She was the heart of our team and the only living human. She is audacious yet funny, kind, and brave."

Alpha turns his magnificent face to meet Sir Winston's eyes, nods, and sympathizes, "Winston and Abigor, I can feel your deep emotions because you value her greatly. Your heartfelt grief speaks well of you. As discussed, Bones has now died three times, which is rare for humans and indisputably traumatic. We cannot continue to allow her to die every few weeks. It is not healthy for Bones—especially for her psychological well-being. You are at a delicate place in your mission, and I want to be of assistance, as does Omega."

Alpha pauses as if a new thought occurs to him. "I shall do this for your team. Sophie can bring Bones back to life again. Yet, she must be sent back to her former life at the end of your mission, and we will wipe her memory. Of course, she will remember nothing of this life and you. This is for her benefit and ours. We must insist on this provision. What do you say, Winston and Abigor?"

Winston speaks up quickly before Alpha can change his mind, "Yes! Yes, we sincerely appreciate your assistance, Alpha. We will return immediately to tell Sophie. She will be greatly relieved and joyous. Please share our gratitude with Omega, too."

Abigor says nothing and simply bows. When he hears Bones would live, his joy is overwhelming. He trusted Sir Winston to speak for them, the most celebrated diplomat of WWII, which was good enough for him.

They leave.

David refused to leave Bones. He sat there on the cold, unyielding ground with her lifeless body cuddled in his lap. Sophie, still whimpering, put her wet nose to Bones' face.

They all stayed in their places, waiting to hear from Sir Winston and Abigor. A great sadness descended on them like the shadow of an enormous black Condor circling overhead. No one spoke. What was there to say? The only sounds were Sophie whimpering and David weeping softly, with his lips pressed against Bones' glossy raven hair.

Sir Winston and Abigor return finally, both high on rapturous joyfulness. Churchill, smiling ear to ear, says to Soph, "Alpha and Omega have given us a wondrous gift. They granted you the power to bring Bones back one more time. Please do so at once."

Sophie jumps up and yelps in happiness. The huge Dane immediately begins to rub her warm nose on Bones' face. Little by little, she can see Bones' color change. It turns from deathly gray to her natural light brown color, her Native American ancestry ascendant in its dark beauty again.

David is so overwhelmed by exuberance that he is stunned and speechless. Abruptly, Bones sits up, puzzled, and glances up at David, still holding her in his lap. "Sweetheart, why are we sitting on the ground, and why is everyone looking at me? Never mind, I am starving. I must go to the Hummer and raid the picnic basket again." Surprised, she looks around at the men and Sophie. "What is going on? You all look overwrought. Are we in Xanax territory? I bet it is the stupid machine again. What happened?" They crowd around her to give her welcome-home hugs. Bones is genuinely perplexed now.

Red asks her, "How are you feeling, Bones? You look as gorgeous as ever. I can see that with only one good eye."

Bones looks at him and replies, "I feel great Red. Why do you ask?" Red winks at her and strolls toward the tunnel, whistling a jaunty tune. Angus gives her another huge hug as a telltale tear runs down his craggy, Dirty Harry face. Bones is now unquestionably all in for the Xanax prescription.

David hugs Bones close to him and suggests, "Why don't we take a walk after you eat, my love? I have a story to tell you that won't take long. Soon, you and Abigor will visit the enigmatic Admiral and the angelic Miss Dove. Come, sweetheart, let me help you up. Yes, I am sorry, your heel is broken. You brought another pair of red high heels, correct? You understand what is essential to your work. We will get your shoes out of the Hummer, too."

David had never been happier except maybe the first time he gazed into those intense, mesmerizing cocoa eyes with the intriguing gold flecks.

Sir Winston and Abigor walk over to Dr. Einstein, who is so relieved and delighted by Bones' return that he cannot stand still. After Bones and David go to the Hummer, he says to Winston, "What happened? How did you talk them into allowing Sophie to bring our Bones back? I was in despair that they would not assist us. Abigor, you look troubled. What have you not told me yet?"

Abigor nods to Churchill to answer Albert's question. Churchill coughs, clears his throat, and turns serious. "Albert, there are strings . . . Bones will have to leave us after this mission, and her memory will be wiped clean. She will not remember anything since joining us. Worse, much worse, she will not remember the men who love and admire her. The Powers are concerned that her mental stability might be affected because of the numerous traumas she has experienced. They reminded us that she had died three times. They seemed to believe that was an unusual number of deaths for humans. I assured them, as did Abigor, well, he nodded, that she is a lioness. Bones is as tough, if not tougher than any man on this team. That girl has cast-iron grit and boldness." Sir Winston roughly blots his eyes again as tears start to well as he considers the deal they struck.

Abigor said, "They would not relent on the strings, but we want her alive for now. Thank God they granted our request. We wilt argue the details later. We thought it would be better to tell her and the others, especially David, about these, uh, stipulations in yond future. What dost thee think, doctor?"

Dr. Einstein adjusts his jacket, takes out his pipe, and reluctantly agrees, "We must use our few hours well, with as little emotionality as possible. Let us save this sad news, which could change, until after the mission. That said, I cherish truth and transparency. I have always said, 'Whoever is careless with the truth in small matters cannot be trusted with important matters.' However, waiting is now the more rational course to take." The two spirits and the angel shake hands. The die is cast.

Chapter Ten

The Military Archives

Dr. Einstein and Churchill tell the others they are leaving immediately on their mission to the Military Archives and will return as soon as possible. Abigor will wait for Bones to interview the reticent Admiral Stallings. The two elder gentlemen shake hands and take their leave. Seconds later, they are at their destination, the enormous building that houses records from WWII.

They start digging near the file cabinets where they found the Doomsday Machine blueprint. Whoever stored the documents had made little attempt at organization. They find records everywhere, and just because paperwork is in proximity to other documents does not mean the content is related in time or topic. But Druid said he would guide them, so they continue to search. After several minutes, Dr. Einstein pulls out a document from one of the hundreds of WWII-issued gray file cabinets, studies it, waves it in Winston's face, and enthusiastically shouts, "See this, look what I have found! I believe this may be about the Fantastic Machine." The document heading reads,

Top Secret
Owl Mountain

We have been advised that rebellious Jewish Scientists created a machine to counteract the Doomsday Machine, theoretically a horrific weapon capable of tremendous destruction. Our source said the lead researchers were Drs. Rosen and Goldmann but did not give their first names. There is reason to doubt the veracity of this information because he also made an incredible claim. He said the function of the

Rosen and Goldmann device is to take resisters back to the date the Doomsday Machine was programmed, December 23, 1944.

Einstein stops reading and stares open-mouthed at Churchill, astonished by what he has said. The former Prime Minister uses his linen handkerchief to wipe his dusty hands. He shakes his head in doubt. "Albert, this is fanciful and entirely unbelievable. Shall we continue to look?"

The dismissive words do not deter the scientist. "Winston, hear me, I know these names, Rosen and Goldman. They were brilliant scientists focused on the distant future, decades ahead of their time. My research began the entire time travel question when I theorized that speed could affect time. An astrophysicist in America, a professor at the University of Connecticut, has spent his entire career researching scientific equations and principles to make time travel a reality. He is not the only scientist working on time travel. One theory is a bit concerning—time travel may be limited to one direction."

"Yes, we shall keep looking, yet this discovery is highly informative, and I believe it is the data for which we are searching. The plan now merges into something that makes logical sense in a futuristic way, and now I understand why it was called the Fantastic Machine." The document visibly energizes Einstein, evidence that time travel might be fact and not simply science fiction nonsense. Churchill starts chomping on his Cuban cigar and continues to search.

Quite surprisingly, a tornado arises in the room. It begins to circle the office, swirling documents overhead in a paper storm. The two men duck out of surprise, not that evolving paper or anything else could harm them. The room was chaotic before, but now it is in full disaster mode. Documents are piled everywhere in great heaps. As the tornado winds down, a single sheet of paper lands on Dr. Einstein's fedora. He pulls it, squints, and reads:

Top Secret

'This Top-Secret message is for your eyes only; **redacted***, do not share this information with anyone under any circumstances. Be alert for spies posing as loyal Germans, especially to be feared are Churchill's SOE agents. The subject of this intel is the Doomsday Machine.* **URGENT***: You must keep troops away from Owl Mountain in Poland. You know the area to which I refer. You and I were there a few months ago. It is the most powerful weapon ever invented. Its power can cause unimaginable damage, much more than the atomic weapons we are also developing. We have been told by* **redacted** *those two knobs and a lever "control" the machine. Our source is extremely high up in the government and thus well-informed and credible. They emphasized that the machine can be activated under certain unspecified circumstances and cannot be deactivated. If someone pulls the lever, the device may react in unimaginable ways. The hours left before detonation are displayed on the screen.* **Be aware** *that the source said that once activated,* **it cannot be stopped***. Per our source, it will target the vulnerable tectonic plates as it was designed to do. This surge to the plates will impact earthquakes and volcanoes in the target area and then worldwide.* **Under no circumstance is this machine to be found***. It is too destructive and resistant to recalibrating or attempts to destroy it. We are told* **it cannot be destroyed***. This extremely dangerous weapon must be kept a secret, hidden away to protect our country and the entire world. Only two people of whom we are aware, now living, know where the machine is hidden. I am not one of those people. The Fuhrer knows, as does Reichsfuhrer Himmler. Clearly, we see the writing on the wall. Our military efforts to conquer Europe have failed miserably. After you*

read this message, destroy it. We, the two of us, shall discuss this in person next month at the meeting in Berlin if we are still alive. If we are not, well . . . There is another machine I wish to discuss with you, too, which is more fantastic. Do you remember Goldmann? A genius who invented **Redacted***. My source said he might be involved in creating one of these devices. We will plan to fill in the tunnel entrance to the weapon when we meet. There are rumors of an antidote to the poisonous machine. I know nothing about that. That warning may be a reference to the Goldmann invention. Or, another horrific possibility, if God help us, the Fuhrer decides to use the weapon. Heil!*
Destroy after you read this.'
Signed **Redacted**

After reading the top-secret messages, Dr. Einstein's brain skips quantum leaps ahead. Is it possible, and can it be true? He is thrilled by the possibility of a Time Machine. He cannot contain his excitement as he paces across the document-covered floor. He shoves the document in Churchill's face and asks, "Do you see this, Winston? My dream of living to see the day we could travel as freely in time as in our cars on the highways may come true. Well, not exactly living, but you know what I am saying, my friend. We have a name, Goldmann. He was a splendid scientist, and I am not surprised he might have grabbed the gold ring."

The British statesman is not convinced of anything and cautions Einstein, "We have two documents, Albert, with no evidence to prove their authenticity or validity. We are no further along in our investigation than before papers assaulted us. We both know Druid said he would assist us in our search. Thus, I am inclined to believe these are the documents he wanted us to read. If we knew who wrote the messages, we might be able to validate their reliability. We will never find anything of value in this trash heap now. Shall we return to the chamber and share our findings with the others?"

Einstein nods toward Churchill, neatly folds the documents, and puts them away in his jacket pocket. The two geniuses, like old soldiers, fade away.

Chapter Eleven

The Futuristic Machine

After my walk with the jubilant David, I was alarmed and confused. I do not remember anything after going to the Hummer for food. Sophie healed my injury, so I do not even have a scar to make this nightmare feel real. I am overcome with gratitude that so many people genuinely care about me. Their happiness at my unexpected return is heartwarming. Sir Winston and Abigor courageously faced the Powers, one of the Powers, to plead for my life. I cannot begin to express my heartfelt emotions to my friends. I seem to remember little bits and pieces of David sobbing and calling my name. I do not know how that is possible. From what he says, I was playing a harp in the Heavenly orchestra by then. I cannot remember anything about Beyond either. I hope I saw my beloved Padre!

David is an extraordinary man who loves me, making me the luckiest woman ever born. I have a fresh appreciation for my dear gang. David told me how they grieved for me, even Druid. I did not know the giant even liked me. To my shame, I misjudged him. I will do better when we meet again. Dr. Einstein told me, "However rare true love may be, it is less so than true friendship." I saw the pain in his warm brown eyes. His life has been complicated.

I hug David and whisper in his ear, "David, because of you, I laugh a little harder, cry a little less, and smile a lot more." I read that somewhere. I suppose dying for the third time makes one sentimental. Sniff. Sniff.

I hate to leave David again, but we have a world to save. I search for Abigor and find him in the Weapons Room, examining the annoying contraption. When I walk in, he looks up and greets me, "Oh, hello, dear Bones. I am trying to find something we might have missed that gives us a way to neutralize this monster. I cannot imagine this sophisticated technology available to the loathsome beasts in 1944. Yet, obviously, it was. Here it sits. Still, it puzzles me, and I am not comfortable with it. I would be interested to know which scientists worked on this massive project. They must have been the most brilliant minds in the Third Reich. Of course, the Fantastic Machine may be even more highly sophisticated. It appears that we shalt soon find out, Bones. Art thee ready for our journey into the darkness chasing we know not what?" Abigor looks at me with warmth in his extraordinary eyes. I have a new appreciation for the guys, so I smile and accept his friendship without questioning it.

I nibble on my apple with peanut butter and chocolate as I chat with him. "Abigor, we are going to visit Admiral Stallings in London. That is our assignment. I wonder if I could tag along with you rather than flying first class at Beyond's expense. It worked with others. Besides, David flew with me in tow to the airport in Poland when our plane fell apart. It should be safe for me. It certainly didn't kill Franz. Oh, I heard from Dr. Einstein that Franz has passed away, as we would expect, from a heart attack. That century-old faulty ticker finally failed him. I would be sadder if he had not tried to run me down, shoot me, and garrote me to my detriment. If it had not been for Angus, he would have shot me again, too. The murderous cretin! Undoubtedly, he shares war stories with Dr. Mengele and Hans in Hell. It gives me a warm feeling knowing the old deviants are getting the sizzling band back together again." Abigor observed me for a long time without blinking, trying to understand what I was saying. I shrugged.

On consideration, Abigor seems to be genuinely alarmed by my bloodthirsty attitude. He recovers and says, "I think I will drive you to Poznan Airport. We have been there before, and it is near. We can arrange a commercial flight to London that takes less than 4 hours. Beyond can create a powerful tailwind. Indeed, we will have to pull some strings to get thee on a flight. Beyond has its mysterious ways of getting things done. I do not believe the team would be willing to risk your life so soon after just getting you back from beyond the veil. I know David would not, and I do not wish to incur his wrath again. I will meet thee at Heathrow with a rental, and we shalt drive to Old Naval College to meet with the goodly Admiral and his saintly lady. It has been a long time since we chatted with the Ancient Mariner." I reluctantly agree. I want the adventure of traveling on the wind as Abigor does, but I suppose I will have to settle for the wind beneath the wings of a 747. Oh, yes, he is seriously right about David. Abigor reaches out and hugs me to him for just a moment. When he backs away, I see tears. Again, I accept it as the love one feels for a friend.

When we return to the chamber, we are excited to find that Churchill and Einstein have returned from their adventure in the Military Archives. Naturally, we all want to know what wonders they found in the stuffy old building. Churchill perches regally like the royalty he is, on the gold throne, talking to Red, Angus, and David. He shows them one of the two documents they found. Einstein practically hops with joy over the document he grasps in his hand. I want to know about that one! Churchill carefully explains the Doomsday Machine intel and the challenges we will encounter. "Gentlemen and Bones, we now have rather reliable information that the Machine cannot be controlled or turned off."

Red is more scarlet than ever before, certainly feeling guilty about engaging a weapon that could destroy our planet and kill all life forms. Actually, he only cut the time. The weapon was already activated. Still, my guilty secrets shrink in comparison. Sir Winton doesn't notice Red's discomfort and continues, "According to the document, which we assume Druid put in our path, there is nothing we can do to stop the weapon's impact. Nonetheless, we cannot drown in negativity. The document says there is a remedy to the monster contraption. I shall ask Albert to tell you about that, uh, interesting information." We turn toward Dr. Einstein and give him our focused attention. I feel like I am in the front row of a blockbuster movie. My brain is tingling in anticipation. David puts his arm around my shoulders and the rest of me tingles.

Dr. Einstein jumps up, pipe in hand, eager as a scientist with a new theory to tell us about every single detail of the fantastic machine. He hands the document around, and I must say with complete confidence that we were blindsided. H.G. Wells? Time Machine? The Fantastic Machine is a time machine? I cannot argue with the adjective "fantastic" that I assumed was merely hyperbole. In fact, I would say fantastic is not nearly hyperbolic enough. We all start shouting questions at once, except Sir Winston and David. I know Churchill is skeptical, and David is always suspicious without indisputable evidence. Dr. Einstein raises his hand, "Please, one question at a time. I am afraid I do not have inexhaustible answers. I have this one document, and I plan to research the scientists. Therefore, it is possible I may know more soon. Bones, you shall go first. What is your question?"

In fact, I don't have a question. I have only a "you have got to be kidding me!" exclamation! I thought for a minute, trying to process what I had just heard, and asked, "Do you know these scientists, Dr. Einstein? Are they legitimate scientists capable of such extraordinarily advanced work? If this technology is available, if they managed this monumental feat, why has no one else done it?"

The Genius wipes his glasses clean, ponders, and answers, "Dear Bones, your questions are excellent. I know of them and their reputations. They are undoubtedly brilliant and innovative. I met Goldmann twice at conferences. Rosen, I know only by reputation. I wish I had an answer to your questions—if they can create a time machine, why has that feat not been repeated? It could have been a fluke, and that fluke has never come together again. You would be surprised how often luck or, perhaps, divine intervention provides the spark for marvelous discoveries. Look at the discovery of penicillin. If there is a time machine, the knowledge may be locked up in the Dark World and has never seen the light of day. I assume the two scientists are long dead because I have heard nothing about them since WWII."

He grins and adds, "I was somewhat indisposed from 1955 until recently." He shrugs and finishes, "I regret I have only suppositions for you, Bones." He grits his teeth as he says the distasteful word suppositions. If the great genius Einstein cannot answer my question, there is no answer.

He looks at me as he pushes his startling white hair out of his face, "I will investigate the scientists to determine when and if they died. They were relatively young when I knew Goldmann. I suppose there is a slight chance one of them is still alive. If not, I will look for other scientists who knew them. Also, there may be research notes somewhere. Truthfully, Bones, I doubt the Nazis would have allowed the scientists to live if they participated in such a world-changing discovery. Their incredible breakthrough has been called an antidote for the Doomsday Machine. That implies Goldmann and Rosen developed it to stop the Nazis. We do not know if they had access to the Time Machine, if it indeed exists, or if they created it for this precise reason. Neither possibility would have been prudent."

David sits back, listening and grimacing. His handsome face says, he is unconvinced. He crosses and recrosses his long legs, an unmistakable sign that David is exasperated and growing restless. He sits on the edge of his chair. He says, "Dr. Einstein, respectfully, we are spending precious time discussing something extraordinary that may not, probably does not, exist while our time continues to evaporate before our eyes. We are down to a terrifyingly short 30 hours until detonation. Our time might be better spent determining how to stop the monster weapon. Just because an intel document from psychopathic liars states the timer cannot be stopped does not mean it is a fact. Significantly, that information was from an anonymous source. I prefer to work on neutralizing the weapon while anyone who wishes to do so can chase a time machine." I understand what our ever-grounded former MI5 Deputy Director-General thinks. David will rule out all the ponies before he starts looking for a unicorn. Red and Angus are nodding their MI5 agent heads in agreement. I am torn because I believe in Dr. Einstein and his excellent brain.

Strangely, I shudder as I remember that a surgeon removed the good doctor's brain during his autopsy. Beyond evidently replaced it for him before sending him to save the world. His original brain waits patiently in a jar at the National Museum of Health and Medicine and the Mutter Museum in Philadelphia.

I also believe in Sir Winston's ability to make excellent decisions and his intuitive critical thinking skills. David, Red, and Angus are intelligent, capable men. In most cases, I would side with them, especially David. For whatever reason, call it psychotherapist's sixth sense. I am leaning toward Dr. Einstein's Time Machine theory. Abigor listened carefully, nodding when he concurred, but did not express an opinion. I notice he is looking at me, probably wondering where I stand in this battle of the geniuses. He silently moves over to me and whispers in my ear. I can feel his warm breath on my skin, "Bones, I thinketh thou side with Dr. Einstein, and I agree. I knoweth the Time Machine exists. I can envision an image of it in my brain as if I have seen it before somewhere. That is not possible. Is it? We must leave soon to discuss this fantastic machine with Admiral Stallings. He knoweth something. I can feel it." David observes us and stalks over to see what dangerous mischief Abigor might be trying to get me involved in.

David puts his arm around me, hugs me, and then suggests, "I suppose it is time for you and Abigor to take a trip to the Old Royal Naval College and visit our favorite Ancient Mariner. He will be able to help understand what is going on with these bloody machines! I shall work on the monster weapon with Red and Angus to determine if we can open it. It was opened and closed at one time. Why not now? Dr. Einstein will work on his project. We shall see what we can bring together to solve our problem." Incredibly sexy lips kiss mine and leave me reeling. He winks at me and returns to Red and Angus. Still swaying, I wave to them.

Dr. Einstein will begin his research on the two scientists, Goldmann and Rosen. He is determined to learn more about the mysterious machine and patch together a likely scenario. I whisper to him, "I am confident you will prevail, sir." He just wiggles his eyebrows at me. Giggle.

Abigor and I tell Sir Winston we are leaving for Poznan Airport. The Great Statesman wishes us Godspeed and sends his respect and regards to his old friend Jeffrey Stallings. They have known each other for eighty years or longer. Churchill has great admiration for the courageous Admiral. He and his intrepid boat crew saved many doomed Jews from Hitler during WWII. He was also one of the Captains in the Miracle of Dunkirk boat rescue of hundreds of thousands of Allied service members.

Chapter Twelve

Professor Otto

I told Abigor I need to buy food while at Poznan Airport to replace the food the Padre and I ate. I want sandwiches, fruit, coffee, tea, and desserts to last 30 hours. After that, it won't matter. I will be dead if we don't find a way to stop the hideous weapon. It is rare for human beings to know how many hours they have before they stop living. I can't say I am thrilled about foreknowledge.

Abigor has been particularly quiet since we left the tunnel, and I want to discuss a plan to tackle our sailor (who reminds me of Clark Gable) when we reach the Old Royal Naval College. I lean over and break the unnatural silence. "Abigor, what are your thoughts on approaching the Admiral?" Confused, He stares at me, "Bones, I doth not know what thee ask. The Admiral is not a man who can be led and certainly not pushed. When speaking with us, he will rely on his intelligence, experience, and instinct. We are at the mercy of his generosity to help us as much as possible. Historically, he has been generous, considering his constraints. One doth not play fast and loose with the Powers in Beyond. We owe much to that goodly man and his lady."

I am not pleased to hear we cannot influence the Admiral to help us with essential information to complete our mission. Realistically, he may not know anything useful. These damnable machines seem to have been secret squirrel stuff to which no living person is privy. Come to think of it, most of our Team members and Stallings are not alive.

We arrive at Poznan Airport and check in to see if my ticket to Heathrow is waiting for me. The chic red-haired lady with bright green glasses at the Lot Polish Airlines desk looks at her computer screen under my name and finds a ticket. She prints the ticket and points me in the direction of Security. Joanna, her name tag tells me, suggests I head to security with my one small carry-on bag and purse and assures me they will help me. Abigor will take my food provisions back to the chamber after he returns the Hummer to the National Car Rental desk while I deal with Security. That may sound simple for the average person. Alas, airport security agents worldwide have been a problem for me in the past. No matter how many highly suspicious-looking men appear, they pass through the process without anyone giving them a second glance. Agents stop me and demand I take off my belt, shoes, and hat if I wear one. They have OCD in looking through my carry-on and purse, prompting me to muse to myself about what might transpire should I pack nothing but frilly, lacey, transparent panties someday. Then, I am patted down by several agents. They always seem desperately disappointed that I am not a significant player in illegal drug cartels in various terrorist countries. I asked David about this issue. He has been in intelligence for seventy years. So, David, why me? His reply was incomprehensible. "Don't wear leather." What? Leather?

I am lucky today as there are only two agents on duty. A tall, middle-aged male resplendent in his official blue uniform and a blonde female agent who looks acutely alert, constantly scanning the area. They are the only ones handling the crowd passing through security today. Oddly, I feel neglected when they tell me to continue my journey, and they hope I enjoyed my stay in beautiful, historic Poland. Then, I see Abigor standing on the other side of the metal rail that separates security from the rest of the airport, observing the show. Hmmm, I wonder if I just had a little divine intervention.

After successfully navigating security, the ticket agent told me to go to Gate number 22. Abigor carries my bag to the Gate, placing an avuncular kiss on my forehead. He advises me, as Sir Winston always does, to be cautious, be aware of my surroundings, and not to be bold.

They are exhausted from constantly bringing me back from behind the dark veil. He reminded me that he would pick me up at Heathrow in a rental car, and we would drive to the Old Royal Naval College as soon as I landed. Abigor assures me that Beyond has arranged my flight back, which will be an effortless pleasure. Right. I have been with the team too long to believe in sweet fairytales.

They call my plane as I arrive at Gate 22. The voice on the intercom shouts, "The flight to Heathrow in London is loading passengers now." Fortunately, they shout out directions in both Polish and English. My Polish is a bit rusty. I run down the cattle chute to the waiting jet. A tall, brunette young woman in a navy-blue uniform and a matching smart blue hat stands back to allow me to enter. She closes the door behind me. I peer at the ticket for the first time and am shocked to see I will sit in first class! I thought Beyond would be thrifty (vow of poverty and all that) and put me in the economy section, barely inside the plane. I look at my seat number and see I am next to the window, the second row on the right. The older man in the aisle seat stands and bows slightly as he lets me in. I apologize for inconveniencing him. He looks down at a large book in his lap. I suspect he is quite elderly, or, I suppose, he could have been in a rock band like Mick Jagger. His hair is purest white, and his skin is weathered and wrinkled, perhaps because of enduring life's frequent storms. I sit down and put my small bag under the seat in front of me. I learned a long time ago to travel light, and all I need to carry are jeans, red high heels, and a black T-shirt or sweater. I keep a change of red underwear, a toothbrush, a giant Snickers bar, a brush, lipstick, and a nightgown in my oversized leather purse, just in case.

After I settle in, I take another look at my traveling companion. I would guess he is in his late eighties. He must feel my gaze on his face because he turns toward me and smiles. His smile is contagious, and I grin back. His eyes are the palest shade of Robin's eggs blue. I see keen intelligence and a naughty twinkle in those light eyes. I introduce myself to my new bud. "Hello, I am your seatmate, Bones."

I hold my hand out to shake. He shakes my hand and asks, "Bones, did you say Bones, young lady?" I laugh and nod. He teases, "An odd name for someone so pretty. My name is Otto Wolffe, and I am honored to meet you, Fraulein Bones. I look forward to learning more about you on our sojourn together. So, tell me, what do you do? No, let me guess. You are a journalist on television." I laugh again. Otto is absolutely delightful. "No, I am a psychotherapist in the United States, and I am visiting friends in London and Poland. So, tell me, Mr. Wolffe, what do you do? OK, let me guess, you are an international jewel thief looking for wealthy Countess Agnes and her million-dollar emerald necklace? I bet the police on several continents are hot on your trail!"

Pleased by my guess, he cheerfully tells me he is a scientist. This is quite a coincidence since scores of scientists populate my current cataclysmic mission. I stopped believing in coincidences long ago after Dr. Einstein told me, "Coincidence is God's Way of remaining anonymous." I believe in the Good Doctor and am determined to learn more about this intriguing scientist. His last name drew my attention, too. Another coincidence? I push a wayward strand of hair out of my face, smile, and inquire, "I have always been fascinated by science. I almost opted to be a biologist instead of a psychotherapist. My favorite professor taught biology in undergraduate school. Oddly enough, he was of German heritage and named Otto. In what area of science are you involved, sir?" Everything I said was true, but those tidbits are not why I am so interested in his area of expertise. He chuckles and replies, "Bones, you should have stayed with science. It is the language of the gods. I have spent 78 years immersed in research to understand Dr. Albert Einstein's Theory of Relativity and where that takes us in this universe and perhaps farther. I had some of the best professors in the world at Humboldt University in Berlin. I sincerely believe we were on the edge of amazing discoveries. Then, that horrible war happened. Hitler happened!"

Suddenly, I am all ears. Humboldt University is why I am sitting on this plane, in this seat, next to Otto on my way to London. I resumed learning about Otto and sipped the diet root beer the flight attendant gave me. "Your career following Dr. Einstein's world-changing theory sounds thrilling. He is one of my favorite geniuses. If I may ask, what discoveries were you pursuing?" The elder scientist is getting more enthusiastic by the moment as we discuss his lifelong passion.

Our conversation is interrupted by the uniformed flight attendant I saw when I boarded. She cheerfully serves a delicious meal of Bigos and Golbkis, a wonderful cabbage dish served on real plates. She had covered our trays with white linen napkins, and now, with a magician's flourish, she removed the napkins to reveal our gourmand-worthy meal. I thank her effusively because I am overwhelmed. Generally, in my air travels, dinner is a pack of peanuts thrown in my general direction.

After our mouth-watering repast, we return to chatting. It is a pleasure to see Otto enjoying our conversation so much. He picks up his book and says, "Do you see this book, Bones?" He doesn't wait for an answer since it is rather obvious that I see it. He pushes on, "This discovery answers many fantastic questions. I know that sounds unbelievable to you. Yet it is true. It was written by two geniuses who trained my favorite professors in the 1940s. The university published the book and never made it available to anyone outside the system. I think the loathsome Nazis prohibited its distribution. I wondered why they feared this book, but I don't have an answer for that question." I have an answer: the Fantastic Machine and its world-saving task. Now is not the time to go into that with the friendly professor.

Otto overlooks my hyper-vigilance as he pages through the book and continues his story. "It was buried under other books in a closet at the University. I found it a couple of weeks ago when I searched for something else. Although I have the honor of being a Professor Emeritus at Humboldt, I seldom teach anymore. Let us be honest, Bones. I am no longer young, and my time on this planet is short."

At this comment, I think to myself, *you have no idea, professor. Don't feel bad. We will all go together.* Oblivious to my thoughts, he continues, "I want to use my time in research, not teaching. A few students are interested, but most look at their ridiculous phones. But I digress. Where was I? Oh, yes, I was asking if you see this book?"

He hands the book to me. It is in German, so seeing it didn't help me much. I am startled when I saw the authors' names, Fredrick Rosen and Erick Goldmann. Well, we know their first names now. The title is *Zeit und Raum*. The sweet professor continues, "I have not finished reading it, but it essentially says that Einstein's time and space theory led to a new understanding of the concepts of past, present, and future. They reasonably say that only something in the past can cause something in the present, and only something in the present can cause something in the future. They also theorized that if it were possible to send out signals faster than the vacuum speed of light, we could receive information from the future and send data into the past. As you clearly understand, Bones, this is the basic foundation of time travel. Sending information into the future is time travel. It does not have to be a human. Recently, scientists at the University of Queensland said time travel is possible according to their calculations." He looked at me as Dr. Einstein often has looked at me, expecting a light to come on, only to find me one filament short of a bulb's illumination.

I shake my head and bravely admit." I have no idea what you are talking about, Professor. I must have been sick and missed that class." He stares at me for several seconds without blinking.

Finally, he says, "Bones, I think it is better you became a psychotherapist." My feelings are not easily hurt, so I burst out laughing. I pat his hand and tell him, "I am delighted to be a counselor." If he thinks time travel is complicated, he should try understanding the human brain. Of course, I don't mention my part-time job as a superhero—well, sorta.

Shock! Something catches my eye across the aisle. Big Soph sits in the window seat. She wears goggles, a red scarf, and an obsolete pilot helmet. Yes, I am as amazed as I get. Otto follows my glance and does not react. Evidently, I am the only one who sees her. Whew, that is a relief. Soph nods, does a thumbs up, grins at me, and then turns to look at the clear aquamarine sky beyond her window. Otto asks me if something is wrong, and I don't answer: 'Only a ghost, Great Dane, dressed as Snoopy.' I take a deep breath and stop myself from laughing hysterically like a lunatic. Barely.

With great effort, I gather my wits. So, now we have a link to Rosen and Goldmann and the book they wrote. Dr. Einstein will have to take possession of the book, and we don't have much time to do it. That means Abigor and I will have to kidnap, well, not precisely kidnap, more moderately, appropriate, the good Professor and take him back to Poland. I hope Abigor has an idea for that little challenge. Otto may know more than he realizes, and once the super scientist starts questioning him, we may learn more. My plan is beginning to sound like a crime spree. In our favor, we are running out of minutes. Abigor will have to transport us the way he and the guys travel. We don't have the time to fly commercial.

I decide to change the subject and gently pounce. "Professor, why are you traveling to London today? Do you live there now or have family in the UK? I am meeting a couple of friends in London to discuss a mission. We live in London most of the time, and I traveled to Poland to study an anomaly with my team. A team member is picking me up at Heathrow. I am confident he would be happy to take you with us." Otto is cheered by my invitation. He was not looking forward to finding a 'hackney carriage' in crowded London. At my perplexed look, Otto enlightens me. A hackney carriage means a taxicab. He doesn't have tremendous confidence in my intelligence at this point in our relationship.

The professor straightened his askew purple tie and answered, "I am going to London to talk to a group of scientists at Imperial College who are incredibly interested in seeing this book." My 'red flag' meter goes up. OK, call me paranoid, but you have not experienced my degree of monsters in your life. He is enthusiastic, thinking about their eager anticipation. "Yes, Bones, they are breathlessly waiting to read this extraordinary book. I can't go into what they said, but it is my life's dream."

We must learn who knows about the book and if the Neo-Nazis could have discovered its existence. I keep my voice neutral as I probe. "Professor, I am sure the reality of the book is a thrilling development in your professional circle. Undoubtedly, everyone wants to see it, write a paper on it, and discuss it with you." He is enthused about the book and its extreme rarity and gushes, "Honestly, I have not shared it with many in my professional circle. I shared it with two old and dear colleagues at university, my brother in London, and my department's head. Dr. Schmitt was as amazed as I was to see what may become the Rosetta Stone in our field. I have not shown it to anyone. I merely spoke to them about it." He continues to try to outwit his tie.

I jump in my seat when he says the name Schmitt. I know that name, Hans Schmitt, the other Mengele colleague who died trying to kill me. I wonder whether this could be a relative of my favorite blood-thirsty centenarian Nazi? Perhaps a younger brother. And what about the Professor and his name? Again, the possibility of a younger brother? I don't think either had children, but I cannot be sure. OK, stop, Bones. Your imagination is running amuck.

Otto observes me as I tune out, internally digesting this explosive information. However, I don't have time for an extensive analysis. It won't matter unless we survive the next (I stare at my watch) 27 hours. My heart palpitations are booming, and that very organ is threatening to escape the confines of my chest. Ouch!

Abigor will help decide how best to handle this eleventh-hour treasure trove of information. He can contact Dr. Einstein and Sir Winston for impressive wisdom and instructions.

Bones does not see a dark shadow on the wall separating the cabin from the cockpit. The Shadow travels to New York but will help guard Bones until Abigor takes over when they land in London. The Shadow has a promise to keep with a group of elite troublemakers who finance Neo-Nazis and other destructive misfits. One of the London Neo-Nazis killed Bones, and he promised David that righteous retribution was coming. He knows Weber Weber will be at their meeting. Perfect.

Chapter Thirteen

Seth and the Vultures

NGA Committee members Annette Simmons-Wright, Juan Diez, Emerson North, and Julian Chan meet in Seth's cold and sterile office to celebrate. The office could serve as a morgue with little redecorating. No personal items warm the frosty scene, and no photographs of loving family members clutter his desk. The glaring white is unbroken by cheery colors, and except for a few rugs, his art choices are modern and morbid. The artwork conveys the harshness and finality of death and dying. Seth has quite the macabre sense of humor and often chuckles when he looks at the pricy pieces of art. One wonders why Seth would be at home in such a ghoulish atmosphere. One would be right to wonder.

Seth's willowy executive assistant, Heather, strides into the room in her 5-inch heels and brings elegant grilled tomatoes, chevre, thyme baguette sandwiches, and Dom Perignon Champagne. She serves each guest on bone china plates, pours champagne into crystal goblets, and leaves sandwiches and several bottles of champagne in case members want refills.

After they partake in the pricy delicacies, Juan, the darkly handsome television personality posing as a journalist, takes the floor. He is resplendent in his costly black Zegna suit and Versace V leather shoes. He enthusiastically shouts for himself and his topic, "We have finally come to the finish line in our enormous task. I don't believe any other group of individuals could have accomplished the transformation of nations around the globe as we have. Dr. Herman Wagner tells us he is on the brink of cloning the heart and soul of our movement, Adolf Hitler. Wars are breaking out in countries we have manipulated from behind the curtain of secrecy. We have bribed politicians and influenc-ers to do our bidding. The Demon Aaii has the power to depopulate much of the planet. Only the fake Churchill group has been able to hinder us in reaching our ambitious goals." Juan stops for effect. His audience scowls upon hearing the hated name. He returns to his topic. "I am pleased to announce we have pushed them against the ropes! Weber Weber from the London Neo Nazi camp reports he has recently eliminated one of their members. No, I did not stutter. His name is We-ber Weber. I suggest not mentioning that to him. He is sensitive about his name. I have been told he is also a psychopath. Be assured that I am inclusive and not biased against psychopaths. I only warn you for your continued good health. I am excited to announce that Weber will join us later in the meeting to tell us the details of his adventure. Sadly, the news is not all good. The London Neo Nazis lost their esteemed leader, Axel Fischer, who was murdered in a battle with David, a dan-gerous member of Churchill's team. Weber will tell you more about that, too." Everyone looks aghast. They grimace and make little tut, tut sounds upon hearing the monster Axel has been lost to their world.

"Seth, will you tell us about the devastation in the world econ-omy?" After hearing Juan's delicious news, Annette, Emerson, and Julian applaud and laugh. Seth stands, brushes crumbs from his Ralph Lauren navy-blue suit jacket, and holds up his hand to silence them. There is something about Seth. Something menacing emanates from him like a troubling scent that makes one's nose tickle. He outclassed Juan, leaving him behind in the dirt with his Lucchese Baron Alligator boots. His boots cost thousands of dollars, but he was pleased with the free shipping.

He smiles his friendliest snarl and winks at the members. He is now in financial mode. "I will hit on the worst of the worst issues in the world economy. Lebanon's horrific financial woes have not been seen in one hundred and fifty years. A supply chain crunch that we thought to be temporary will continue for quite some time worldwide. Venezuela, Zimbabwe, and Sudan are supposed to be at a high misery level. The international pandemic lockdowns cost trillions of dollars and caused the worst recession since the Great Depression. With shocking news over the horizon, housing markets are in flux with significantly higher prices, higher interest rates, and a scarcity of building materials. Inflation is out of control in the United States. Food prices are squeezing the poor, as are the highest prices for gas in our history and the world's peak medication costs. I have mentioned only the highlights, and the world economy is worsening. Soon, it will collapse, and we can buy anything we want for pennies. We have had spectacular success. Bribing politicians to vote with us has paid off richly."He stops to enjoy the moment and chuckles—what a wit. He wipes his eyes and continues, "We have reason to celebrate the chaos we created, which will enrich us and further our political agenda. Again, the worldwide economic crisis will only worsen as the months pass. Let's drink to that! Weber will be here soon and has exciting details to share." Right on cue, Heather calls Seth to tell him Weber has arrived. Annette, Julian, Emerson, and Juan clap appreciatively.

Heather escorts Weber into the office, licks her lips, and withdraws as silently as a wraith. Everyone stares at Weber partly because he is a bear of a man, tall and bulked by an obscene obsession with the gym. Meds probably play a part in his bulk and his fits of rage. With his slicked-back blonde hair, hazel eyes, and chiseled features, he is a remarkably desirable man if one ignores his reptilian glare. His suit reminds Seth of Tommy Lee Jones in Men in Black. Seth does not know that is the London Neo Nazis' uniform, except for the lower-ranking members who wear WWII Nazi uniforms when on duty.

Seth introduces Weber to his guests. "We have been waiting for Mr. Weber to arrive, and here he is. Please introduce yourselves." Everyone stands to say hello and shake hands with the psychopathic killer. Annette is visually drooling as she shakes Weber's manly hand. The men are both fascinated and repelled by him. Seth asks Weber if he would tell them what happened to Capt. Fischer.

Weber seems uncomfortable addressing the small group of sophisticated people. He looks like he wants to drag one foot and say, "Ah shucks." He wipes sweating palms on his black pants and stammers, "Uh, yeah, they got Capt. Fischer. He was a good guy, well, not good, but he could shoot. You know what I mean? We think David, the guy in the bomber jacket, got him. David is one bad dude! We found Axel's body with a hole between his eyes. He was dead before he fell. But I got even! I killed the woman, Bones. I shot her, and she was bleeding out when I left. Some spooky guy in black robes, who was floating about three feet off the ground, came after me and I left in a hurry. I was finished anyway." His audience is enjoying the ghoulish tale and wondering about his sanity. Psychopath, remember . . .

Abruptly, the room turns pitch black, though there is bright daylight outside. Everyone screams! Lightning zigzags all over the room, making a thunderous crackling noise as each bolt whizzes past. They cry out in abject terror! Chillingly, a booming, chainsaw voice bellows, "Weber, you tried to kill Bones! You Godless creature! The rest of you were cheering him on! Yes, you were! You will not survive your wickedness and depravity. I shall end that! Your time is brief before the Sword of Righteous Retribution smites you. You will not know the day or the hour of your destruction, but verily, I am coming for you! If you have a soul, fall on your knees and pray for salvation. It may not be too late for some of you. I will be back! Watch for me when the night is the darkest. I am His Sword!"

Mass hysteria follows. They run toward the door, knocking and shoving each other in their haste to escape their Armageddon. Annette is trampled underfoot but manages to rise to her feet, shod with unstable heels, and shakily stumbles out. Their screams echo off the walls as they run helter-skelter for shelter.

Heather sticks her head in the door after they have fled and asks Seth if he is safe.

She is shocked to see Seth laughing hysterically. He waves at her to close the door.

Seth sits at his enormous desk, rumbling in a drawer, and finds a Cuban Cigar and a silver match holder. He sits back in his lush ergonomic chair, lights his cigar, puts it to his nose, sniffs in the aroma, puts it in his mouth, and takes a lusty drag. He glances up, and in front of his desk stands a giant with wavy blonde hair in a weathered black suit and a bowler hat. Seth stands up, bows to the giant, and reverently crosses himself. Druid touches the tip of his hat, nods, and walks out through a wall.

Druid is headed to London to help Abigor and Bones with the professor and his fantastic book.

Chapter Fourteen

The Admiral

Our plane finally arrived at Heathrow. After waiting for our turn to exit the aircraft, the Professor and I disembark and walk down the cattle chute into the crowded international airport. We make our way through the crowd toward the central area, which is open to travelers who have yet to go through security or visitors waiting to pick up passengers. Sophie is walking in front of us in her Snoopy outfit. The immortal Dane has flair. No one sees her, and I know this because there is no mad rush for the exit doors. We wander around, looking for Abigor. I see his gorgeous eyes before I see his face. He runs over to greet us and takes the professor's bag, including the book. Naturally, he knows precisely who Professor Wolffe is and why I have committed a subtle kidnapping. I introduce them, and Abigor, always the perfect gentleman, shakes the scholarly elder man's hand and welcomes him to London. Abigor looks young but is more senior than the professor by eons.

The professor is charmed by Abigor. He takes a seat for a moment's rest after our hike and looks at the angel. "I am so pleased to meet you, Herr Abigor. It is kind of you to offer a ride to a stranger in this magnificent country. Fraulein Bones assured me you would be hospitable. I am grateful for your assistance getting to my destination since I do not know the city." Abigor puts his hand on the good professor's shoulder and presses down slightly, and Otto sways and rubs his eyes with his hands. I am baffled by what is happening to Otto. Abigor and I step a couple of feet away, and I ask him what just happened. He confides with a lowered voice, "It is a technique for helping a mortal relax. He will come with us now and not realize he had not planned to do so all along. The technique will last for 24 to 48 hours. He can accompany us to visit the good Admiral because he will remember little that happens in this altered state."

I am still concerned about the Professor and probe further, "Abigor, is this a technique you can perform as an angel, or is it left over from your demon days?" He laughs at me and answers, "Our heavenly stupor wilt not harm the goodly gentleman. We, messengers of God, use it for the mortal's welfare in cases such as this. We know naught about the men he was going to meet. Verily, yes, I know about that plan, and it also raised red flags with me. He art safe with us, but we must quickly take him and the book to Dr. Einstein. I shalt confer with the geniuses about travel arrangements to Poland since our time is precious. Thou ought not to worry, dear Bones. I shalt not harm him. I have sent Dr. Einstein a message and await his reply. Now, shalt we drive over to see Admiral Stallings and his lady? I borrowed a friend's 1939 Rolls Wraith for our short trip. Come, we must go!" Angels have friends?

That gets my attention. Another 1939 Rolls-Royce shows up in our story. David had a 1939 Rolls Phantom before he died, and the Director-General of MI5 wrecked that gorgeous car, killing himself in the process.

I turn to the Professor and urge, "Professor, are you ready to leave now? Abigor will carry your bag. Is there anything you need before we leave the airport? Food? Coffee? I would be happy to get whatever you need." He answers my query, "I am fine, Fraulein Bones. Thank you for asking. You are truly kind. I am getting a little hungry, so perhaps we should eat dinner soon. Also, for some reason, I am quite sleepy." I sent the food I bought at Poznan with Abigor, and it is waiting for my new friend Otto and me at our temporary headquarters in Poland. I hand the Professor the large size Snickers bar from my bag. I must say, I appreciate and miss the luxury and comfort of our suite at the London

Savoy more every day. I still feel guilty about the whole Vulcan nerve pinch thing.

We escort the now compliant Professor Otto to the magnificent 39 Rolls Royce and store our bags in the back seat with him. I will say one thing about my job: the cars are extraordinary! The dear man has enough room for colleagues from the Physics Department at Humboldt University back there. He seems fine, and I don't see anything I should concern myself about. His eyes are clear, he walks well, and he understands and answers my questions appropriately. I suppose I could ask him the date and the name of the German Chancellor.

I keep a close eye on Otto in the backseat, and soon he falls asleep. My comfort level with the nerve pinch is still low, and I need more clarity. "Abigor, how long will this voodoo thing last? Are you sure it is only one or two days? Will it leave any permanent, residual side effects? Otto seems well, other than being hungry and sleepy."

Abigor glances at me while still trying to navigate through London traffic alertly and reassures me. "The Professor is fine, and he will have no adverse effects now or later, dear Bones. That is more than thee can say about many commonly used medications and alcohol. Otto will be compliant, but other than that, his memory is intact before and after his visit with us. His cognitive abilities art not affected. The 'voodoo' will pass soon. But I am more concerned about the time we need to complete our mission. We have 24 hours before we succeed in our mission, or thee and the rest of humanity will cease to exist."

My heart skips a beat as it always does when the reality of our calamitous situation is pressed in my face. We are almost at the Old Royal Naval College. Suddenly, I am incredibly anxious to get there and question the Admiral about the Doomsday Machine. I cannot believe I am also thinking about the strong possibility of a time machine. Hopefully, we will soon learn from these geniuses if we have their permission to ride the wind to return to Poland since flying a 747 is out of the question. I see no other option.

As we park at the college, I am again amazed by the beauty of the surrounding area. The campus sits snuggled up to the Thames River. Gardens and parks with lush plantings are everywhere the eye wanders. I wish I had time to enjoy it. More importantly and grimly, I pray it is still here tomorrow. Seeing all the families laughing and having a joyous visit today with no clue about the danger that threatens their survival fills me with sorrow. They believe this is just another day in their lives and are confident that tomorrow will come. They are carefree as they take in the majestic façade of the college, visually absorbing the magnificent paintings and tucking away the maritime history to savor at their leisure. I feel compelled to sound an alarm to make them understand that these remaining hours are precious, yet I cannot. Who of them would believe me?

Abigor lays his hand on my shoulder. He knows the futility of what I am thinking. Professor Otto has never been here before and is excited to visit the college. We allow him a few minutes to drink in the magnificent artwork in the lobby before heading to the secret stairs and the ship's cabin on the third floor. Here at the college is where Abigor and I met when he was still a demon and where he attacked Angus and me on the secret stairs. The Admiral, David, Sophie, Sir Winston, and Dr. Einstein stopped him from killing us. I try not to hold a grudge.

The climb is a bit intense for the aging German. We must stop and let him catch his breath a few times. He finally asks me, "Fraulein Bones, why don't they install an elevator? This hike is comparable to climbing Mt. Grober Muggelberg near my home. My older brother Franz and I climbed it when I wore a younger man's clothes." Shock! Well, well, the good Professor is full of surprises—Franz is his brother, as we suspected. Or just another coincidence? Abigor whips his head around when he hears the familiar name, and we stare at each other as we try to process that last bit of information in that eureka! moment. The professor is busy trying to breathe, so he does not notice our astonishment. Now is not the time. Abigor and I will get into that bizarre coincidence later. Yes, I know, there are no coincidences. We continue our slow climb to the Admiral's landlocked office.

Finally, we arrive, and poor Otto is so thrilled to have finished the climb that he chuckles, and I giggle with him. Abigor is focused on our mission and overlooks our merriment. I am eager to see the number on the door since it keeps changing. Today, it is 13:10-12, and I have no idea what that means, but, of course, Abigor does and is visibly shaken by its hidden meaning. After our chat with our sailor, I will ask him about it.

We stand outside the door until a booming voice says, "Come in, Abigor, Bones, and Otto." What? How does he know Otto's name? On cue, the door begins to open slowly.

It is dark in the ship Captain's cabin (on the third floor) with white shiplap walls, a battered old desk, a few ancient wood chairs, and an oil lantern hanging from the ceiling. If the lantern is meant to hold the darkness at bay, it fails miserably. Several yellowed maps hang on the walls, echoes of distant places visited and perhaps forgotten in the fog of time as it marches forward to other destinations. The compelling seafaring Admiral sits at his desk. He is an imposing figure, even if one ignores his swashbuckling 1940s movie-star face. There is something mysterious about the Admiral, but one subconsciously feels it and is careful to be respectful and walk softly.

Admiral Stallings, as always is unflinchingly bold, barks at us to sit, then welcomes Otto, "Professor Wolffe, what a pleasure to meet you. I believe you taught for many years at the prestigious Humboldt University in Berlin. Welcome to London and the Old Royal Naval

College. It is good of you to join our little meeting tonight." He offers his most engaging smile to the enchanted Professor.

Otto stands and thanks him, "How generous you are, Admiral. Though we have not been formally introduced, I know your name from the war. My father was a great admirer. I was an incredibly young man then." The professor pauses as if working through a conundrum that refuses to be resolved. He finally reluctantly asks, "Just as a matter of curiosity, how are you still so young?" We all laugh, realizing this will be a tricky question to answer. Abigor and I look to the Admiral to provide that answer to our new friend. Our sailor gazes directly at Otto and says with solid credibility, "That is a good question, Professor Wolffe. You are undoubtedly aware of time travel and its influence on age. I participated in some experiments many years ago."

The Admiral stops briefly and tilts his head as if to gauge Otto's reaction before continuing, "As you know, and the 1971 Hafele-Keating experiments proved, dilation is real, not just a concept. Also, if one travels nearer the speed of light, he will not age as fast as humans on Earth. I will elaborate for Abigor and Bones since I would not consider lecturing you, Professor. The faster you go through the three dimensions that define physical space, width, breadth, and height, the more slowly you move through the fourth dimension, time."

The professor adjusts his horn-rimmed glasses and stares at the Admiral. He is reeling from the tsunami of information coming at him and manages to ask, "Are you saying that the reason you look young, much younger than you should, is due to high-speed travel in space?" And there you have it, a stalemate.

But Stallings merely gazes at him and says, "I did not say that, did I, Dr. Wolffe? I merely explained how less aging could occur using your area of research. Now, shall we continue with the meeting?" Game. Set. Match! "How can I help you, Bones and Abigor? I see proverbial question marks hovering over your heads?" I try to appear utterly at peace with his outrageous explanation to Otto. Outrageous, right?

I nod at Abigor to run with the ball, and I will carry the water bucket. Abigor jumps right in, anxious about our dilemma. "Admiral, we must learn more about the Doomsday Machine and its alter ego, the Fantastic Machine. We have only a few hours to complete our mission, or we shalt lose all. How can we stop the Doomsday Machine?"

Stalling's face is grave as he considers this explosive question. Finally, he says, "I understand your sense of urgency. It is appropriate, Abigor. However, you know my limitations over which I have little power. Beyond sets the rules, and I am their servant. Thelma has been terribly concerned about this end-of-the-world scenario. She is quite fond of Bones and does not want her or any other mortal to die. She has unrealistic hopes that David and Bones will have a life together." My heart stops for a beat or two when I hear Thelma's hope. I can't even imagine such a wondrous life. The Admiral ignores my reaction. "Therefore, I want nothing more than to help you in your mission, for you and my lovely lady. However, I must be bold and say this: remember, we have talked about the Doomsday Machine. You cannot destroy the machine. I believe they had help from a demon in protecting it, probably Aaii."

The admiral holds up a hand to forestall any argument from Abigor. "I know you thought it was too advanced for that time, Abigor. The designers were the most advanced minds in science. Exceptionally talented men and women. Some were forced to work on that project. Two courageous, brilliant Jews, Rosen, and Goldmann, were among a small group of scientists who learned about the Doomsday Machine and sought a way to stop it. They were decades ahead of the science of that time, hence the Fantastic Machine." Abigor and I are intrigued by what the Admiral is saying. I ask him to slow down, "Are you seriously saying that the Doomsday Machine is demonic or, more precisely, shielded by a demon? We considered that theory. If we were to accept that, can another demon, or former demon, change the way the machine works? I understand that humans and former humans cannot open it or deactivate the timer." Stalling shakes his head and answers, "Abigor is probably better qualified to answer your question, but I understand that only the demon who protects it can make changes. As you know, much information is floating around, and it evolves."

We all look to Abigor for his expert opinion. Abigor gestures and responds, "It hurts me grievously to say this, but that is correct. No one can change something a demon protects other than that demon himself. Verily, we art back to the Fantastic Machine in the Dark World, or we can try to sway Aaii to demolish the weapon of mass destruction. Good works, justice, fairness, or compassion will not sway Aaii. How do we persuade him?" He throws his hands up in frustration.

I glance over at the Professor to see how he reacts to the rash of bizarre ideas circling this room, looking for a place to land. Astonishingly, he appears to be only intensely curious, not as if he might bolt for the door at any moment. What a man! I don't know if the "voodoo" influences his tolerance for the weird and wild circumstances or if he, as a scientist, is fascinated and thus ignores the more bizarre elements of our conversation. Otto has spent his life applying Dr. Einstein's theory of relativity to science as it pertains to the world, time, and space. In his way, the Professor himself is a rebel and a revolutionary, much like Dr. Einstein, except our genius doesn't have a psychopathic brother who tries to kill me whenever he is bored. We will learn more about psychotic Franz later when Dr. Einstein can help us with the interview.

I return my attention to Abigor and Admiral Stallings, but I am exhausted and have not slept in at least 36 hours. Truthfully, I have lost track of the last time I dozed off. The only meals I have had lately were at Poznan Airport and on the plane. I realize I am not at my best, so I step back from the conversation. I desperately need sleep, but I don't foresee it in my immediate future.

Abigor, looking desperate, pleads, "Admiral, is there anything else thou can suggest that might help us complete our mission? Time is draining away at a dizzying rate, and we have few viable solutions." Abigor looks so disconsolate that I forget the professor and I are the only ones in this group who Doomsday will negatively impact. We will die. But at this point, I am too exhausted to care. Probably due to the voodoo, the professor doesn't seem particularly concerned either.

Admiral Stallings sits erect and sturdy with sympathy carved into his stone face. He understands our plight and the constraints of the steadily ticking clock. His eyes are sad, and I am grateful for his friend-ship and concern. After composing himself, the Admiral reflects, "We have discussed certain options of which we are all aware. But there are probably options that are still unknown to us. I have always lived by the dictum that every problem has a resolution. When my crew and I were discovered and killed by the Nazis, I wondered if there might be exceptions to that rule. Never mind that. Let us discuss the options. First, you can enter the Dark World hoping to find and use the Fantastic Machine. However, that option is dubious since we do not know if it is there or how to find it. Then, we have other issues: how does it work, and will you return? Truthfully, I am beginning to doubt its existence. We discussed neutralizing the demon-protected machine, but we now know that only the demon who casts a spell could negate his magic. I have a question, Abigor. Could you locate Aaii and persuade him to cooperate? Is there anything he fears or desires that you might use as leverage?"

Abigor is unprepared for this question. He presses his lips in concentration and stares at the hypnotically swaying lantern for a full minute before tackling it. He turns to Stallings and hesitantly says, "I am unsure about a response to thy questions. I could probably find Aaii using the demon stream of consciousness or other ways. Those ways can be time-consuming, and I have nothing I can use as leverage when or if I find him. He has not been especially fond of me since I changed sides. Wait!" Abigor silently considers something. After deliberation, he eagerly says, "That art an excellent question, sir. There is one being who terrifies Aaii and all demons. If I could locate him and acquire his assistance, we could probably bend Aaii to our point of view. The more I consider thine option, the more confident I am it could work! Again, the only objection is deciding if we have the time to find both Aaii and the, uh, anti-demon. I devoutly wish right now that we could slow time." I am on the edge of my seat, embracing Abigor's eager semi-confidence. I feel hope surging.

The Professor pops up like burnt toast, which brings me out of my hope splurge. Otto jumps around from one foot to the other, shouting, "I know how to slow time! Moving faster than the speed of light slows time!"

"As you know, the speed of light is 299792458 m/s. The closer we get to that universal number, the slower time moves. Remember, we discussed that earlier?" I vaguely remember. Good, I am not the only one losing their mind! And as usual, I do not know the speed of light was whatever he said, nor have I ever needed that number.

The admiral surprised me by paying serious attention to Otto and his declaration of a viable solution. Our Old-Salt leans toward Otto and says in a measured voice, "How exactly can we use moving toward the speed of light to wrestle our planet from the jaws of death, Professor?" The professor stretches up to his full height and proclaims, "I understand we have more powerful friends, much more powerful than humans. Am I correct in this assumption? If that is correct, can we increase the speed of the earth for a brief time? That would give us more time, not a lot more, but every minute counts from what I am hearing."

We are startled by this simple statement of a staggeringly ridiculous idea. It is an outrageous idea. Right? We turn to Abigor for an answer. He appears as dumbfounded as we are. He blinks fast, trying to digest the statement and its tremendous implications. That is not hyperbole. The idea is tremendously fantastic. Abigor is not about to get caught up in this idle distraction, yea or nay. He circumvents it with, "This is a question for Sir Winston and perhaps for Alpha and Omega. The result of increasing the earth's rotation rate could be catastrophic. We have no data to consult to understand the consequences of such a radical, unimaginable change. We may have to consult with the Powers in Beyond before we can even understand the question, much less formulate an answer. I have no idea what to tell you. If we could change the rotation speed, we do not know how much time it would gain for us. Unless this option created a significant gain, it would not be worth the risk."

I chew on my bottom lip as I attempt to stop my tired brain from spinning out of control. I am not impressed with Professor Otto's idea as I understand it. Too many variables are involved, many of which we cannot even begin to imagine. Of course, I am not a genius and lack essential knowledge in theoretical physics. Abigor is looking at me with question marks in his eyes. I gradually move my head. He nods to signal, "Roger that." The Professor is so euphoric that I hate to see his bubble burst. Still, we should be discussing options that have a chance of working without sending Earth and its inhabitants spiraling off into the deepest reaches of the Milky Way and on into infinity.

The Admiral is distraught that he cannot help us in our desperate need. He says gruffly, "You know my commitment to your team and your mission. I have told you everything I know and can surmise. I suggest you immediately talk to Dr. Einstein and Winston and focus on at least one plan. The Professor's book may tell Albert something only he can understand. Aaii is a viable option. I suggest you immediately explore persuading him to cooperate. I wish you Godspeed." The Admiral stands to signify that this meeting is over. "It was a pleasure meeting you, Professor." He walks around his desk to embrace Abigor and me. He kisses me on the forehead. I see little hope in those fathomless eyes, and I shudder.

As we walk to the door to leave, it opens on its own as usual. The stunningly angelic Thelma is standing there with her golden curls encircling her tranquil face. The Professor had never seen Thelma before, and her loveliness dazzles him. His gaping mouth is a dead giveaway. She approaches me, puts her arms around me, and whispers." You will be safe, dearest Bones. I have prayed for you, and I felt an answer. Do not worry, my dear. Please tell David you will have a life together. You are very precious to me. One day, we shall sit and chat just the two of us." Then Thelma fondly embraces Abigor, the former demon whose soul she saved for all eternity by interceding with Beyond on his behalf. She takes the professor's hands in hers and wishes him God's blessings. I am a little confused by her optimism and emotional attachment to me. She is a unique, brave, angelic woman, but we have never been close. There has never been a time we were not in one crisis or another.

I feel I must try to get information from her. "Thelma, last time we spoke, before the battle in the Demon Cavern, you gave us vital information from your vision. Have you had a vision about our success in stopping the demon machine? Anything, no matter how insignificant, would help us." She looks at me with serene eyes and pauses, then says, "Yes, there was something, but I don't know if it was about your mission. My vision was quite vivid. I saw a massive dog and a huge wolf standing nose to nose. Both were snarling and growling, showing their teeth in an aggressive threat. Suddenly, an enormous blonde man appeared. He walked between them and laid his hand on each head. The dog was calm and at peace. The wolf howled, snarled, and bit at the man, then turned and ran away. I am sorry, that is all I saw. I wish I could help you, Bones, and Abigor." I jump and yell because Sophie appears beside me out of nowhere! Thelma is tapping my shoulder and pointing at Sophie. I hugged Soph and tried reassuring Thelma that Soph was with us. Then, it occurs to me. She has not met our ancient entity. I introduce them, "It is OK, Thelma, Big Soph is one of the good guys."

Thelma still looks astonished. She chokes out, "No! That is the dog I saw in my vision! So, my vision must have been about your team. But I still don't know what it means. I felt at peace when the blonde man arrived. Up until then, I was shaking with fright." The Admiral appears at the door and watches us. He sees two mortals, one Great Dane, and an angel, all giving Thelma our complete and focused attention. He puts his arm around his lady, and her face is serene once more. I look back at them, the couple who had planned a life together before the war. Sadly, a life that never happened. War and death occurred instead. Will that be David and me one day?

Sigh.

I sense Thelma's overall aura of saintliness, holy, Godly, and pious. It emanates from her like the fragrance of newly mown sweet summer grass and spicey cloves—an irresistible fragrance. We thank Thelma for her concern and blessings and walk through the door that closes behind us. I wonder if I will ever meet Admiral Stallings and Thelma Dove again. During our many meetings and joint efforts to stop Dr. Mengele and his supporters, they have become team members.

Darn, we don't have time to discuss Thelma's fascinating vision now. We'll tuck it away until we join our Team. Sophie trails along with us toward the real world. I hug Thelma's vision for David and me close to my heart. If only.

The third floor doesn't exist outside these walls except for the few of us who have been here.

Abigor and I look at the numbers on the door since we are accustomed to iron door embellishments changing of their own volition. The numbers still proclaim 3:10-12, and Abigor stares gravely at them. I am amazed when he snarls viciously as if they were rattlesnakes about to strike him. The Professor stands behind us, staring into space, still in a daze after meeting the incomparable Thelma. I'm anxious to understand why Abigor is snarling, so I ask, "I am puzzled. Why were you so angry with the numbers 3:10-12? They seem inoffensive to me."

Abigor looks at me as if I am a raging lunatic. He pushes his hair back and says, "Bones, do thee know nothing of the Bible? The number is an awful sign if I interpret the message accurately. It is from 2 Daniel, and it reads: 'But the day of the Lord will come like a thief, in which the heavens will pass away with a roar and the elements will be destroyed with intense heat, and the earth and its works will be burned up.' He is waiting for the meaning to dawn on me. I wipe the perspiration forming on my forehead and answer, "Well, I admit this does not sound good for us, but the door is constantly changing numbers. This could be temporary and not a forecast of things to come. I am going to remain optimistic." Abigor just shakes his head. With the Professor in tow, we move toward the secret stairs.

As we descend the seemingly endless stairs, I ask the Angel, "Do you plan to try to locate Aaii and whomever he fears? I assume that is Archangel Michael. Is it feasible, or should we focus on the intangible and questionable Dark World? That would not be my first choice if I could avoid it, but I will not shirk from my duty if it becomes our only option. The Admiral appears to doubt the Dark World and its significance now." Abigor looks back at the Professor. He obviously does not want to discuss this with our guest within earshot. I nod my understanding and let it go for now. I am sure we will be discussing demons with our team as soon as we return. Suddenly, I remembered that we had to return to our team. How will Otto and I travel?

Abigor knows I am curious about our travel arrangements. He answers my unspoken question, "I have heard from Sir Winston and Dr. Einstein, and they think since I am an angel, I should be able to transport thee safely and Dr. Wolffe without harm to either one of thee. That is not necessarily the case for David, Sir Winston, Red, Angus, and Dr. Einstein. However, we know that when the jet bringing thee and the team from London to Poland broke apart, David transported thee easily. Sophie is a unique entity. She insists she will transport thee, and Professor Wolffe can take his chances with me."

Sophie grins at me in satisfaction. Otto looks up at Abigor with his eyebrows peaking upward. I also notice a slight tremor vibrating his portly body. Since the "voodoo" thing rendered him submissive, he is horrified by what he hears, but he does not protest. I assure him we will take excellent care of him while he is under our protection, and he has nothing to fear. His eyebrows relax slightly, and his shaking subsides. He is trusting, considering he doesn't know me from Adam's house cat. I am telling the truth about the dangers we can control. We cannot prevent earthquakes and volcanoes.

As we continue to descend the endless stairs, Abigor tries to answer my question about Aaii, "Bones, I do not have an answer for thee. Aaii may be easy to find, and that option then becomes viable, or he may not. I am more optimistic about locating the entity that strikes fear into the brute's heart." He rolls his eyes and glares before saying, "I suppose

Aaii needs a heart first. We will discuss this with the team, Bones. Do thee have the compass with thee?" I pat my purse and reluctantly say, "I will do whatever is necessary, just as you will. I am waiting for Sir Winston to say, 'Now is the time.'" This superhero stuff is draining.

We walk back to the 1939 Rolls Royce to grab our bags. Abigor's friend will pick up the stately Rolls. Abigor takes the Professor's hand and disappears. The last thing I see of them is Otto's mouth open wide. I think he was mouthing, "Oh Hell," But I can't be entirely certain. I put my arms around Big Soph's neck, and we melt into space.

Chapter Fifteen

The Other Wolffe

Within minutes, we will be with the team in the Demon Chamber. Professor Wolffe, my bags, and I are safely back on solid ground. The first face I see belongs to my beloved David, and I waste no time running into his open arms. He swings me around as if we were ice skating for the gold. We are both grinning. As soon as he can breathe again (Yeah, he does not really need to breathe, but he likes to pretend), David says, "I am thrilled to see you, gorgeous! It seems like weeks since you left on your mission to London. I missed your sweet smile and bright eyes. How did the mission go? Was the Admiral able to help us with either machine? We have not had any luck trying to open that bloody thing. It appears to have never been opened. I can find no way to do it, even though common sense tells us it had to be when the Nazis constructed it. We will keep trying." He hugs me tighter this time and my blood pressure soars into the stratosphere! OK, Bones, get it together and tell the Team what we learned—remember clock-ticking time bomb.

I hug the others: Dr. Einstein, Sir Winston, deadly Red, and dear Angus. Sir Winston, the perfect leader, welcomes us back. "Abigor and dear Bones, how good to see you. I am pleased you brought a guest to our humble abode. How do you do, Professor Wolffe? It is indeed a pleasure to meet you." The great man transfers his iconic Cuban cigar to his lips while he shakes the professor's hand. Taking a quick puff, he deftly returns it to his hand and informs Otto, "I believe I have met your brother Franz. Have you talked to him recently? Oh dear, please excuse my poor manners. May I introduce you to Dr. Einstein, Air Marshall David Smythe, Agent Angus Snowden, and Agent Red Biggers?"

The entire time Churchill talks, Otto stares at Dr. Einstein, trying to decide if this is his hero—who should be quite dead. However, he remembers meeting the Admiral, who should not be so young and alive.

Poor Professor Wolffe is ecstatic. The man he has spent his life following in academia stands before him. It is too much for him, and he buckles to the floor. We rush over to help him. Dr. Einstein looks him over, and as far as we can tell, Otto is fine. We help him up, and David pulls a chair over while I run to get some tea from my thermos stash. I also bring a nice zapiekanka, an open sandwich similar to a pizza, from Poznan Airport. All our food bounty is here in the cave, thanks to Abigor. While I have an opportunity, I grab a turkey sandwich with hot mustard and a piece of Szarlotka pie. The Professor slowly returns to his full faculties and simply accepts Einstein.

The geniuses interview the professor about his infamous brother Franz. They hope he will know something about the weapon. Franz was in Hitler's inner circle and could have been aware of the Doomsday Machine. It is unlikely he would have shared this top-secret information with his younger brother, but it is worth pursuing. Dr. Einstein leaves Otto with Sir Winston and David and starts reading *Zeit und Raum*, the Rosen and Goldmann book we brought with Otto. Since the book was never circulated, Einstein didn't know it existed. It could prove informative.

Otto tells David and Churchill, "I seldom saw Franz during the War years. He was terribly busy with the monsters he supported, and I was on the other side. Like many Germans, I hated Hitler, who was a bloodthirsty, psychopathic tyrant. When Hitler came to power, he tried to appear to be a patriotic German who desired to help the people after the devastation of WWI. Slowly, he took control, and his dark side began incrementally manifesting. By then, he had millions of followers, and his Brown Shirts bullied any group who disagreed with his murderous philosophy. His early vehicle to power was the National Socialist German Worker's Party. His skill as an orator expanded the Party, its coffers, and political power. As he grew in influence, he marginalized, then viciously attacked various groups such as communists, Jews, disabled people, and Gypsies."

The professor's reverie seems to transport him back to that time and place without the benefit of a time machine. He mutters, "It was a dreadful time for the German people to see their country become divided and harshly punitive. Later, as you know, the violence worsened as Hitler sank into drug abuse and psychosis. The courageous tried to stop him and paid the price. Germans were fearful of each other as neighbors turned against neighbors. As the years passed, I learned much more about the nature of the horrors than I knew as a 10-year-old." Dr. Einstein embraces Otto as he remembers the friends he lost during this heartbreaking time in his birth country. A tear trickles down his wrinkled face. He coughs and asks the Professor to continue.

Otto sniffs and says, "You can be certain Franz would not have told our parents or me anything Hitler was doing. Franz was the oldest of the ten children, and I was the youngest. We were desperately poor. My father was a factory worker. Between 1944 and 1945, the Allies dropped 45,000 tons of bombs on major cities in Germany. It was terrifying, and we didn't know what to do, so we could only hope that someone would oust Hitler so we could live free again. Franz visited once in late 1944 and bragged that we would win the war or Hitler would get his revenge by catastrophic global destruction. He said it could be years later, but it would happen. Franz said doomsday was waiting like a giant spider underground for someone to awaken it. Hitler and his followers were raving mad, gentlemen." Otto stopped his story and looked into Churchill's eyes, the abject panic still there after 80 years. The elderly professor took a deep breath as he relived the fear of that 10-year-old boy in 1944. "My mother and father thought the weapon was just silly bravado. I did not doubt the truth of what Franz said and lived in horror for many years waiting for the world to end."

Sir Winston is also emotionally transported back to his days of dread and desperation during the War. He puts one plump hand on the Professor's shoulder and gently asks, "Did he say anything else about the machine? We need specific information, Otto. We must stop that monster. Think, Professor!" We could not ignore the sound of desperation in Churchill's last two words. Red, David, and Angus are sitting close by, listening to every word, hoping to hear a tidbit or a morsel they could use to manipulate the Machine. Red wants to reach out and gently shake the man. Sophie has her great head cocked. She is almost sitting in the professor's jacket pocket. He should appreciate that she is not in the Creature from Hell mode.

Otto is tired, but at least he has hearty Polish food to fuel his body. I hand another cuppa to him and kiss him on the forehead. I hope the caffeine will keep his neurons firing. Sadly, Otto reminds me of our beloved Padre, and I pray he will continue to live. After taking a few sips of his tea, the dear man scratches his head, adjusts his wayward tie, and meekly suggests, "I may know something helpful, yet it means nothing to me. I am probably wasting your time with these reminiscences. Franz said something that struck me because it sounded bizarre, and, of course, he had been drinking. He looked at our mother and babbled, 'A woman could stop us. A woman not yet born, an American with turbulent dark hair and a strawberry-shaped birthmark on her right wrist, and behind her stands the shadow of a giant. Hitler was obsessed with finding this mysterious woman." Otto stopped, and with a meek smile, he looked at us apologetically. He pressed on again, "Franz also said, and this was particularly odd, that a high-ranking English Naval Officer was their nemesis, and he had saved the pests, Rosen and

Goldmann, from execution. Later, I was privileged to meet scientists at university whom those talented scientists trained."

"Franz said a magician told them to continue watching for the girl's appearance and to destroy her. I know how this seems, but I trust my memory. I have almost total recall. That was all Franz told us, Sir Winston, nonsense, of course." Abigor whips around. His body is stone as he stares at Otto in horrified disbelief. Then Abigor stares at me and strides toward me. David watches the former demon and intervenes. Abigor grabs my right hand, and David slaps his hand away and shoves him backward with enormous power. I am confused and looking back and forth between the former demon and the ghost, trying to understand what is happening.

Dr. Einstein and Sir Winston step in, and David pushes past them. He asks Abigor what he thinks he is doing and tells him he must explain what he knows about the woman with the strawberry birthmark. David is scowling at Abigor, and his eyes are bright sapphires.

Sophie is looking at Abigor and growling low in her throat. I am utterly baffled now. David knows, as I do, that there is a strawberry birthmark on my wrist. My grandmother loved to share Native American lore with me, and she said the Iroquois tribes associated strawberries with love and happiness. I do not know what is going on, but whatever, it doesn't seem to revolve around love and happiness. Sophie is observing. She knows something.

Sir Winston stares Abigor down and demands, "What does your behavior mean, sir?" Abigor holds his head down, shuffles his feet like an English schoolboy caught with the headmaster's grade book, and mutters, "Thou knoweth I did many evil and wicked things in my previous life. I am not proud of mine past, but I cannot change it. Many of my former demon days are simply gone, and I have forgotten those painful memories. That art a mercy. To use a modern example, many of mine files were deleted when I transitioned back to an Angel. The Professor stirred a long-dead memory. I participated in designing the Doomsday Machine project." At this revelation, we were all staring in dead silence. He continues, "My part was relatively minor. I chose the target to hit when we finally activated the machine. After looking at the original research article, Doctor Einstein told you about the target area, which was what I did. While planning, Aaii said he had peered into the future, which is exceedingly difficult to do, and only a few high-ranking demons have the sophisticated ability to prognosticate. His interpretation is not a perfect peek into the mist of time because God gave us free will. Something in the chain of events could change. He saw a woman, as described by Otto, somehow rendering the machine impotent. I never thought of Bones as "the woman" until just now. The description is vague, and I had forgotten about that episode in my life. I am sorry I did not remember immediately. Yet, I had nothing that took us any further, even if I had recalled sooner."

Dr. Einstein listens with interest and muses, "If the woman is Bones, that explains numerous mysterious aspects of our mission. Let us listen carefully with open minds. We are simply analyzing the data, and we must develop options. From what Abigor and Otto tell us, Bones has an inexplicable resemblance to the description of the mystery woman. We are also told she must be here to destroy the machine. Whether the stories are accurate or not, we are lucky Bones is here if we need her. I have always wondered about the story of the book *Gathering Storm*, which selected her to be on the team. There was no definable reason, so the story was questionable logic at best. Please indulge me for a moment while I hypothesize. What if the Doomsday Machine was always part of the mission? Alpha and Omega could answer this question for us. Reflecting on this, Bones was important enough for them to return her to life three times. What do you think?" The physicist sits down and stares at Sir Winston.

Sir Winston, as always, jumps into leader mode without a second of reluctance. He stands and walks around pondering and caressing his father's gold Breguet pocket watch before he answers, "Albert, this interpretation is quite interesting. I agree. The book story was too much of a fairytale to satisfy my logical mind. I am intrigued by the enormous blonde man Thelma described from her vision and the giant Franz mentioned. We want a conversation with the only giant blonde we know. If this was decided before Bones was born, the connection was to her grandparents or great-grandparents. Why would such a promise be made? The only possible powers behind such a promise are the Powers in Beyond. Bones, we know your father was Native American. We will talk about your mother later when there is more time."

I nod as the story plays out. We are glued to our seats, wondering what and who we can trust. Churchill removes his linen handkerchief, wipes his hands, and continues, "I have no further information, yet I am not inclined to discount Otto's story without data that strenuously contradicts it. As David and Albert know, because they were there, Alpha and Omega gave us the parameters of this mission and specifically said our assignment was to stop Dr. Mengele. They also referred to my book, *Gathering Storm*, and its part in the drama. Yes, it sounded extraordinary, but we did not question them. David, dear boy, do you have something to add?" Churchill sits on the throne and sighs.

David is visibly upset. His face is a dark tropical storm about to break in Poland. He spits out, "I think we should have known this alternate reality long ago. We may be wasting time discussing it, yet it might be pivotal in dismantling the weapon. I want to talk to Alpha, Omega, Druid, and Aaii. Why is Bones suddenly an essential element of the takedown of the weapon? Why is Druid involved in the 'background?'" He bangs his knee with his fist and shouts, "Were we the only ones who did not know about Bones, Druid, and the machine? What about Abigor, Bones, and the Dark World? Does the book in which I wrote the code mean nothing now? Those versions appear to be just wild fantasies!" David is getting louder and louder. Then he turns his eyes to Abigor.

David steps toward him and challenges, "Abigor, you must have heard something that would help us stop this devil machine. They would have discussed more than the woman Aaii foresaw and the target area. Do you remember anything about controlling the device or the power source? These bits of information could help us end this part of our mission. Concentrate on your time with Aaii working on the plan here in this chamber."

Abigor, looking extremely embarrassed, says, "David, I have been trying, and nothing else came to me. Possibly something will, but we knoweth one thing: Bones is the key to stopping the monster. I don't understand Druid's role any more than you. Undoubtedly, Aaii is the 'magician' Franz mentioned to his family."

While we try to digest what Abigor told us, he plows on. "I have not revealed this to thee yet, but when we talked to the Admiral, we discussed hunting down Aaii since he can destroy this machine. He protects it so no one else hast the power. Verily, I have questions to ask him about Bones, too." At this point, I am bewildered about my purpose and why David and Churchill were misinformed about our mission. My brain is processing at warp speed. Nothing.

Abigor continues, "I will need leverage since we are no longer on the same team. There is one entity of whom he is deathly afraid, and you saw the entity in our battle to secure the chamber. He wast beaten by that Angel and retreated to Hell to lick his wounds. I would have to find Archangel Michael as well as Aaii. I can leave immediately to begin mine hunt, but keep in mind that I have no idea if I can accomplish these tasks in the time we have left. I believe we art now at 18 hours and 27 minutes. Well, what think you?"

Otto listens to Abigor, trying to understand his English, but he needs to comprehend that Abigor speaks broken Shakespearean Old English. Our angel is slowly pulling himself into the current century, but he is a work in progress. Shakespeare once warned, "What is done cannot be undone." I hope the Olde Bard is mistaken this time.

Dr. Einstein swoops in with this brilliant suggestion. "Abigor, I think we should try all possible options since we have no evidence proving one is superior to another. I think Professor Wolffe will agree with me on that." The Professor was thrilled to be included by his hero, and he lights up like one of Aaii's massive chandeliers. He vigorously nods his complete agreement. Dr. Einstein continues, "All in favor of Abigor hunting for the missing demon and Archangel Michael, please indicate by raising your hands." All hands went up and waved briskly. I waved both of my hands. I want to do something to stop this maniacal machine.

Red asks if he can accompany Abigor on his reclamation journey. Our former demon waves him on as he starts toward the tunnel. Sir Winston calls out, "Abigor, you must be back no later than 5 hours to detonation. If the Aaii/Michael plan does not work, we may, in desperation, return to the remote, unlikely possibility of Dark World, and you must be here for that operation. Yet, I am relatively sure that story is imaginary, too. While you are gone, perhaps we shall have a visit from Druid, and we can discuss Franz's tale about him and Bones." Abigor bows to the former Prime Minister and disappears into the tunnel along with Eye Patch Red.

It is my turn to report on our visit to the Admiral. I push wayward, black strands of hair from my eyes to see. Yes, I need a haircut, but getting an appointment here is problematic. I whistle to get everyone's attention. "Gentleman, we discussed various possibilities with the Admiral and Thelma. She arrived just as we were leaving, and she was a delight as always. She seemed optimistic about our mission and told us about her recent vision. As you remember, her previous vision gave us information on how many demons would confront us in the rumble for control of the demon chamber. Recently, she had a vision in which she saw a large harlequin dog-like Soph and a wolf facing off, angry and threatening. She was frightened until an enormous blonde man appeared. She said he patted both animals on the head. The wolf was still aggressive and bit at him but then ran away, and the Sophie-like dog immediately became calm. Thelma felt at peace then. She doesn't know what the vision means. I wish Thelma would just send a text with bullet points to make our lives easier. Her mood was optimistic." We are all musing about the possible meaning of the vision and trying to gather helpful information from the little morsels Thelma gave us.

Sir Winston was the first to venture a guess. "Of course, Thelma's description is quite limited, and it is impossible to extrapolate meaningful facts from it. We can surmise it refers to our mission because of Soph's presence. The blonde man is perhaps our own inimitable Druid. She felt frightened, but then she was calmed by the blonde man's presence." Turning to our Dr. Einstein, Sir Winston pressed upon him, "Dear Albert, you often say, 'imagination is more important than knowledge. Knowledge is limited. Imagination encircles the world.' Would you share your imagination with us? We are in dire need of a plan."

The genius stands, adjusts his jacket, and pulls on his unlit pipe, "Winston, I am flattered and gratified you have hung on my every word. Yes, I can see that knowledge has a limited ability to help us with Fraulein Thelma's vision. One, we don't know if it means anything.

Two, if I were to let my imagination run unfettered, I might wonder if one of the two canines represent the evil villains poised against our Team and us in the person of Sophie. In that case, does the blonde man, perhaps Druid, come to our assistance, and we save our mission and our world? Also, if I remember correctly, Miss Dove's vision changed last time. She gave us a very dark interpretation the first time. Later, she had a more optimistic vision, which was more accurate. Even imagination must have some facts on which one can build." He starts looking for Otto's book and momentarily forgets about us and our dire predicament.

David speaks up, growing frustrated that we are still dealing with murky possibilities instead of a definitive, defined plan. He rubs his eyes and says, "I see one plan at the moment that gives us a path to follow. Abigor and Red are looking for Aaii and the mighty entity he fears. If we can leverage Aaii to stop the machine, we will be finished and can go home to London triumphant and ready to finish the Mengele part. We still have . . ." He looks at his watch to verify the time and announces, "Seventeen hours before blast-off. If an evil spell protects the machine, we cannot touch it. I wish Father Antonio were still with us. He was a valuable team member, and he could have addressed the spiritual aspects of our dilemma. I realize we have Abigor, but he is busy with two plans. There was something solid and undeniably holy about the good Padre. I have thought about going to his cathedral to pray and see what happens."

David resumes his habit of pushing around his hair with his fingers while considering his options. "Bones, are you up for a ride in the Rolls? I had it delivered here in case we needed it. There have been a few, uh, enhancements since we last rode in it. The James Bond novels had Q, and we have the original Charles Fraser-Smith. I knew him, as did Sir Winston and Red during his lifetime. He was the genius behind Sir Winston's Secret Service gadgets. Beyond sent him back to help us.

He souped up our fine old lady, our "newest" 1939 Rolls Royce." David looks at me and winks. Heart be still. He says about the Rolls, "She will have us there in about 30 minutes, Sweetheart. The old gal can fly and float when needed. Are you ready for a quick drive? It will be a bit chilly. You may want your sweater." Of course, I jumped at the chance to spend some alone time with hunky David, especially now when my life might be measured in brief hours and minutes. I grab my black cardigan and throw it on.

Sir Winston, Otto, and Dr. Einstein are still throwing around theories to fit our various stories on overcoming the demon machine. Otto is understandably ecstatic about theorizing with the most brilliant scientist of the 20th century. I consider their personality types and what they contribute to our team. Dr. Einstein is probably an INTP on the Myers-Briggs Personality Inventory. They are formidable, analytical people. Churchill is likely an ENTJ, and they excel as the heavyweight champions in leadership. No surprises there.

Sir Winston verbally jumps in, clenching his fists. "Charles Fraser-Smith, what an amazing man! I must drop by his lab and shake his hand. Did you know Ian Fleming based his character "Q," at least partly, on Fraser-Smith? I wish Red were here, as they were great friends in the SOE. When Smith created gadgets for SOE, his designs were seldom in writing, and he stayed behind a curtain of secrecy. I remember his brilliant hairbrushes, shaving brushes, and even inoffensive dominoes were much more complex than they appeared to be. He modified those innocent items to hold escape files or maps. Also, he provided the Minox cameras, which were so invaluable to secret agents seeking to take photographs under the enemy's noses. Special Air Service and SOE benefited from his long hours cutting red tape and applying his ingenuity. I am so pleased he is back with us again!" We agree that Fraser-Smith is astonishing, and we are privileged to have him on board. I had not realized Fleming based "Q" on an actual person.

Chapter Sixteen

The Priest

David and I wave goodbye to the guys. David whispers in my ear, "Well, gorgeous, shall we take the updated old Rolls for a ride to St. Albans and see if prayer in the Padre's Cathedral brings blessings?"

I couldn't wait to see what the souped-up car can do now. We drove at astonishing speeds and used the flying mode when needed to save time or when we hit water. I wondered if anyone on the ground saw the regal car flying like something out of the fantastic musical Grease or Harry Potter. I have never had so much fun in my life. It is magical, flying with David, the top down, looking out at the world below, the brightly lit houses, streetlights, and cars. I am reveling in the enormous, dreamlike full moon above us. I am disheartened to leave my fantasy world when we reach the charming village of St. Albans. The Cathedral is easy to find since it is enormous and stands majestically in the village's center. As we walked to the front entrance, I asked David what people would think when they saw the flying Rolls. He hugs me and chuckles, "Beautiful lady, Charles did not want to start any crazy rumors, so he made the car invisible from the ground using a special cloaking device. He said it was not that difficult. I will take his word for that."

I think about something I had read and tell David, "I read something about specific materials' electromagnetic properties that could make some objects invisible if applied from the inside. It requires that no distortions of the light waves are detected."

David looks at me and breaks out laughing. He sputters between laughs, "You are not only gorgeous but also brilliant. How did I get so lucky as to come to your office in North Carolina looking for Winston?

I thank God every night that Sir Winston's book, with the secret code chose you to be on our team. From what Abigor said, we are not sure the book story is what happened now. Beyond may have always meant to give you to me with a slight direction change to destroy a monster weapon."

We approach the church's front entrance and pass through the massive doors. We stop for a minute to kiss. I suppose it is not sacrilegious to kiss in the narthex of the Cathedral. We walk reverently toward the nave, cross ourselves, and genuflect. We chose a bench in the front that devout believers have worn smooth and glossy after many decades of sitting in church services. As soon as we sit, weightlessness comes over me, and I feel as if I could float in the air. My body, mind, and spirit are at peace, not encumbered by the enemies unbeknownst to us in the malevolent fog that shrouds our lives. Yes, we have a heavy burden that must be borne until victory removes the Herculean weight from our shoulders. Yet even that seems a little lighter. I pray for guidance, strength, and courage to stop the devastation that threatens Earth. David is also deep in devout prayer. I look toward the magnificent old altar with its scarred wood cross, and I am shocked to see a column of light moving slowly toward us.

I nudge David. The hair stands on the back of my neck, and I feel the tingling of chill bumps. David is a rock and is nonplused, as usual. We stare, fascinated by the moving light, and it stops before us. We gaze at it, and it seems to regard us with mild curiosity. I think I see pale blue eyes. Indeed, it is a spirit, but is it our spirit? St. Albans holy Cathedral is many centuries old. Construction began in 1077. It is probably crawling with dead priests. Then I hear a soft, melodious voice, "Yes, it is I, your loving friend Antonio. I have missed you and our afternoon teas, dearest Bones. David, I sense that events have not been going well since I left you. Tell this old priest what you need." I cannot speak, yet you would think I would be comfortable with ghosts by now. David is a ghost, so the strangeness is minimal for him. He casually answers the Padre, "We miss you too, Father Antonio. We are desperate, which I acknowledge is not unusual for us. We cannot neutralize the Doomsday Machine. The demon Aaii protects it with a supernatural force field. Even Abigor cannot destroy what another demon has created. Besides, he is no longer a demon. He is searching for Aaii now. He tells us there is an entity that Aaii fears, and he is looking for that entity for leverage. If that plan does not work, we may be left with only the implausible journey of searching for the Fantastic Machine. You know the ambiguities and dangers inherent with that option. I do not plan to lose Bones in what may be a black void."

A thought strikes me, and I shudder. How do we know we are talking to Father Antonio? I must always be mindful that powerful forces of darkness are pitted against us. Would David know if evil beings were playing us since he returned from Beyond as much more than a human? David looks at me as if he hears my thoughts and nods slightly. The faint movement would not have registered with me if I were not in tune with his body. I think we are on the same page. His intuitive ability is much more acute than mine. I will leave the analysis of 'the Padre' to him. I wonder whether I am becoming paranoid.

Father Antonio is sympathetic. "I understand, my son. These are almost impossible decisions since so much hangs in the balance. I am sure you have consulted with your other eminent team members. What does the brilliant and oft-tested Sir Winston say? David, have you considered that all of this about a Fantastic Machine is a sinister plot to have you chasing fantasy rather than working on your other tasks? Also, you cannot know what the weapon can or cannot do if activated. Demolishing the diabolical scientists and vicious Neo-Nazis is of the utmost importance. I am aware that if the weapon is as powerful as you have been told, it will take care of the scientists and everyone else. Be wise and pray for courage and discernment. Hark, look to Druid for guidance. Dearest Bones, seeing you blooming with robust wellness is marvelous. Last time I saw you, I was terrified that we had lost you to that murderous beast."

Tears well in my eyes, and I utter, "I am in debt to you for so much, Father Antonio. How can I ever thank you for frightening away the monster, Weber, and comforting me as I lie there in pain?"

David says through his teeth, "Weber will pay for his brutality soon. I promise! My dearest friend, I owe you for being there for Bones when I was not. Father Antonio, I will bless your name until I face my maker, uh, again." He stands and bows to the padre.

David pauses for a moment, gathering his thoughts before he says, "In answer to your question, Churchill has directed us to look at all possible options before choosing a path. Naturally, Dr. Einstein and the others agree. We are not committed to anything other than the need for measured haste now. I understand what you are saying, and it is certainly possible, Padre." I notice that David is being more general and evasive in his answers now. It cuts me deeply to doubt Father Antonio. If he is my beloved Padre, I am being ungrateful and disloyal. Sir Winston and I love Cicero, who wrote, 'Nothing is nobler, nothing more venerable than loyalty.' I value the virtue of loyalty above all other virtues. And now, I question my doubts. Am I being faithless to someone I love dearly? I choose to believe in Father Antonio.

While I am having this pointless conversation with myself, David and the Padre are still chatting. David is ending their chat. "Padre, thank you for giving us the gift of your wisdom tonight. We are indebted to you and will return if the world doesn't go poof. You were a cherished member of our Team, and we miss you terribly. We must return to the others. Our time to stop the annihilation is dwindling." David turns to me, "Come, Bones, we must get back." I awkwardly echo David's words to the column of glowing light and pass through the historic cathedral. I am so deep in thought that I don't even notice the incredible architectural beauty around me. St Albans is famous for its exceptional medieval wall paintings, quality, and quantity. I did not see a single painting. In my defense, I was a bit engrossed in pressing matters such as survival and loyalty.

We return to the souped-up Rolls. As David holds the door for me, I burst out with questions like, "What do you think? I love the Padre. End of conversation."

David kisses me because he wants to or to stop my questions. He furtively surveys the area and whispers, "We shall talk in a few minutes when we return to the chamber of horrors. Be patient, my love." He says louder, "Are you comfortable, Bones?" Now, I want answers, and none are coming my way. Being in the dark is maddening, and squirming around in my seat is the best I can do for now. What is going on?

We are playing Chitty Chitty Bang Bang again and drinking in the glory of the incredible harvest moon. It seems to watch us impassively with little interest in us or our mission. I remember some scraps from my high school astronomy class. A full moon is opposite the sun in its orbit around our planet. Astronomers define a moon as full when it is precisely 180 degrees opposite the sun. OK, I am a nerd with nothing better to do than reminisce about a class I hated. Thank God we finally arrive back at the Tunnel after a night of magic and miracles.

David gets out of the Rolls and walks to my side to open the door for me. Yes, he is an old-school gentleman, and I bask in it! I practically attack him with a bombardment of questions. He puts his arms around me and explains, "My love, I am not certain what happened at St. Albans. Something indefinable was unquestionably off, so I cut our chat short. I have never seen a returning spirit from Beyond look like Moses' burning bush. Maybe that is standard with dead priests, but I was not convinced, and I know you were also wondering. If he is Father Antonio, I owe him a tremendous debt."

We talked as we strolled down the damp, foul-smelling tunnel to the Demon Chamber. Our Team members, minus Red and Abigor, are assembled and discussing Druid, The New Global Agenda, and Dr. Wagner and his mad scientists since that is our next adventure if Abigor is successful with Aaii.

Dr. Einstein says, "We must be ready to stop Dr. Wagner as he draws closer to cloning the Nazi monsters. That was our original mission, gentlemen and Bones, and we have lost our focus. Realistically, if volcanoes erupt due to massive earthquakes, Dr. Wagner will be the least of our problems. Still, we must have a strategy while waiting for Abigor. Therefore, we have time to discuss options. When we neutralize the Doomsday Machine, we must be ready to act immediately! When we see Druid, we can ask him about Bones' role. Amazingly, she was chosen before she was born. Just in case, I suggest David and Angus continue to try to open the machine."

Sophie is watching the genius and nodding her great head in agreement. She is naturally optimistic and helps me stand on the side of light. I remember something Soph told me after our first mission. During that conversation, she was another creature and could speak to me through her thoughts. Soph also said I was born for this team, and she helped prepare me for my role. I just remembered that! How could I forget that? I am not going to share that until I talk to Soph.

Sir Winston is lighting his cigar and clapping Albert on the back. Churchill believes in the power of optimism and action. As soon as he took the reins as Prime Minister in 1940, his electrifying energy shook up Whitehall. In Geoffrey Best's Churchill and War, I remember reading that the new Prime Minister took out his engraved silver match-box and set Whitehall on fire, figuratively speaking.

Churchill's inexhaustible energy was felt immediately in Whitehall. Government departments, which under Neville Chamberlain had worked at much the same pace as in peacetime, began to run rather than walk. Soon, they awoke to the realities of war. A sense of urgency was created over a few days, and respectable civil servants were seen running along the corridors. Telephones quadrupled their efficiency. The Chiefs of Staff were in almost constant session, regular office hours ceased to exist, and weekends disappeared.

The Powers in Beyond knew our immense challenges. We desperately needed the fireball known as Winston Churchill. The portly man with the umbrella, round glasses, and a Cuban cigar is our only hope for success. My optimism is rising to new heights as I remember what Sir Winston has accomplished in his extraordinary life. Hey, we've got this! I hope.

Chapter Seventeen

Weber and the Giant

Druid plans to terrorize Aaii into cooperation, but currently, he is busy in London as he promised he would be. Druid knows he must return to help the team soon, so he can only choose one miscreant to visit today. After little consideration, he decides on Weber Weber. Druid had promised David that revenge would be visited upon the murderous Neo-Nazi. He keeps his promises.

Weber does not exert the worldwide power of Annette Simmons-Wright, Juan Diez, Emerson North, and Julian Chan. Their organization has thousands of influential members worldwide with the objective of Elite rule over the peasants. They foresee and work toward the New Global Agenda, where countries will no longer be independent and self-governing. To accomplish this assault on liberty, they will vigorously punish noncompliance and censor opposing voices. These despicable humans plan to handcuff the planet to a totalitarian regime run by a newly branded and re-packaged Adolph Hitler. Druid will get to them later. They can depend on his retribution. First things first, Weber shot Bones, so he earned the number one spot on Druid's hit list. Naturally, Druid knows where to find Weber.

Weber had rented a house in Whitechapel Gardens close to the location of Dr. Mengele's lab before the Team found it. Hurriedly, Mengele and his brutes fled for their lives. Druid is impressed by Weber's good taste in housing. He rented a pricy end-of-terrace brick house with a garage. This general area was the hunting ground for Jack the Ripper in the 1880s. Some residents say the shadow of the fiend still hangs over Whitechapel. Residents and visitors alike do not tarry alone in the dark alleys after sunset. Several pubs add their festive aura to the area, and the streets ring with cheerful chatter late into the night. Yet, when a lone woman walks these streets, she is alert and watchful until she is safe among trusted friends. At times, a peal of chilling laughter rings out near the White Hart Pub, where the Ripper's victim, Martha Tabram, drank her final toddy.

Druid is waiting in the garden behind Weber's rental house. The blood-red climbing roses along the fence are magnificent and glow in the moonlight. Druid wonders idly about the gardener who planted the showy flowers. He knows the over-bulked thug will be home from the gym soon. He has made it his business to learn Weber's schedule. Weber has lived here alone since his psychopathic pal, Axel Fischer, died. Axel tangled with the wrong person. David Smythe killed him as he was attempting to crush Bones' hyoid bone. Druid must agree with the Powers in Beyond that the woman is attacked and dies a lot.

Druid hears Weber's car pull into the garage. The grim giant walks into the kitchen through the locked backdoor. He waits for the brutal Neo-Nazi to turn on the lights. As he flips the light switch, Weber jumps back and almost falls over a kitchen chair when he sees his uninvited guest. He yells out, "Get out of my house. I know who you are, and you don't scare me like you did Seth and his sissy friends. I said, get out!" Muscleman Weber shakes, and his voice cracks when he speaks, belying his false bravado.

Druid shakes his head and cautions him, "Why are you surprised, Weber? I promised you I would come for you. You shot Bones, an innocent young woman. Do you deny that, blackguard? I heard you brag about killing her in Seth's office! You may be interested to know you failed, sinner. Bones lives. I found her after it was too late for me to help, but others more powerful than me saved her. I have given you time to seek redemption and save your miserable soul. What have you done?" Sinner seems downcast to learn he is a failure. Pity.

Weber grows more combative as time passes. Relying on his steroid-soaked brain, he stupidly thinks he can take this giant. He yells at Druid, "I don't know what you are talking about! Get out, scumbag! What if I did kill her? She weren't nothing to me. You are lying! She were dead! Come and get me if you think you can!" With jaw clenched, chin tucked down, knees bent, and rear lowered, he braces for a physical attack by the giant that will never come. He cannot brace for what is in store for him.

Druid reaches under his long black duster, drawing out a glowing sword with intricate carvings and brilliant jewels. He swings it around his head with blinding speed. It is a mighty and tremendous blade given to him by God Himself.

Then Weber makes a fatal mistake. He draws his revolver from his waistband and shoots Druid three times. Bang. Bang. Bang!

The Giant looks at his duster. So, what if it has a few more holes? As Druid swings the sword for the last time, he booms, "I am His instrument, the Sword of Retribution, sinner!"

Weber tries to run as Druid lets the sword take flight and it spins toward Weber at lightning speed. The blade cleanly separates Weber's head from his body, and both fall separately to the floor. His journey to Hell is over. The floor opens . . .

Blood splashes on the white tile. Weber's eyes are still open and disbelieving. He crosses into the world of hellfire, where the living cannot enter.

Druid holds up his enormous hand, and the sword flies back to him as if it were a lethal boomerang or Thor's hammer, Mjolnir. He grabs the sword by the shaft and tucks it back under his weathered duster. The giant picks up his well-worn bowler and puts it back on his head. He looks at Weber and says in a quiet, gentle voice, "I gave you precious time to repent. You chose to continue in your sinful ways. May

God have mercy on your soul." Then he says in a less reverent voice, "Say hello to Beelzebub for me. I look forward to grappling with him again someday." Druid breaks into a brilliant yet terrifying smile as he says these last words.

The Sword of Retribution walks through the kitchen door into the garden. There, he pauses to bask in the fragrance of the glorious flowers. He picks one red rose, rubs it gently against his face, feels its satiny smoothness, and strides into his destiny.

Chapter Eighteen

The Insane Asylum

We are back together except for Abigor and Red, who are still tracking Aaii and Archangel Michael. The team jumps into what we do best: brainstorming. We have discussed Dr. Wagner and his wicked associates and how we will permanently neutralize their evil plans once we finish this part of the mission—keeping the world in one piece. Assuming we will conquer the bewitched machine gives us a bump in morale we desperately need. Agatha Christie's Team tipped us off that the medical maniacs were returning to London from France. They will join Dr. Mengele's mad scientists. The plan had always been to combine the two teams when Dr. Mengele thought they were safe from the assassins who stalked them. Of course, that would be us.

Dr. Wagner believes it would be more efficient to join the larger group of scientists living in London, where they have a sizeable Neo-Nazi contingent to protect them. Wagner looked for property suitable for their needs and ultimately decided on an old Insane Asylum sitting deserted and decaying since the 1960s—quite fitting, I should think. It sits in the middle of several acres in a small village far from prying eyes. It is called Quietude Asylum near Leicester. The property has been abandoned since the institutional hospitals for the chronically mentally ill were shuttered because of concerns about inhumane treatment. Treating the mentally ill in community centers while allowing them to live at home was considered an excellent, less restrictive, and more humane idea. Most Western nations, including England and the United States, followed the "more humane" plan. Paradoxically, deinstitutionalization is frequently cited as the primary reason for the enormous, burgeoning homeless population. Many homeless individuals have an addiction and/or at least one mental illness diagnosis. There is nowhere for the chronically mentally ill or their families to turn for long-term treatment now—unintentional consequences.

The buildings and grounds will be adapted for Dr. Wagner's purposes, and then they can triple the number of scientists working on their projects. He also plans extensive experimentation using, ironically, homeless individuals as subjects. Since Dr. Mengele's Youth Formula has not been tested on women or older individuals, he must begin the lengthy testing process. Most of their elite New Global Agenda patients who seek to recapture their fading youth will, naturally, be older men and women. The Youth Drug has only been administered to a few individuals. They were all psychopaths in their prime of life. In fact, the list of subjects is incredibly short: Drs. Mengele and Wagner, Hans Schmitt, Franz Wolffe, and Edward Wentworth. All are dead except Dr. Wagner. Although the Youth Drug is highly effective, most have died of heart disease. The drug did not protect their hearts. Ironically, those organs continued to deteriorate with every beat.

Mengle was never able to eliminate that pesky glitch. The subjects who died of heart disease were approximately 100 to 110 years old. The subjects looked precisely the same as when they received the drug treatment in the 1940s. Even considering the fatal heart glitch, extending life by 20 to 30 robust years was a miraculous accomplishment in and of itself. After treatment, subjects were tougher than before the treatment and remarkably resistant to illnesses. Because of a recent improvement in the formula, subjects heal like lizards. Another small group received the Drug. They were specialized former SS, an elite group of paranoid, skilled assassins. Consequently, no one knows how many survive. Psychopathy is also a resultant side effect of the Youth Drug if one is not already a psychopath. Naturally, Dr. Wagner doesn't consider psychopathy undesirable. He, always the optimist, embraces the "positive" traits, charisma, charm, coolness under pressure, and a lack of conscience. The deviant doctor often quips, "What is there not to like about psychopathy?"

Since their sample of subjects is ridiculously limited and homogeneous, they cannot generalize the data to a larger population. Dr. Wagner will start at the beginning of his research design to overcome small sample bias and study reliability. His ambitious plans will require a heavy dose of financial support from his villainous friends at New Global Agenda.

Wagner's team enthusiastically anticipates cloning the arch-Nazis Adolph Hitler, Heinrich Himmler, and Joseph Goebbels. He expects to complete that cloning process soon after moving into their new home in England. The Demon Aaii had promised to top off the three Nazis. He will do this by returning to them their original personalities, knowledge, and the essence of their beings. They will be the unique fiends they were in life.

Wagner had hoped to find an estate in London, but Leicester is only a couple of hours' drive to the east midlands of England. The Mad Scientist had to adjust his location requirements to acquire the perfect property. Large, secluded estates in London are not as easy to find as they were in Dracula's time.

Wagner still holds Dr. Suggs as a captive, uncompensated employee without the usual employment benefits and vacation days. The Team will liberate the dear man as soon as the blow-up-the-world thing is over. His expertise is essential for the success of Wagner's plans. Thus, Suggs will be safe and well cared for until we take him home to his family and laboratory. We are anxious to see that happy reunion. Regrettably, the impact of the emotional and psychological harm to Dr. Suggs may be severe and long-lasting.

Dr. Wagner has many variables to consider as he moves forward with cloning the three Nazis. One of those variables is the New Global Agenda (NGA). They plan to use the vile monsters to subjugate humankind under NGA's iron fist. They are confident that Hitler is the ideal lunatic with his oratorical skill, brilliance, and psychopathic charisma to lead the radical movement. They chose Himmler because he was instrumental in growing the Nazi Movement and believed he could repeat the black magic for their movement. NGA recognized what Goebbels brought to the movement: propaganda and marketing genius. Goebbels wrapped Nazism in glowing, impressive, appealing words. He was a star at twisting words to hypnotize the masses at home and abroad. Goebbels used propaganda as his canvas to paint "reality" to enhance public acceptance of the Nazi Party. He spoke of a National Community and spelled out who was and was not in the National Community. Division was a powerful and corrupting tool in their plans. Hitler appointed Goebbels to head the Reich Ministry of Public Enlightenment and Propaganda.

Nazis believed controlling information was essential to shackling the German people and placating the rest of Europe. Every form of communication, radio, newspapers, school textbooks, and films were designed to support the Nazi Party and its Hellish philosophy. There were no differing views because Hitler had abolished Freedom of Speech, the foundation that maintains a free people. The German language was manipulated in a very dark way to villainize Jews and other marginalized groups under the National Socialist German Workers Party. When reality turned unfavorable for the Nazis during the War, Goebbels pulled out his old standard—lies. Also, significantly, he hinted at a secret miracle weapon.

Contrary to his usual lies, he might have been telling the truth if his miracle was the Doomsday Machine. Soon after the "secret miracle" weapon was touted, Hitler committed suicide. The next day, according to records, Joseph Goebbels and his wife Magda murdered their six young children and then committed suicide. Soviet troops found them. Thus, the reports of their deaths may not be entirely accurate.

Hitler was portrayed as a charismatic nationalist leader. Goebbels was the star-maker. Heinrich Himmler was the Monster Nazi Enforcer. He greatly expanded the vile Waffen-Schutzstaffel as a strong arm of Nazism. Himmler was an inflexible slave to fanatical organization and numbers. He combined an obsession with philosophical mysticism with a cold-bloodedness rivaled only by Vlad the Impaler. Himmler had a leading and shameful role in the Nazi's reign of terror, and not surprisingly, he also committed suicide.

The NGA Committee admired these vile humans and believed they would succeed in controlling humanity this time, though they failed in the 1940s. The NGA tasked Wagner with cloning the worst of the worst from the nightmare, which was Nazi Germany.

Wagner and his minions keep their new location a deep, dark secret to avoid unwelcome visitors who might threaten their existence. I am proud to say that would be us. Since Beyond has Teams worldwide, keeping us in the dark is much more challenging than Wagner had anticipated. The purchase of the old property is big news in the area, and we have attentive ears close to the ground. All the locals are talking about and guessing who Dr. Wagner is and how he will use the old building.

His cover story is that they are scientists working on a cure for fibrodysplasia ossificans progressiva or FOP. This is an extremely rare disease in which the body's tendons and ligaments undergo a strange metamorphosis, essentially a transformation into bone. Only a couple of million patients suffer from this disease. Dr. Wagner hopes the dreadfulness and rarity of the disease will discourage unwanted curiosity and prying eyes.

His large estate and remote location will provide the privacy he cherished in France. The French estate was walled, and armed guards were scattered about, adding another layer of beyond-the-pale security. After the Team learned Dr. Wagner might be working with the Evil Mengele, Dr. Einstein was dispatched to France to investigate. Observing closely, he was shocked to see the razor wire topping the old Roman-built stone wall surrounding the estate. One could overlook the excessive secrecy unless one is incredibly observant. Our genius was suspicious when he saw the high level of security not generally utilized by a legitimate research facility. Dr. Einstein reached out to Wagner, posing as an editor for a highly regarded international medical journal. The genius requested an interview with Wagner, and the arrogant cretin rudely refused Einstein's invitation. Genius, stung by the rebuff, knew Wagner was not a credible scientist. Medical researchers never have the financial security to reject an opportunity to be heralded in an article in a distinguished journal. Researchers dream of professional recognition, the bump it brings to their prestige, and the lifeblood of research—donations.

Wagner was on our radar after Dr. Einstein's visit. Now, we have him again. We shall visit when we have the time to give him the attention he deserves. Hang on, dear Dr. Suggs, the cavalry led by the courageous equestrian Sir Winston Churchill is on the way! Lt. Churchill received his commission on February 20, 1895. He sailed for India in 1896 as a proud member of the Queen's Own Hussars. He began his military career on a steed and is still quite the horseman.

Dr. Wagner's Asylum: Seth Watches

Dr. Wagner sits in the ancient conservatory in his new estate, sipping vodka and talking on his iPhone 13 Pro. "What are you talking about, Seth? I told you we would be moving to England per Dr. Mengele's plan. I will admit that the opportunity came together faster than I had anticipated. I had to move quickly when I found the perfect property for our new, vastly expanded research projects. I signed the contract and called our Neo-Nazi Neanderthals to help us with the heavy work, and we relocated here. As you are aware, our human subject capacity must be significantly expanded. We need room for at least a hundred new researchers and as many research subjects. We will also be investing in high-performance computing resources." The Doctor babbles on with more good news, "I am excited to tell you we have identified work in synergistic cellular pathways for longevity that could amplify the lifespan. Our hackers monitor their work, and we may have to extend an invitation to one of their key scientists." Dr. Wagner laughs darkly as he says these chilling words. Shades of Dr. Suggs?

The egotistical doctor returns to his story. "I am terribly busy with our many projects, Seth, and I don't have time to report to you as often as you would like."

Seth breaks in, "I look forward to visiting you soon with the NGA Committee members. We have been neglectful and must catch up on your work." Dr. Wagner blinks, frowns, and retorts, "Yes, you are quite welcome to visit our new facility with members of the NGA in tow. After all, they support our work and have been quite generous. I am sorry. What did you say?" Dr. Wagner looks up to his butler, who delivers another vodka and spinach quiche with fruit. He nods to him, possibly a sumo wrestler, and rudely dismisses him. Hmmm, where have I seen that bulk and face? Of course. He is a member of John Kennedy's Team. Nice!

Seth repeats his question. "I said, when will you begin to, uh, re-cruit subjects for the Youth Formula experiments? I believe you said you would use both male and female homeless subjects to verify how the formula will perform on middle-aged and older subjects. I assume, for obvious reasons, you will be finding these subjects far from your facility. We cannot afford to call attention to your work." Dr. Wagner rolls his eyes and glances at the old rose garden, now gone to decay. The garden seems sad, with only a few brown sticks left of what was once a magnificent spot alive with dazzling colors. What the good doc-tor does not realize is that I can see everything he is doing. I have pow-ers the doctor cannot imagine.

Wagner replies, trying to keep his voice even, "Of course, we will hunt afar. And we will procure a few subjects from each area. No one will miss them. Why would homeless people be missed? No one has been concerned about them up to this point. They are parasites on so-ciety. They should be grateful that we will give a purpose to their mis-erable lives." Seth must take a breath and count to ten. The doctor chatters on, "Also, we will begin the cloning process as soon as our equipment is set up and tested. I am studying Dr. Mengele's journal to avoid a misstep in removing the nucleus. As I have explained to you, this is exceptionally delicate work, and we have only one chance be-cause we have one cell from each candidate. If we fail to remove the nucleus cleanly, the cell is destroyed. Naturally, I will not allow that to happen." On the other end of the line, Seth smiles and must control his laughter by biting his lip. Right, Wagner, you keep believing in your success.

Seth pulls out his silver matchbox and says, "I wish you enormous success, Doctor, and I look forward to seeing you in a couple of days. No doubt, you shall triumph in your numerous world-changing pro-jects. Be assured that the NGA Committee members support you completely. Now, I must join them in a virtual emergency meeting. Goodbye, Doctor." He hangs up and laughs until he is rolling on the floor, unable to control his merriment. Yes, doctor, my friend Druid will be seeing you soon. Enjoy!

Dr. Wagner feels an acute discomfiture after his conversation with Seth, and he cannot pinpoint the reason. Oh well, he tells himself he is probably just exhausted from all his monumental projects. He turns his attention back to the rotting rose garden.

When Seth gathers himself together again, he tunes in to Annette's virtual emergency meeting. He is the last to join the discussion. He sees the others brought to him by their computer cameras. Seth notices the distinct look of fear, disbelief, and anger reflected on each face. Annette begins by screaming into her speaker. She is radiant in a blue silk robe, diamond earrings, and a white neck brace. Charming.

Seth turns down his audio because Annette is blowing out his speakers. She screams, "What was that? What was that in your office? Did it threaten us? Yes, it did! I know it did! Why did everyone step on me? Do you see this neck brace? I was in the emergency room at Presbyterian Lower Manhattan for hours. They ignored me because I did not have bullet wounds like everyone else! I demand to know who trod on me as I lay helpless in your office!"

When she stops to breathe, Seth asks her, "Annette, my dear woman, how are you? Will you be all right? I am so sorry. I would have sent flowers had I known." Seth almost chokes on his words.

Julian is the next screamer. "Never mind, Annette! I want my questions answered immediately! What did we see? Are we in danger? It said we would die or some such thing as that! What are you doing about this outrage? I demand justice!" Julian is not his usual, perfectly groomed and dressed self. He needs a shave, his hair is mussed, and his eyes are twitching.

Emerson is lost. He looks as if he has not slept and has been boozing. He keeps lifting and dropping his hands as if he does not know what they are supposed to do.

When he speaks, his words are slurred. Seth wonders about Emerson's wellness and sobriety. He sees a nurse in pink scrubs hovering behind him.

Emerson lifts his right hand and looks at it, puzzled. He says, "I aamm not suuurre . . . who are yooouu? Angel?" He turns away from the computer and wanders off the screen.

Juan is the worst. He sits in his desk chair, staring at the screen. Seth asks him, "Juan, are you all right? How can we help you? Juan?" Juan is not dressed. Seth is thankful he only sees Juan's face and neck. Seth sees Juan's butler in the background. Evidently, he tuned into the virtual meeting. Juan could not have performed that complex operation.

Annette screams again, "Seth, do something! For the love of God, do something! Julian, shut up!"

Seth mumbles, "I didn't realize Annette was religious."

Julian, turning red with rage, yells, "Annette, you egotistical, ugly cow, go away! Seth, what about me?"

Seth promises Julian and Annette that he will do something.

Seth turns off his computer and muses that Druid does not need to visit them. Their belief that they could do any vile and evil act against humanity, even collaborating with a demon, and never pay the price for their wicked behavior, is shattered. They are now mere shells of their former selves. When a narcissist runs headlong into reality, it is a devastating blow to their ego. Because narcissists' fantasies are rarely factual, it can lead to frustration and anger when their egocentric visions blow up in their faces.

Regrettably, it is not over for NGA. Other snakes will slither in to replace them.

Chapter Nineteen

The Hunt for Aaii

Red and Abigor return to the Savoy in London to make their plans. The luxury suite serves as their headquarters when they are not in Poland dealing with monsters. Abigor looks at his watch. They have 15 hours left until detonation. Red is pacing the enormous room as time presses against him. He is a warrior with no obvious opponent.

Abigor goes into the study to concentrate on the stream of consciousness. Understanding the voices and seeing the images as time passes becomes more challenging. Eventually, he will no longer gain any information from the stream. After all, he is no longer a demon and has joined the opposition. Soon, his connection with demons will break entirely.

Abigor sits at the vast partner's desk in their English Gentlemen's Club study and closes his intense green eyes. After a few minutes of concentration, he picks up bits and pieces of the demons' thoughts. He has no control over what he hears. It is entirely random. Precious minutes pass, and he continues to grasp for something that will help him find Aaii. He hears the demon Belphegor think about banquets, and he is busy seducing people with promises of great wealth. He advocates laziness and sloth—couch potatoes, nothing to interest Abigor. Then, he breaks into Shaitan's thoughts. He infects human minds with evil suggestions. Humans have no idea Shaitan exists or controls their thoughts. Next, he hears Beelzebub, associated with the Canaanite god Baal. He has the dubious honor of being one of the seven princes in Hell. He is thinking about or imagining his power in Hell. This is definitely not what Abigor needs.

Then suddenly, a familiar voice whisks by . . . is it . . . can it be? Yes, it is Aaii! Abigor is all attention now as he strains to absorb every bit of information. He could lose the connection with Aaii at any minute. He is picking up tidbits, suggesting that Aaii is in Leicester, just a short distance from London. It is not that distance matters even if Bones were with him since she can transport now. His thoughts turn to the raven-haired warrior, and he wishes she were with him, and he suffers a jab of sharp pain. He jerks himself back to the present.

He reminds himself that he is there for a reason. Get back to Aaii! He can see the enormous old house where Aaii is hiding. Wait! He sees someone else. Dr. Wagner is there, too. He recognized him from Dr. Einstein's thoughts when he was in France. Excellent!

He calls Red to join him in the study. "Come in, Red. Guess who I have located?" A huge smile brightens Red's face, and his good eye twinkles with delight. "So you found the slithering snake! Excellent job, Abigor! I cannot wait to see him again after all the trouble he has caused us. Maybe he can make up for some of his mischief by destroying his infernal weapon. Had he not protected it, we would be working on our primary mission instead of running all over the globe chasing shadows. I owe him for that, too." Red slams his fist into his beefy hand, demonstrating what he would like to do to Aaii.

Abigor admires Red's courage and confidence, but he reminds him, "Aaii art still a powerful demon. We hast only so much control over him. That control comes from Michael. Thus, we must also find our winged warrior friend. We have Aaii in our grasp, and now we can concentrate on finding Michael. I am going to have to think about that. How does one find an archangel? Who does one ask? Perhaps Father Antonio could tell us. He is our authority on all things angelic." Abigor pauses in thought, and he stares at Red. "Wait, thee predicted that Druid would come to the chamber to help us when we fought Aaii.

Druid never came. I would like to hear more about that, Red. What part dost Druid play in all this other than yelling at us? Can he help us find Michael?"

Red looks surprised by Abigor's question. He adjusts the patch over his eye and answers, "Druid and I hung out some when I was trying to win my way back into bloody Beyond after I shocked their sensibilities in the War. I was more violent in fighting against the Hellish Nazis than the Powers thought was mannerly and British. Hell, it was not afternoon tea with the Queen! I was not as gentle as Beyond would have liked. Because of this difference in opinion, most of my Team and I survived the War. Since we are working together, Abigor, you should understand who I am and that I do not regret anything I did in the war years. Survival and defeating the enemy were our primary objectives in SOE. Many more good folks would have died if I had been less aggressive. We sent dozens of women to France to fight from the shadows. I trained women in hand-to-hand combat, guns, explosives, surveillance, evading capture, complex codes, and radio operations. I tried not to weep when I handed them suicide pills in case the worst happened."

Red pauses to compose himself. He coughs gruffly and returns to his story. "Tragedy struck in February 1944 when 19 SOE operatives were captured and executed. Germans had confiscated a wireless and notes that gave them the location and time of the parachute drop. Yes, I was vicious, combating the monsters who would shoot women in the back of the head. Anna Gant was one of the women I trained, and we fell in love. We lay on the ground under the stars, dreaming about buying a small farm on the East Coast on many blissful nights. Anna had enlisted in the First Aid Nursing Yeomanry to give her cover. The SS caught her in their web when she parachuted in on that darkest of nights. My beautiful, intelligent, brave, funny, and hot-tempered redhead was gone. A grateful country posthumously awarded her the Victoria Cross." Red reaches into his jeans pocket, pulls out the medal, and lovingly caresses it. Abigor pats his shoulder and wipes away the tears that roll down his face. Yes, Abigor understands his pain, and it breaks his angelic heart. Red explains why he wants to go to Beyond, "I wouldn't care, and I would accept my fate like a man for my ruthlessness, but I want to be with Anna." Red stepped neatly around Abigor's question about Druid.

Abigor looks away for a moment, blinks, and says." I am a former demon. I have no right to throw stones. I do not judge thee, Red. Thee did what thee believed was right at the time. I am deeply sorry for the loss of thine beloved Anna. I understand more than thee know." Red stares at Abigor, wondering what that means. Abigor is an angel. He does not feel romantic love. Or does he? He thinks of a woman with luminous brown eyes.

Abigor returns to their mission. "Thank thee for allowing me to see who thee art, Red. As I said, we must find Michael, and as a recently reclaimed angel, I dost not know the secret stuff yet. Four friends who might be able to assist us come to mind: Father Antonio, Alpha, Omega, and the Admiral. The Admiral and Thelma are right here in London, Father Antonio is near, and Alpha and Omega are a hop away. I would rather not involve the heavenly duo. I never know how that will turn out—besides, they art not particularly fond of thee now. My instinct tells me to talk to Father Antonio if that is possible. Bones and David were going to visit him, but I knoweth not how successful they were." Abruptly, the room shakes, and the windows rattle. A fascinating heavenly fragrance permeates the room. The enigmatic Druid, in all his glory, black suit, dusty huge boots, and bowler, stands before them like the fabled Colossus of Rhodes.

Druid booms out. "Well, Abigor and Red, what are you doing? Waiting for room service? Don't you have a deadline?" He looks at his massive wrist, which is not wearing a watch, and shouts, "I think it is 15 hours before detonation, and here you stand exchanging stories?" The room rumbles again with the Mach 1 wave clap of Druids' voice. They struggle to remain upright, bracing against the vibration—Red and Abigor miss David, who always goes toe to toe with this potentially catastrophic mighty force.

Finally, the room stops shaking, and Abigor responds, "Druid, we art very much aware of the time and half of our mission is complete. We found Aaii in an estate outside Leicester. We must locate Archangel Michael, for he is our leverage. We need Aaii to remove his protective force from the machine, and he fears only Michael. We also discovered that Dr. Herman Wagner is at the estate, too. I assume this is his new laboratory in England. We knew he planned to reconstitute the mad scientists' teams from France and London somewhere in England. He must have found a property large enough for spacious laboratories, numerous scientists, and subjects for his research. This is a gift, so we will not have to find Wagner. Thus, no Druid, we have not been standing around telling war stories. Art thee here to help us? While discussing duties, why the Hell were thee not in the Chamber when we fought against Aaii and his devils? Thee told us thee would fight with us." Red looks at Abigor with his mouth hanging open. He didn't know angels could say Hell or sling rebukes at their betters. This is indeed a shocking revelation!

The Giant sits down and begins laughing, which turns into a foot-stomping, knee-slapping, rocking back and forth until tears rain down his handsome face guffaw. This explosive levity lasts for several minutes while Red and Abigor fear this might be a psychotic break. Abigor wishes desperately that Bones were here to diagnose Druid. The building is shaking as if an earthquake were erupting under the Savoy. Red ponders what the other occupants think.

Eventually, the Giant stops laughing, focuses his startling blue eyes on the angel and the dead MI5 agent, and asks, "Abigor, look at me, and think. Who am I?" Abigor does not know what to make of the question. He looks at Druid and thinks as Druid asked him to do.

Abigor squints and stares. Nothing registers. Druid removes his bowler and says, "Look with your heart and soul, man. Listen to your spiritual voice."

Abigor squints harder, tightens his jaw, cocks his head, and—still nothing. The Giant is about to pound on the angel's head to loosen up his gray matter. When suddenly, Abigor jumps up and yells, "I know! I know! Why did I not see it? It is obvious when one's mind is open. Of course! Thee art Archangel Michael! Oh my God! May I shake thy hand?"

The only Archangel mentioned by name in the Bible reaches out to shake Abigor's hand. Red has always known the truth, so the time has come to reveal it? Red learned long ago how to keep a secret. The whole 'loose lips sink ships thing.' However, he asked Bones if she knew who Druid really was. She did not. Red is bewildered. Can angels say, "Oh My God" and "Hell"?

Druid remains in costume, the weathered black suit. No need to show massive, feathered wings now. He says to Abigor, "I am ready to go to Dr. Wagner's new estate soon. However, we must discuss something first. We are not ready to deal with Dr. Wagner, his scientists, the Neo-Nazis, and NGA. They are all connected in a web of evil and deceit. Their time will come. I have warned the NGA Committee to allow them time to repent. I staunchly suggested repenting. Weber Weber was at the NGA meeting and verily, he was duly warned of the consequences of his wickedness. I decided to visit Weber Weber first. He shot Bones, and she would still be dead if it were not for Alpha and Omega. I promised David the villainy would not go unpunished, and I kept that promise. Weber did not use his time to repent and was wicked until his last breath. He lost his head, literally, smote by the Sword of Righteousness. He shot me! Three times. He was punished." They look at Michael in amazement. He said he cut Weber's head off with a sword and didn't seem to be at all remorseful.

Unrepentant Michael says, "I suggest we take Aaii to the Chamber and deal with him there. We will return to the doctor when we are ready to sort out the entire interconnected group. Wagner will be given the same warning as Weber Weber to allow him time to repent. The Neo-Nazis will also receive a final warning. At present, I have no interest in the lesser scientists—that can wait. I have little hope the Neo-Nazis will use their time on their knees asking for forgiveness. Another, higher than I, oversees forgiveness. I am the Sword of Retribution!" He throws his right arm up as if holding a sword.

Abigor nods slowly in agreement, "We must kidnap Aaii, warn Wagner and the Neo Nazis as you reminded us. We are racing the clock. We are down to a few hours, and if this does not work, I must return to the Demon Chamber. If possible, we must find the Time Machine. From what Franz said and what I heard when the machine wast created, Bones is pivotal in this operation. I do not know who created the Grand Plan, but it seems to have come full circle with Bones in the midst of it all. Shalt we go to Wagner's estate now? Michael, thee art the only one who can conquer Aaii and bring him to the Chamber. Red and I could warn the varlet Wagner and yond Neo-Nazis that they must repent or be destroyed? That is thine forte, but thee shalt be busy with a demon."

Michael considers Abigor's suggestion as he turns his dusty bowler around in his hands. "The warning must come from me. I am the Sword of Retribution. We shall stay together, warn the sinners, then escort Aaii to the Chamber. Red, are you ready to capture a demon?" Red claps his hands together and smirks. "As I told Abigor, I have been itching to get even with Aaii. I blame him and Axel for Father Antonio's death, and I want revenge. I could be all proper and say I want justice, but I would be lying. I am ready to go, mates!"

Two angels and a ghost MI5 Agent pop over to the insane asylum to pay a visit to the new owner and his demon buddy, Aaii. They land in front of the old mansion and look it over. Red walks around the estate, checking for guards or ill-tempered and armed Neo-Nazis. He returns in a few minutes to report. "I looked in every corner and hidey-hole, and I didn't see anything to worry us. We don't want gunfire with so many mortals in the house. I did not even see a slightly petulant calico cat. What do we do now?" Abigor looks to Michael. Whenever an Archangel is in attendance, he is automatically in charge of the operation. Few entities outrank Michael. Sir Winston believes he outranks everyone no matter how exalted their Holy title, and Churchill may be right.

Chapter Twenty

The Sword of Retribution

Red, Michael, and Abigor are outside the old asylum, preparing their assault plan on Dr. Wagner's new laboratory. Michael believes in action, not plans. "We are ready to enter the mansion. The evil doctor is in the library with the demon Aaii. We shall go forthwith. They were naughty not to invite us to their meeting. Shall we enter, Red and Abigor?"

Immediately, they are in the mansion outside the door to the library. The room is an outstanding example of a mid-19th-century English Library with a rolling ladder, an enormous globe, and oxblood leather club chairs. The room is two stories tall, with thousands of books and dozens of sculptures. Whoever designed this library was a true bibliophile. The three intruders are oblivious to the beauty of the room. They see Dr. Wagner seated at his rolltop desk talking to the demon Aaii, who sits in a club chair with his back to them.

Dr. Wagner says, "We appreciate your assistance with this project. We could not reach our goals of returning these three great men to life without your contribution to the projects. We do not want three . . ." He stops mid-sentence when he sees Michael dressed as Druid, standing just a few feet from him.

Dr. Wagner also sees Red and Abigor as they stroll into his office. Druid is a sight to behold, but the other two intruders look normal enough except for Red's pirate eyepatch. Both men wear faded jeans and black T-shirts. Even Druid looks boringly normal compared to Aaii in his usual jousting amour. The doctor was utterly astounded when he first saw the clinking and clanking demon.

The evil doctor jumps up from his chair and loudly demands to know who they are and why they are in his office. He is annoyed by the interruption because he does not have tea with a demon in full armor every day.

Michael is running low on patience. "Sit down and do not shout at me, mortal! We are here to offer you an opportunity to save your eternal soul. You are meeting with a demon who would be happy to harvest your soul and carry it to the depths of Hell. You have a choice to make."

Wagner is standing staring at the three men in amazement. He rouses and screams again, "I do not know who you are or what you are babbling about, but you must leave at once, or I shall call security and remove you." Aaii has not bothered to turn around. He makes himself as comfortable as possible in his painfully unforgiving metal armor. He knows who is speaking and can do nothing to improve his situation. The demon is outgunned, and he knows it. He could tell Wagner he is not playing this hand right, but why should he bother?

Wagner grabs his phone and calls security. "Get to my office at once, and I need all of you. NOW!" He throws his phone on the oak desk and believes, foolishly, that he has solved his problem. The intruders wait patiently for the security detail. Something is amiss. Their complacency stuns Wagner. He does not see weapons. He feels perfectly safe, not realizing appearances can be deceiving.

Suddenly, a dozen men rush into the office with guns drawn. Druid steps closer to them and shouts, "Nazis, throw down your weapons before you accidentally shoot each other. I get in trouble when that happens on my watch." He knows they are Nazis because they wear WWII uniforms with the Nazi belt buckle and carry Lugar P08 pistols. The tall, dark-haired Nazi in an officer's uniform is surprised by this behavior. He shouts back, "Who are you to tell us what to do? Are you crazy?" Looking at Druid, he has reason to wonder. He tells a stocky redhead and a broad-shouldered soldier with horned rim glasses to handcuff them. They take out their handcuffs and move toward the intruders as ordered. Abigor slowly raises his hands in front of him. Poof, all their guns and handcuffs disintegrate and fall to the floor as inoffensive gray dust. The Nazis stare at the floor and their once-solid Lugars in abject horror.

Mass pandemonium ensues! Dr. Wagner cannot believe his eyes as the Nazis run into each other, trying to get away! Abigor waves his hands again, and the doors lock. They, the predators, are caught in a trap by their prey. Aaii is still sitting with his back to Michael. He is studying his fingernails and humming Ninety-nine Bottles of Beer under his breath. I do not know why.

Michael steps into the middle of the room, and, surprise, his suit is gone! He now comes equipped with a 15-foot-wide set of wings, a girdle, a cloak, and a sword. He turns around, looks directly at each creep, and demands, "Verily, I say, listen to my words, mortals. I am here to take the demon Aaii sitting there in his jousting armor." He points out Aaii as if he is not the only one in jousting armor. Michael mesmerizes his rapt audience. "I have a gift for you." He smiles sweetly, "I know your sins against mankind, and I offer you salvation. You can save your eternal soul and avoid the everlastingly, consuming fires of Hell. I shall return in 48 hours, and if you have repented, you will be forgiven, not by me, but by One who is merciful and Divine. My advice? Be on your knees when I return. I shall have your guts for garters if you have not repented." Again, he smiles benignly at them as if he expects gratitude. Not this time.

Archangel Michael looks at Aaii and says, "You look ridiculous in that costume." Aaii just stares at him. He knows he can do nothing. Why bother to speak? He wants to say, well, big boy, those wings are rather showy too!

Two young, bulked Nazis try to break out through the French patio doors to the garden. Red stops them by throwing them toward the high ceiling. One ends up hanging from the railing on the second floor. They stare at Red, shocked and dismayed by his prodigious strength. He grins at them. "Mates, let me give you some advice. Listen and behave yourselves or bloody bad things could happen." He is enjoying this mission way too much. He can visualize Alpha and Omega's faces if they are watching. He grins again.

Except for Aaii, everyone is now hanging on Michael's every word. He instructs, "I have told you what I can do for you. You have free will. Use it wisely." The security detail is in various stages of debilitating fright. The officer is still acting big and bad, yelling insults at Michael. When the archangel moves toward him, he falls over in a dead faint. Obviously, he is not leadership material. Dr. Wagner sits at his desk, yelling for the Nazis to do something. Quite reasonably, they can do nothing since their guns disintegrated. They ignore Wagner.

Michael decides to leave them with a little demonstration he had used in the NGA Committee Meeting with electrifying effect. He lobs lightning bolts around the room, and Abigor joins in for fun. The room is crisscrossed with ribbons of light, and the sound of crackling and hissing voltage fills the library. That final exhibition of power sends a couple of the Nazis into a comatose state. Others suffer severe horror and panic. Two Nazis clutch their chests in pain, believing they are experiencing cardiac arrest. One tall, slim man with tattoos dissociates and stands, staring at his comrades with dull, glassy eyes, perfectly still.

Dr. Wagner slowly crawls across the antique Persian rug toward the door, mumbling to himself. He may be experiencing a severe psychotic break.

Aided by the Neo Nazis and the NGA, the doctor has committed sins against humanity and plans to use experimental, possibly deadly drugs on homeless study subjects—shades of the concentration camps and the evil Dr. Mengele. He also plans to clone monsters. Hark, retribution has arrived.

Michael grabs Aaii from his seat and jerks him to his feet. He addresses the Nazi guys for the final time. "Remember, I shall return in 48 hours. Be prepared!" Two angels, a demon, and a ghost MI5 agent disappear into the lightning bolts.

Chapter Twenty-One

The Demon and Bones

Sir Winston decided we would benefit from warm, dry air and genuine leather sofas, so we took 'flight' for London. Otto and I are thrilled to have the utterly thrilling room service again! While we wait for Abigor and Red, we might as well wait in luxury. Big Soph beams at us triumphantly, taking an entire sofa for herself.

David and Angus had been laboring in the Weapons Room in Poland, where they futilely struggled to unlock the machine one last time. Disappointed and frustrated, they finally gave up and joined us at our Savoy HQ. We enthusiastically showered them in welcome-backs, hoping to dispel their dark mood. Demon field forces are tough. Ya know?

Suddenly in a din of irritating clatters and bangs the travelers return with their reluctant package; the bunch from the Leicester Asylum have arrived. The Team is positively ecstatic to see them and particularly to see the reluctant, elusive demon.

Churchill, always the gentleman, greets them. "Gentlemen and Aaii, how wonderful to see you. Aaii, you cannot comprehend how devilishly excited we are to meet you again! You are the answer to our prayers."

David starts chuckling, "I bet this is the first time this disgustingly evil abomination has been the answer to a prayer." Judging from his demoniacal glare, if Aaii had the power to defeat us, we would now be sizzling in Hell's inferno. He does not.

Aaii must be satisfied with looking devilish daggers at David. We roar with joyous amusement. The team is profoundly relieved to see our mission approaching an end. Ok, part of our mission. I could dance with delight. Instead, I grab David for a cardiac-arresting, oxytocin-soaring bear hug!

Sir Winston takes charge, sniffs his brandy, and commands, "Gentleman, Bones, and Soph, we will now return to Poland with this diabolical guttersnipe. Who will transport Bones and Otto?" Big Soph grabs me, and we wing our way to Poland. Abigor transports a confused Professor Otto. He should be there to witness the end of this adventure since he provided us with valuable information about the weapon and me.

Before I can blink, Big Soph and I are standing in the Demon Chamber. The others arrive a minute later. Then we move to the Weapons Room as one triumphant mass. It is a little crowded, so Angus and Abigor stand in the passage.

Sir Winston is ready to destroy the weapon as quickly as possible. He asks Michael, "How do we raze this horrifying blot on God's earth? What is the procedure?" Michael, back to Druid, pushes Aaii toward the machine. The demon clanks along until he is standing within inches of it. Speaking for the first time, he says, "I do not have the power to destroy it myself. Wings boy here knows that. This is one of Beyond's annoying little miracles, so we must follow their absurd rules. Beyond is all shalts and shalt nots. Spells are so much cleaner." Staring at Archangel Michael, he blurts, "Would you like to tell them?"

Aaii grins wickedly at us—a daunting sight. We wait for Michael to explain Aaii's babbling as I suspiciously wonder if it is a stalling tactic. Our Archangel touches my arm and speaks quietly, barely above a whisper, "Bones, the time has come to tell you the truth. Our mission was in part miracle and part a promise kept to a blessed lady, your great-grandmother." Michael bows his massive head in respect. He snarls at Aaii, who enjoys the discomfort, and tells us more. "Aaii cannot destroy the machine without a blessed person touching it first. That requirement is an essential part of the miracle." I am astounded! What is he talking about? What great-grandmother? Everyone starts protesting at once.

David shouts, "What are you saying? Why should Bones touch that Tin Man monstrosity?"

Dr. Einstein hisses, "I do not comprehend this 'miracle' at all. We must know more. Could you proceed with your explanation?"

Sir Winston commands, "Wait, I am not happy with this. I must have some facts to assess. What you are saying does not fit what we have been led to believe. Is this another secret to which I have not been privy?"

Michael looks at Aaii, who also knows the entire story behind the miracle used to destroy the evil that was Nazi Germany. Aaii says, "Well, are you telling me Michael and I are the only ones who know about the promise, the miracle, and Bones? Now, this is just terribly delicious, I know more than Churchill and Einstein, and they are so amazing and exalted in the feeble human world. Even the silly girl who keeps getting killed does not know the story, and it is her family. This is hilarious!"

He looks around at all of us, and as we stare at him in confusion, he giggles—a grotesque sound to hear from a demon. Michael thunders. "Aaii, shut up or suffer the consequences!" He is Archangel Michael again, and he is feather-ruffling furious. Aaii just chuckles with devilish glee. Michael grabs for him with his huge hands and then stops short.

Sir Winston chews on his ever-present cigar and suggests we all calm down. "Let Michael tell us, since he seems to be the only one who knows what is going on other than the guttersnipe devil."

Michael is uncomfortable, quite aware that we should not have been blindsided at the last minute. However, in his defense, the choice of secrecy was not his. Sir Winston is outraged at the Powers' audacity. He knows they are the only ones with the authority to make this decision.

Still looking distressed, Angel pushes forward. "A promise was made, and a miracle was ordained many years ago. It has now come to pass, and the only way we can eliminate the weapon is if a blessed person touches it to remove the evil. Then and only then can the demon protector destroy it. Beyond deprived him of the power to accomplish its destruction alone. I cannot emphasize that point too much. I will not go into details since that is not my place, but Bones is the Blessed One. When she touches the machine, she will remove the evil." He nods at the count-down meter on the piece of unholy junk, and it loudly shouts DANGER. It reads 10 minutes until all is finished for me and everything else still alive on Earth.

I do not know what to think, but whether as Michael or Druid, he has always been there for me. I trust him with, well, my life. I deliberately take reluctant steps toward the monster and warily stop in front of it. I can hear the others reflexively trying to hold their breath. I reach out, then instantly draw my hand back. My amygdala is screaming—no! I take a moment to gather my courage. I reach out again and smack it hard with all the pent-up rage I can muster. The timer stops at 5 minutes. My Team shouts in jubilant celebration! Aaii is quiet now and pouts. Michael propels him toward the weapon with tremendous force. Aaii strikes a monstrous hellfire reverberating blow. The machine and the chamber begin to shake and rumble in protest. Perchance, the entire Owl Mountain range shudders in alarm.

Suddenly, the vile device that has been our personal Bubonic Plague and bloodsucking nemesis crumbles into dust at our feet. The danger is gone! We all laugh and hug each other in rapturous celebration. There is much slapping of backs and shaking of hands. For me, I am hugging everyone—except creepy Aaii.

Part two of our mission is now back on our radar. We can return to our original mission—the raid on Dr. Wagner, Neo-Nazis, and deviant mad scientists. We can also return to the Savoy's luxurious rooms and room service. Otto and I hug with joy at the thought of delicious food at our fingertips. YES!!

Chapter Twenty-Two

The Resignations

"There is a fine line between coddling and holding someone down so they can't get away." —Churchill

Seth is getting his marching orders from Druid. The rumpled, dangerous monolith, in a suit and hat, stands before Seth's desk and says, "Seth, as you know, we are in the final stages of our mission. From the beginning, we guided and nudged Sir Winston's formidable team from inside the distorted mirror. Often unseen, we were there every minute, yet we were unsuccessful at times. Weber shooting Bones was one of those times. He has been chastised for his wickedness. You have been an immense help to me in identifying and controlling the National NGA Committee. I have another task for you. Call them together, the ones who can still function. We must keep them close to us. I have made a promise to them, and I shall not waiver. We have completed only half of this task. A loathsome human being holds the reins of the International Association. He has hidden behind many fictitious names, and I must find him and make the same promise to him that I made to the national committee. I will be engaged with the vile Dr. Wagner and his team for a while. Find out where the snake's head of this worldwide association lives. He is next on my visit list."

Before Seth can answer Druid, the giant is gone. Seth can have only one answer to Druid's "request." Waiting for an answer is socially polite but unnecessary. Seth begins making his plans.

Seth is ready to complete his task. He is communicating with the despicable members of the NGA Committee in New York and the

International Organization in Germany. Seth set up another meeting with Julian, Annette, Juan, and Emerson. Seth is not terribly surprised to hear Emerson will not be joining them. His executive assistant Carmen called Heather and informed her, in the most dramatic terms, that Mr. Emerson North is undergoing treatment for his nerves at a small private hospital in the south of France. His brilliant and pricy psychiatrist insists that no one should disturb Emerson under any circumstances. No, she does not have a phone number for him. Seth checks Emerson off his list. This should be final.

Seth tunes into their Zoom call right on time, and as before, the others are already checked in, eagerly awaiting his presence. Seth welcomes them. "It is such a pleasure to see each of you today. You have been on my mind. My dearest Annette, how is your neck? I see you are still wearing the brace." As is her charming habit, Annette begins to screech at a glass-breaking pitch, "What are you doing, Seth? We are in great danger from that horrible brute! He is probably outside my door at this very minute! I am afraid to go beyond my apartment! I had to hire two pricy, stupid, muscle-bound Neanderthals to protect me."

Seth sees two bald, 300-pound men wearing khaki pants and tight black t-shirts standing behind Annette. Their lowered brows, thinned lips, and pulsing red faces suggest they might be angry about something. Seth takes a deep breath, shakes his head, reduces the volume on his speakers, and replies, "Dearest Annette, I am not leaving a single rock unturned. I have the very best security professionals in the world on the case. Their fee is horribly high, but you are worth it. I suggest you move to an undisclosed location and stay there until this is over. I would also suggest that Juan and Julian do the same. We cannot be too careful with your lives. We have no way of knowing what this maniac might do."

Julian is still crimson with indignant rage from the last call. "This is on you, Seth! He came to YOUR office! I see no reason why I should hide like a common criminal! Where are the Police? We pay dearly for their protection, and I shall call the mayor. I donated generously to his reelection fund. I heard Weber is dead! Is that true?"

Before Seth can answer, Annette stands and starts screeching again. "What? What? He killed Weber? We will all be murdered in our sleep!"

Seth remains calm. "I have heard ugly rumors that Weber died. I have not seen his body.

"I have no way of knowing if the stories are true. Our security experts are looking into that and searching for the man who assaulted us. The police have been informed, but they have nothing to go on. He left no fingerprints. The security cameras malfunctioned that day. I was stunned and speechless! Let's take reasonable precautions and wait for this monster to be apprehended. If you should decide to move to a secure location, give Heather your contact information in case I need to reach you with new developments in the case." Seth wants to be sure Druid can find them if necessary.

Seth turns toward the on-screen Juan. "My dear fellow, how are you? So pleased to see you looking so well." Juan opens and closes his mouth, and nothing comes out. He blinks wide, dark eyes. Again, his butler in a tailored gray suit stands behind him, hovering and wary. Seth pauses and decides to move on. "As you have noticed, our colleague Emerson is not with us today. He decided to take a little holiday in the South of France. No doubt, he will return soon. I think we all need a holiday. Oh, just one more thing before we end today: the police told me they are concerned about the safety of others in the NGA. A specific threat was made against the head of the International Organization. I must get in touch with him to set up security services."

Annette waves her ring-filled hands around and, gaping at Seth, shrieks, "Why do we care about Fritz, that arrogant old fool? We are in danger! That is the issue! Are you not paying attention, Seth?!" Her voice rises to new frequency heights approaching 20,000Hz.

Seth turns his head to avoid laughing in Annette's face. "My dear, I understand perfectly. Please help me locate him, and I shall make security arrangements. That will only take a couple of hours, then I shall turn my full attention to protecting you."

Julian jumps in now. "We care nothing for Fritz Helms. He must be 100 years old and a nasty old snake. Did I tell you he tried to stick it to me over a mere nothing last year?"

Seth shakes his head in mock sympathy. "You must tell me about that when next we meet, Julian." Julian is now purple in the face and spluttering, "I need your full attention on MY safety. Do you hear me, Seth? MY safety! I am texting you his address. Don't waste valuable time on that ugly swine." Seth checks his iPhone 13. Yes, he has the address, and it is conveniently located here on Park Avenue in New York City. Seth smiles broadly. He hears a clap of thunder. Perfect.

Julian and Annette are screaming at each other. She calls him a moronic, asinine, toxic male and a psychotic SOB.

Not to be bested, Julian calls Annette a stupid, narcissistic, and psychopathic old shrew. Seth wipes his forehead and says, "I am sorry, Juan, Julian, and Annette, you are starting to fade. I don't know what is wrong. Hello! Hello!"

He has switched off the speakers and camera and grins as he thinks about the meeting. He will report to Druid. They will now work on the NGA International, which means Fritz Helms. Of course, INGA will replace him when he is gone, but it will take the new person years to achieve the same poisonous influence.

Seth goes to his medicine cabinet to grab a couple of aspirins or three. That Annette is a real banshee.

Fritz Helms is the president of the International NGA Organization and one of its founding members. He has been banned from several countries due to his propensity for compromising elections and funneling money to various groups of vicious thugs who create havoc for fun and profit. He is not a beloved human except by his organization (?), ruthless dictators, and whomever he bribes. Fritz ensures vast amounts of money are available to rioting deviants when needed to keep the world in a state of chaos and confusion.

Fritz is shuffling toward his 95th year, and his health is failing rapidly. He was once a large, robust man with dark brown hair, a short beard, and soulless steel-gray eyes. The years have whitened his hair, what little he has, and turned his gray eyes watery. Time and experiences have hardened him, though people who know him would agree that Helms was never agreeable or honorable. He is frail, emaciated, and plods along bent over his expensive jeweled walking stick. His unvarying uniform is a threadbare brown suit with a once-white dress shirt and a blotched tan tie. His pricey ancient Alessandro Berluti oxfords complete his Miss Haversham look of moral and spiritual decay. His butler, Alfred, dresses him in the morning and undresses him at night. Alfred is tall, blade thin, with sandy hair, and looks like he escaped from the city morgue. After seeing the inexplicable things that I have seen, heck, maybe he did. Alfred hates Fritz. Who can blame him? Realistically, there are few butler jobs for men who look like cadavers. Employers can be so demanding. Some "friends" in Fritz's circle have whispered that Alfred might be a double agent. They offer no other particulars.

Obviously, Fritz is not a healthy man. The joys of a delicious meal consumed with a hearty appetite and a peaceful night's sleep evade the leader of the INGA. He feels the effects of an overworked heart, fatigue, and shortness of breath. Regaining his health consumes his waking hours. He has tried all the dubious, exorbitantly expensive, highly touted miraculous cures on the market. Not surprisingly, none have made a microscopic difference in improving his appetite or sleep.

Helms cannot walk from his bed to his luxurious marble bath with gold fixtures unless he rests to catch his breath. His only hope is the miraculous Mengele Youth Formula. He hopes Dr. Wagner will defeat the heart glitch in his Fountain of Youth before he has a massive, fatal heart attack. Tick, tick, tick. Fritz is one of the volunteer subjects at the top of Dr. Mengele's Youth Formula candidate list and has paid generously for the privilege. Being a practical man, Fritz says, what do I have to lose? The old sinner has supported Dr. Mengele and his vile minions since the late 1990s. Due to Fritz's liberality, money has not been a problem for the Angel of Death. He heard about Dr. Mengele through a friend from his old neighborhood in Berlin, Franz Wolffe. They had gone to school together and they happened to meet in a German Restaurant close to Dr. Mengele's laboratory at Whitechapel. The two old schoolmates began meeting once a week for lunch. Naturally, Fritz was extremely curious to know how his old 'friend' could look 35 years old, and he looked every minute of seventy at that time. He continued meeting Franz for lunch, hoping to finagle the truth out of him. The passing years had not aged Wolffe, and there had to be a reason other than good genes, and Fritz meant to learn that reason. Finally, after a little too much Schnapps, Franz told his old neighborhood pal about the Mengele Youth Formula and offered to introduce him to the psychotic doctor.

Dr. Mengele was foaming at the mouth, furious when Franz admitted he had told Helms about the youth drug. Curiously, he softened when he learned the banker had virtually inexhaustible funds. Fritz joined Mengele and Wolffe at their favorite German Restaurant, The Bierschenke, and discussed how they might assist each other. Dr. Mengele had funding from the Neo-Nazi organizations and Nazi sympathizers. Nevertheless, the Angel of Death's expenses were exorbitant. He never had sufficient funds to develop and expand cloning technology and enhance his Youth Formula. Equipment, computers, laboratory space, and salaries were crucial to achieving his goals. He traveled the world consulting with scientists exploring similar technology, and this extravagance frequently left Mengele fighting the growling wolf at the door. The old butcher would go into narcissistic rages because he, Herr Hitler's favored physician, had to scrape funds together like a pauper to continue his world-altering work. He was convinced the world would forever be changed after he completed his life's work. Everyone would remember his name with admiration and envy as long as there was a Germany. Remember? That is true, but definitely not as Mengele imagined his legacy. He will be remembered as the infamous monster, the Angel of Death, who haunts our most terrifying nightmares. We are terrified to know a human being could sink to such depths of depravity. We ask ourselves, from where does the darkness come. The question that logically follows is, what does that say about the darkness hidden within each of us? What would we have done in 1939?

Mengele and Helms's quid pro quo was a partnership born in Hell. Fritz was willing to bring the universal muscle and significant funds of the INGA with him. Mengele was able to work on his research at an entirely new level. He accomplished all his goals except the actual cloning since the technology was not available at that time and, of course, he had not controlled the heart glitch. Mengele became an influential member of the NGA as he brought a new focus to the table and means of achieving the NGA's dream of a one-world dictatorship under their control. If Hitler couldn't do it, who could? He had Hitler in his back pocket.

Seth is now aware of Fritz's role in this fiendish organization. He has targeted the old sinner. He will neutralize the creepy reprobate, or Michael will, after graciously giving him time to repent. Or, since his time is running out, Fritz may catch the Grim Reaper's attention, and Scythe Guy may step in and play his hand. It does not look good for the leader of NGA International. Unknown to Seth, Druid has something different in mind for Fritz. Sophie had an enlightening conversation with him. Sometimes, Druid, AKA Michael, gets too focused and misses opportunities. Yes, Sophie can communicate with Druid.

Many people have died fighting for freedom against Helms and his organization. Honest politicians and journalists have fought to have him investigated and charged for his crimes. They met with bad luck and suspicious accidents, or they mysteriously committed suicide on the way to get a vanilla latte. He bribes dishonest politicians, bureaucrats, and journalists so they will enthusiastically sing his praise and push the NGA militant agenda.

Fritz will receive a visit from the blonde giant soon.

Chapter Twenty-Three

Dr. Wagner's Options

The team is ready to visit Dr. Wagner and his mad scientists. Angus and Red take turns watching the old estate for signs of a hasty departure. So far, on his watch, Red hasn't seen anything suspicious. He is standing on the patio outside the library, looking through the French doors. Dr. Wagner sits at his antique roll-top desk, speaking with one of his ethics-challenged, white-coated researchers. Whitecoat is a man in late middle age and probably of Middle Eastern descent. He stares directly into Wagner's eyes as they speak. His large brown eyes, behind round glasses, seldom blink. Red notices the man is quite presentable, dressed in well-pressed pants with razor-sharp creases running down the front. Still, Red is not favorably impressed with the scientist, knowing he is probably not credible or ethical. Integrity is a deal-breaker when applying for work with Wagner.

Red might also have tagged him as a likely psychopath if he had my training and experience. Sustained eye contact and fewer than average blinks are red flags. Though not conclusive evidence, this is called the predator's stare, a common psychopathic quirk. They are described as soulless creatures without a conscience. The term is colorful and accurate. They can also be perceived as charismatic, smooth-talking, and engaging. It is dangerous to be fooled by their sallow appeal. Approximately one in 22 people would qualify for the diagnosis of a psychopath using the Hare Psychopathy Checklist. The scientists working with Dr. Strange undoubtedly exceed the national average. Oddly enough, doctors, surgeons, politicians (not so odd), and CEOs are more likely to be psychopaths than individuals in other occupations. I am happy to say psychotherapy is not a profession popular with psychopaths. I have no data on superheroes.

Red listened in on the conversation between these two soulless creatures. Dr. Wagner shook his head, indicated Psycho to come closer, and whispered, "I don't know what you have heard, Advik, but I must caution you to ignore outrageous rumors. We are men and women of science. We do not believe in the Boogeyman or John Wick. Every occurrence has a reasonable and logical explanation. Our Neo-Nazi security detail is made up of men who are fanciful and easily manipulated. Believe nothing they say and tell your colleagues to trust only information from one of us."

Psycho moves farther away. "Sir, I understand what you are saying, yet our scientists are concerned about what they have heard about a frightening creature on our campus throwing around lightning bolts like confetti. Perhaps you should address them yourself with those logical explanations you mentioned to counteract what they have heard. No doubt you have such an explanation. Correct?" Psycho gazes at Doc with that lizard-like, unnerving stare. Though the Doc has various psychopathic and narcissistic traits himself, he is unsettled and looks away from Advik to focus on a bust of Hitler sitting on his desk. Psychopaths are everywhere.

Regaining his confidence, Dr. Wagner stands, nods emphatically, and yells, "Of course, I have an explanation! Do you believe this utter nonsense, Advik? Did I err when I hired you to apply your research skills to these critical projects? Indeed, you do not believe in fantastic creatures. Have you never heard of theater? This is no more than theater. The ridiculous morons used elaborate makeup and then threw in fireworks for effect. I am astonished you ever entertained an idiotic interpretation of recent events! Perhaps I should reevaluate your suitability for our research team?"

Psychopaths have a grandiose sense of superiority and can react with a vengeful counterattack to criticism or ignore it altogether as a senseless dribble from a moron. Fortunately, Advik, a brilliant man, remains dispassionate and dismisses the doctor's sharp condemnation. He may believe the scientist doth protest too much. He turns to walk away and says over his shoulder, "I shall do what I can to reduce the confusion and fear in the labs since you have explained theater to me. I shall tell them you will be speaking to them soon." Advik walks out as Wagner splutters nonsense.

Wagner knows he can lie to his staff, but he cannot fully accept make-up and fireworks as the answer to their recent bizarre visitation. Two members of his security squad have disappeared without explanation. Two others are in the clinic under sedation. He had only 19 men assigned to him when he arrived. He has tried several times to contact the NGA Committee members for reinforcements. He called Seth, Annette, and Emerson, and no one returned his calls. Damn it; he cannot understand what is happening. Why has no one replied to his desperate SOS? This is unprecedented dismissive behavior. He doesn't know what he can do to protect his irreplaceable projects. He is not concerned about his staff or the security team. He can replace them if necessary. He chose his staff of scientists for their brilliance, knowledge, expertise, and lack of professional integrity. Truthfully, which he is on occasion, they would be challenging to replace. He stops and smiles as something occurs to him. Still, he could harvest some researchers from other institutions, like the reluctant Dr. Suggs. He hears a noise outside the French doors. Wagner peeks out, hiding behind the red brocade curtain. He thinks he sees a stocky man with red hair and an enormous black and white dog, and then the vision fades away. He wonders if he is losing his mind and honestly doesn't care anymore.

He returns to his thoughts on harvesting scientists, which is undoubtedly cheaper than paying the lab rats outrageous wages. He has two choices: stay and fight or flee with a couple of trusted colleagues, a few security guards, and his research. He can return to his fortress in France. Yet, they would know where to find him in France. Fighting is futile if they are what they appear to be: paranormal freaks. Wagner feels frozen between two very unattractive alternatives. Hmmm, he may have to flee to save himself and stay with friends. The feather freak wants his research, not him. Yes, the winged thing said he wanted them to repent and gave them 48 hours to do so, whatever repent means. He has run out of options and is quickly running out of time.

Strangely, at this very minute, in the historic Savoy in London, the Team is talking about Dr. Wagner and his nest of vipers. Sir Winston had conferred with Dr. Einstein, and thankfully, they suggested we move back to our luxurious suite at the opulent Savoy. It has been our home since we started this journey. There was no reason to continue to live in the Demon Chamber with no cozy accommodations other than a hard gold throne. I did have a small bed that David acquired for me.

We have successfully completed our mission to destroy the monster machine. If the Fantastic Machine is somewhere in the darkness beyond the Chamber, it may stay there for all eternity. Thankfully, we didn't need it.

We packed our few belongings, mostly mine and Otto's bags and tea. Since we have previously survived transportation by Angel and Great Dane, we shall travel the wind currents with them again. It is like First Class without the lines, peanuts, and waiting. We land in the spacious parlor with its gorgeous plush sofas and chairs. I am thrilled to have an opulent bathroom and bedroom, and God bless me, room service. I will order a delicious meal for Otto and me as soon as I take a real shower, not a dip in a stream, a chilling, turning blue experience. I dash into the marble bathroom with the pool-sized tub. Grab my sponge, shampoo, and rose-scented soap, throw my clothes onto the floor, and jump into the shower, turning it to maximum hot! Seriously, heaven can't beat this by much! The glass gets all foggy, and the fog creeps on 'little cat feet' into the vast bath and fills it. After I luxuriate in the shower for a few minutes, I dry off with one of the Savoy's pamperingly plush towels, shake my head to style my hair, throw on clean jeans and a black t-shirt, and my red heels and head for the suite phone to call room service. The professor said to order for him. The poor man is exhausted.

I spent a few minutes savoring the menu. I finally decided on Classic Beef Wellington, pomme puree, sprouting broccoli, Lobster Thermador, banana and salted caramel tart, apple tarte Tatin with vanilla ice cream, tea for Otto, and a coffee latte for me. I think that will be sufficient for now. We can always order more food later. No, I don't know what all this miraculous food costs. Beyond is very generous with its superheroes.

I join the team to discuss Wagner and our plan, which we will implement tonight. Sir Winston insists on moving at once to avoid finding an empty asylum. Red, still at the estate, has reported they are still in residence, and nothing amiss appears to be happening. He is watching the doctor because if he decides to make a break for it, he will take the three monster's cells with him. We cannot allow that. This mission must end with a decisive victory from which the late Mengele's forces cannot recover. We are not taking anything for granted. Otto and I munch on our scrumptious meal while the guys talk about strategy. I am starving.

We will descend on them en masse, except for Professor Otto, who will stay here and rest in our comfy quarters.

Sir Winston lights a cigar and motions for us to gather around him, "Gentlemen, Bones, and Soph, we will attack their old asylum, a perfect place for them, tonight, and I understand Druid, uh, Michael shall meet us there. He said something about his promise, which he must keep. I trust Michael is not planning on a blood bath. That is not our way. We shall see how he proposes to keep his promise. Our mission is to capture Wagner, the viable cells, and his research material, including the journal and computers. We do not need or want to house all of the Neo-Nazis and scientists in the sewer. Between those cells and Milo's accommodations, we can restrain the leading villains. They will have to be questioned. David has talked to Miles about that, and I will let him tell you about their conversation. When we leave, we shall be armed with our pistols." The great statesman bows to our genius and points his cigar at David.

David has enjoyed watching Otto and me devour our food with enthusiasm and focus. I have not experienced such a heart-fluttering delicious meal in a long time. Service was fast and courteous, as is typical at the London Savoy. Swashbuckling David winks at me and turns to the guys and Soph. "Achieving our goal will not be without its dangers, and we must consider the possibility of failure. We can't allow that to happen. You have your 9mm pistols and ammo, and Bones also has her protective gear. Otto will be sitting this one out."

He glances at Otto, who looks crushed by his exclusion from the battle. David returns to the plans. "This may be our last battle, folks. I pray it is so. We must protect Bones. Soph and I will be the first line of defense, though all of us will be involved. We will land in the garden and spread out into the Mansion. Dr. Einstein is with Sir Winston, and Red, Abigor, and Angus will take the upstairs. I will have Bones and Soph with me. We will start in the library."

David offers Otto a part in their adventure. "Your job will be to pray and wait for us to return. As Sir Winston indicated, I talked to Miles at MI5. Miles cannot be officially involved in the takedown because he doesn't have permission. He and his team will be waiting nearby to take the Neo-Nazis into custody. Something is happening at MI5, but Miles did not go into it with me. It seems to be a critical internal problem. Miles sounds as if he is concerned. After the mission is wrapped up and put away, I will discuss it with him."

Sir Winston, drawing on his cigar, asks, "Weren't we concerned about an enemy within MI5 and the sudden death of the Deputy Director-General a few weeks ago? You said Miles was not himself. Something was on his mind."

David faces Churchill and wonders aloud, "I remember and think we were correct. Miles' problem is also a problem for our team because we don't know who to trust. That was why we moved away from working with MI5. Now, we need their help with this large-scale takedown. The only way we could handle it ourselves would be to kill everyone there, which seems a bit excessive. You know Alpha and Omega get excited about creative solutions." I know David is frustrated with our limitations, MI5, and still furious with the Celestial Duo. The creative solution is his law enforcement dark humor. Angus starts laughing hysterically, and Dr. Einstein turns gray from shock. Sir Winston and Abigor pay no attention.

David continues with the plan, "The scientists will only be held for questioning unless they physically resist our, uh, audacious drop-in." Big Soph sits up to her full height and expands her chest as she enters creature from Hell mode. She growls, showing enormous, tearing teeth. Nothing will get past her. God help anyone who tries.

We will leave as soon as I finish eating. David has been thinking about my journey to the Asylum. He mutters to himself, "Bones flew with me from the rigged jet falling apart in the sky. She has not suffered any ill effects from any of the express flights. I think I will transport her the short distance to the Wagner Asylum in Leicester." I nod vigorously in agreement. David is careful about my life. I must admit he has reason to be after suffering through my death-defying history.

David seems satisfied with the safety of my newfound freedom. Sir Winston and Dr. Einstein nod in agreement. Commercial and rental airlines are history! Yes! David resumes his preparations for the assault on Wagner and his minions and looks around at the Team. "Do you have anything to add?" We are in action mode, and it feels awesome to finally come to the end of this exhausting mission.

Abigor scowls, obviously concerned, as he stands to address the group. "Thank thee, David. I am reviewing David's plan to retrieve the research objects and the support material. Thanks to Red and Angus, we knoweth there art probably less than twenty Neo-Nazis and about four dozen scientists and staff in the estate. They are a much larger group than thou faced at the lab in Austria or London. Quite reasonably, Wagner will have screeched to NGA for reinforcements. Michael and Seth hast virtually dried up that source of staffing. It would be a more challenging hostile takeover without their efforts to pave the way for us. I would be surprised if some of the Neo-Nazis present when Michael, Red, and I visited the evil doctor hast not fled back to London shrieking as they ran. We must secure the viable cells and records." Abigor takes a moment to chuckle as he pictures that scene. The rest of us join him. We are so starved for heartening news that we celebrate it when it comes our way. Dr. Einstein and Sir Winston wave pipe and cigar in a here, here! Salute. Sir Winston yells, "The bloody scallywags!"

'Scallywag' triggered reminisces of Operational Bases during WWII, often hastily built bunkers along the coast named Scallywags

Bunkers or Suicide Bunkers. Civilians were trained at Coleshill House to function as weapons in these remote fortified holes in the ground, usually operated by four to eight people per bunker. They were instructed to stop or slow Nazis who might land by water in England. Tough civilians manned the bunkers, willing to put their lives on the line to prevent enemy combatants from reaching the interior of the Island. Sir Winston remembers with sadness that the last remaining Scallywag recently left his post for eternity.

I wave my hand to be recognized, and Abigor nods to acknowledge me. "I have one question, Abigor. Who is Seth? I don't remember hearing that name since I came across it while listening to the dark stream a few weeks ago. I had the impression they were involved in the unsavory. A couple of years ago, Angus heard from an active MI5 agent that Seth was a person of interest."

Angus jumps in to support me. "Yes, I certainly did hear that name at one of my weekly card games with the MI5 gang. I was retired, but the others were active in the agency. The agents told me his name kept popping up in their investigations, but they could not get a hand on him. He was fog. Nothing solid. He was a bloody ghost who faded away every time they tried to follow his trail." We were intrigued by Angus' lurid description of the man of fog.

Abigor squints in concentration as he considers my question. "That is an engrossing question, Bones. I am struggling to characterize Seth. I can say "fog" is not a stretch in describing the, uh, man. Seth hast been working with Michael as an undercover agent. Of course, that tells thee what he did and with whom he did it and not who he is. I am not free to tell thee more, yet Michael might be able to add more meat to the bones, so to speak."

We are staring at him in consternation and disbelief. What is Seth? Wearing his usual three-piece gray suit, Angus sits up straight in the plaid club chair and leans toward Abigor, wide-eyed in confusion. No doubt, I look much the same as I try to process this surprising new information. So, we had another team member we knew nothing about. David looks daggers at Abigor.

Dr. Einstein and Otto discuss the Novikov self-consistency principle, which concerns objects that are transported back in time by a time traveler. They are rudely ignoring us.

After Sir Winston looks around the room at our team, searching our faces, he jabs Abigor's chest. "What are you saying, Abigor? You cannot mean that there was another soldier in our Holy war on evil of whom we knew nothing! I beg your pardon. What do you mean you cannot tell us anything about him? Both you and Michael knew about this 'Seth' and no one shared that pertinent information with me? That is utterly preposterous!"

The great statesman is working up a fit of anger. His eyes budge, he reddens, and his jaw tightens. Yes, we are in for a storm! Through gritted teeth, Churchill thunders, "I am the team leader. Am I correct?" Baby blue eyes skewered the angel.

Abigor stammers, "Of course, thee art our esteemed leader, Sir Winston. I did not participate in the discussion to keep Seth cloaked in secrecy. I probably should not have mentioned Seth. After we complete our mission, no doubt, Michael will talk with thee about Seth and why he was deemed top secret." Abigor does a nice little dip toward the highly miffed former prime minister.

Dr. Einstein said, "I think it may be time we go to Leicester and pay the dummkopfs a social visit. Are we not ready to put our plan into action? Thank you, David, for the preparation. Shall we move forward, gentlemen, Big Soph, and Bones?" Everyone rises, except Otto, to put our plan into action. I shall transport with David. Churchill is back in warrior mode, as are Angus, Soph, Abigor, Dr. Einstein, and I. Angus told Red we were on our way, and our ETA is almost immediately.

Red tells Angus that Michael just arrived, wings and all.

Chapter Twenty-Four

The Bones Solution

Alpha and Omega meet with Gabriel, also known as Gavriel and Jibrail. They sit at the gold table to discuss what they should do about Bones. Gabriel isn't a warrior like Michael but has a high rank in God's world. He is the angel who told Mary she would have an extraordinary son. Gabriel is clothed in blue and white garments and carries a white lily, a lantern, and a scroll. He is mighty as the protector of Israel along with Michael. However, he is in the meeting today due to his communication skills and wisdom.

They are in the same spacious room with many windows, looking out into the lush gardens in paradise, where they have met special guests such as John F. Kennedy and Agatha Christie.

The contrast of many brilliant floral colors would blind a mere living mortal.

Michelangelo rendered his most lauded pieces on these walls. The magnificent artist stands in a corner admiring his masterpieces. He ponders repainting the room. It has been five hundred and twelve years since the last update. The three Holy beings ignore him.

The beings discussing Bones today have seen the room frequently. It no longer makes them catch their breath (so to speak) in pure, joyous ecstasy. This is also where Alpha and Omega met with Sir Winston on his various visits. Churchill is much loved in Beyond.

Alpha begins their informal meeting by telling Gabriel why they are together. "Gabriel, Omega, and I appreciate your time today. We have a confounding decision to make, and we hope you will guide us. You are aware of Sir Winston Churchill and his team of Mysterious Secret Guardians. They recently saved the earth from blowing up. It was not an effortless operation but was completed successfully with remarkable skill and audacity."

"One of Sir Winston's team members is a mortal, a psychotherapist from South Carolina in the United States. She was chosen for the team when she bought the first edition of Winston's Gathering Storms at a bookstore in London. The book had a secure code that Air Marshall David Smythe had written in it for security. The code was top secret, and only David, Winston, and the Director-General at MI5 knew it existed. When a Nazi sympathizer killed David, his possessions were sold or given away. He had no family. This is essential to understand. We told Winston we had endowed the book with the power to find the appropriate human for his Team. That is not the entire story, but it was useful to avoid speaking about something we could not discuss. Bones was chosen to be part of the Team before she was born. However, we did not address that with Albert, Winston, or David. There is a long history to that story. We will not go into that at this moment. The mortal, Bones, is the Team's heart. The other Team members have lost their connection to humanity since their worlds are quite different. She is their connection, a bridge if you will. She has played her part well with compassion, courage, loyalty, and intelligence." Gabriel puts down his lantern and listens with interest to the story Alpha is telling. Bones sounds interesting.

"Sadly, she can be entirely too courageous, if not utterly reckless. Because of this and her circumstances as a member of the team, the dear girl has died three times. Sophie has brought her back, and we allowed Sophie to bring her back one more time not long ago. Sophie had used her allocation of "Lazarus" cards and needed special permission. Winston interceded for Bones and impressed us with how important she was to the mission, and they were at a critical juncture. She has been attacked many times in her brief association with the Team.

Yet, Bones fought back and did some damage to the varlets. Omega and I had decided she must leave the Team and return to her former life before all the dying permanently scarred her. We can arrange that. No one will realize she was ever gone from her new office and home in South Carolina. Oh, and we would wipe her memory. We thought that would be best for many reasons."

"Something happened when Bones joined the Team we had not anticipated. She and Smythe fell in love. That is one reason we would wipe her memory, so she will not mourn that profound loss. The Guardians' current mission should come to an end very soon. We must decide before then. I know it is quite a baffling maze, and we want to make a wise choice for everyone. Oh, one other thing. David will be on trial as soon as they complete the mission. He shot and killed a mortal to save Bones' life. We think his reasoning may have been muddled because of his love for her. It is unclear that the mortal, Axel Fischer, would have killed Bones before David could tackle him, thereby saving Axel's life."

Alpha pauses as another thought presents itself. "I am sorry, there is one other complication. Sophie guides Bones and loves her beyond all measure. Sophie will be devastated by her loss if Bones returns to her former life or if she dies again. We have told Winston that Bones cannot be resurrected again. Omega and I have worried that the pain could cause Sophie, our powerful ancient entity, to go mad with grief if she loses Bones. She could and might biblically destroy whatever she blames for the loss. Then there is David to consider. He would undoubtedly assist Sophie in this utterly cold and vengeful destruction."

Gabriel looks at Alpha in bafflement. Yes, this is a bewildering maze. "Brother Alpha, I am honored you have come to me with this concern. I cannot imagine that I can add anything worthwhile, yet I am eager to be supportive. If I may, I understand you wish to decide whether to leave Bones with the Team or return her to her former life.

You will also be deciding what penance David deserves, if any. I comprehend the complexity of this delicate problem. You do not want her killed again. I should think that dying so frequently could be quite wearing on this young woman. Also, we must consider Sophie and David, who could become epically destructive if they lose her. I must admit, I do not see a perfect resolution. I shall have to think and pray about this. Is there anything else I should know while deliberating?"

Omega speaks for the first time. "Gabriel, we value your wisdom and are thankful you comfort us in our worriment. Our Gordian Knot makes me think of King Solomon. And the king said, 'Get me a sword.' So, they brought a sword before the king. And the king said, 'Cut the living child in two, and give half to one and a half to the other.' But I am afraid that ordering a sword will not suit our dilemma nearly as well. Yet, a sword solved both of those dilemmas. Interesting, don't you think? Thank you, Gabriel. How long will you need to consider our Gordian Knot before we can meet again? Oh, yes, one more thing: We knew Bones would buy the book. It was ordained that she would be on Winston's Team. With or without the book, it could end no other way. As I said, her connection to the Doomsday Machine is old and complex."

Omega feels compelled to explain further. "During the War, a daring heroine, Thelma Dove, fought with Winston's SOE to help the free French make life less comfortable for the Nazi invaders. In her duties, Thelma found two scientists who were hiding in France. Their names were Goldmann and Rosen. She was engaged to Admiral Jeffrey Stallings. He and his crew had saved many Jews escaping the Third Reich. Thelma arranged for the scientists to be picked up by the Admirals' crew and taken to England. Goldman and Rosen were on the Nazis' kill list. Impressive, brilliant mortals, the scientists had worked on a time machine to negate a hideous, wickedly destructive weapon, the

Doomsday Machine. Thankfully, it has been destroyed. Once pro-grammed, no one can control it if it is activated by error or intention-ally. A demon, Aaii, was responsible for this problem. He put a force field spell on it. Of course, you are familiar with his evilness." Gabriel frowns and grimaces. Yes, he is aware of the troublesome demon. Omega scowls in agreement and says, "No one could get into the Weapon to deactivate it. Goldman and Rosen tried to create the Time Machine to take them back to the date the Weapon was programmed and stop the Nazis before they could program it. Since before the war, they had been working on a time machine as they built on Dr. Einstein's epic work. A traitor tipped off the Gestapo about Rosen and Gold-mann's location. They immediately offered a large reward for the sci-entists. It was only a matter of time before someone would turn them in."

Gabriel had been trying to follow the complicated story. He broke in to ask, "If I may inquire, what does this have to do with the woman, Bones? I am confused."

Alpha picks up the story there. "I apologize, Gabriel. We are arriv-ing at Bones now. We owed an outstanding debt of gratitude to Thelma Dove and Jeffrey Stallings for rescuing the scientists who worked to defeat the weapon. We were much saddened when, later, German spies in England killed the scientists. The time machine sits in the basement of Humboldt University in Berlin, unknown to anyone now alive. It was never completed."

Alpha nods toward Omega and takes up the story. "Thank you for your patience, Gabriel. We are near the end of Bones' family history. Thelma and Jeffrey did not marry. Jeffrey was shot by German soldiers while trying to rescue Jews from Germany. Thelma had a baby girl a few months later. Thelma and Jeffrey's baby girl was Bones' grand-mother.

A hush falls over the room at the revelation, and then Alpha continues, "We knew the date the machine would be activated. We don't have magic spells like demons, but we have miracles. We used beatification to reward Jeffrey and Thelma for their Godliness and the many lives they saved during the war. We blessed them, and since both died young, we allowed the blessing to pass to their daughter. She also died young. She was Bones' grandmother, and her mother died, giving Bones life. Archangel Michael blessed Bones at birth. That is one reason he was so protective of her. If not for her blessing, she would still be dead after the black Mercedes ran her down. That was Franz."

Gabriel is confused again. "What Black Mercedes? Franz?"

Alpha shrugs and says, "The blessing will end with her." All three of the Saintly beings cross themselves in solemn respect.

"We brought Sir Winston and his team together to stop Dr. Mengele and destroy the weapon. We were not entirely candid with them when we requested their help. When Thelma arrived in Beyond, we promised to try to destroy the Doomsday Machine. We cannot guarantee success because of free will. For the miracle to work, a blessed person had to be there. As one can imagine, blessed mortals are not in great supply. We knew one. Aaii could not have destroyed the Doomsday Machine alone—we have rules here in Beyond. Demons are cretins with few rules. Just cast a spell, and they are done." He waves his hand to show their thoughtlessness.

"Michael captured Aaii and forced him to raze the machine. Bones was there, and it fulfilled our promise to her great-grandmother, that righteous, saintly woman."

Gabriel rubs his temples and asks, "Does Bones know about her great-grandparents? Is she aware that she is blessed? That is a truly great privilege!" Alpha ponders that question and shakes his head. "If

Thelma and Jeffrey wish to explain their family history to the girl, they will. That is not our place."

Alpha considers and finally concedes, "We cannot bring Bones back again if she is killed, and it happens with great regularity. Resurrection will not be possible again. That is why we are now faced with a problem. What should we do with Bones? We owe a debt to her courageous great-grandparents." Gabriel walks away from the meeting with Alpha and Omega, scratching his head, which is beginning to ache. Odd, he thought angels didn't suffer from headaches.

Chapter Twenty-Five

Asylum Tactical Takeover

Now that the pesky Machine is out of our hair, we can focus on the mission we have been preparing for since our team was created. We are set to leave for the Asylum, armed and ready to roll. David has equipped us well, as he always has.

David reminds the Team, "Folks, we are about to finish our assignment, and this is our last rodeo for Beyond on the Dr. Mengele mission, though it turned out to be much more than that. We still have the NGA to tackle and Neo-Nazis—later. I don't know what Beyond will assign to us when we mop this up. Evil is not in short supply. Job security! Does everyone have their weapon?" We all nod our heads except for Dr. Einstein and Professor Otto. The perfectly adorable professor will not be accompanying us on this mission. I ordered a fabulous dinner from room service a couple of hours ago. Savoy's seafood is to die for! We were lucky to get several hours of sleep last night, which rarely happens in my life. I know Otto will be fine until we return, and I hope to return.

The Team cannot guarantee my survival. They will do their best to protect me, but I am not a fragile flower, and I plan to do my part to rid the world of Dr. Wagner and his evil cohorts. We began the mission with every intention of stopping Dr. Mengele, the Angel of Death, by doing whatever was necessary. He died the night we attacked his laboratory in London. We had nothing to do with his demise. He suffered a long overdue heart attack, and we were not sad at his passing. His heart could no longer carry the burden of the black acts he had committed. Ironically, Mengele's soul was the last Abigor harvested as a demon.

We have the satisfaction of knowing he is in the abode of the damned with his henchmen Hans Schmitt and Franz Wolffe.

The Doomsday Machine then sidetracked us before we could follow the next chapter to Hitler's viable cells and Youth Formula. We discovered the Machine was a Black Swan Armageddon powered by a Perfect Storm, and it could destroy much of the planet and all life forms. That began our quest to stop the machine and the demon behind it. It got highly complicated. We won!

The Neo Nazis and New Global Agenda Organization replaced Mengele with Dr. Wagner. He became our primary target. He is the only subject left alive whom Mengele treated with the Youth Formula. We know little about him, but I assume he is about Mengele's age—just figuring in my head, he is probably about 112. He and his army of researchers have been working tirelessly to bring back the horror that was Nazi Germany in the person of Der Fuhrer Hitler and two of his faithful, heinous lieutenants. Wagner is also involved in unethical, dangerous research studies on homeless subjects. They must be stopped, and we are the team that must stop them!

Sir Winston talks to us about our duty stations when we invade the Asylum. "Red has become familiar with the mansion's layout, which greatly assists us. You will find four labs, a kitchen, a dining area, and the library downstairs. On the top floor are two sleeping areas for subjects, two large suites for the scientists, and Wagner's private quarters. Approximately four dozen scientists and about twenty homeless research subjects live in the mansion. The 17 Nazis have quarters in a barracks outside unless Michael frightened them away. A few staff are here during the day, and three women work in the kitchen. We will be rounding up all the researchers and Neo-Nazis. We shall leave the homeless men and women here and contact local social resources to provide the services they will need. Staff members will be allowed to leave unmolested by Miles's officers. David, my boy, will you speak on the arrangements with Miles and MI5 agents?"

David walks to the front of our parlor at the Savoy and looks over notes. "We have asked Miles to take most of the scientists and Neo-Nazis to their MI5 campus to question them. We cannot question that number of prisoners, and we are not particularly interested in them. Miles will interview them for further information on the Neo-Nazis network and the NGA organization. We will take as many guests as possible, a few scientists, several high-ranking Nazis, Wagner, and Advik, to our cells in the London Underground. We will interrogate them and use the information to strike their regional and national groups. Other Guardian Teams may be involved in the sweep-up duty. Our responsibility to humanity will not end with our assault on the Asylum. We will continue to overcome the cretins wherever we find them until those malignant groups are eliminated from the face of the earth. Beyond will assign our task, but I hope to stay on this until the end. Angus, will you hand out the assignments?"

Angus thanked David and discussed the assignments. "When we enter the mansion, David and Bones will begin in the library. Big Soph will stay with Bones. They will take lab #4. Red and I will take laboratory #1 and upstairs. Sir Winston and Dr. Einstein will take laboratory #2 downstairs. "He looks up to remind himself who is left. He sees our angel. "Abigor will search upstairs and laboratory #3. Assignments may change as the situation develops. We will be prepared to adjust and overcome." He pauses for questions, but none comes. He nods and continues, "The library will be the holding cell for our guests until Miles can grab the prisoners and transport them to London. We will specifically search for the journal, lab notes, viable cells, and computers. Red will transport the computers back to the Savoy. Guys, I am afraid our suite will be bloody crowded for a short while. We will have all the information on what they have done in research and what they plan. Neither the Wagner group nor any other mad scientists will be able to proceed with cloning or the Youth Formula studies. They will need the research notes in their notebooks, journals, and computers to do anything. After that, we will assess the situation and respond based on our evaluation. Any questions?" Nope. We want to get to the Asylum and begin kicking Nazi butt.

I cannot believe we are finally there, beginning the last assault on the Mengele gang. Our original enemies, Mengele, Hans, and Franz are dead. I remind myself that I have believed we were at the end twice before, and the journal and viable cells evaded our clutch at the last minute.

Sir Winston asks, "Is everyone ready to go?" We all answer, "Aye, sir!"

In the blink of an eye, we are in the insane asylum. I have always assumed I would be in one someday. We land in the impressive English library. No one was lounging in a club chair reading a good book, so we decided to visit the kitchen and help Abigor. I love old kitchens, and David told me he likes to cook. This man keeps getting better and better. Three women work in the enormous brick room with floor-to-ceiling windows and polished wood counters along three walls.

Two elderly ladies who look like they came with the mansion in 1965 are making bread and preparing two vast steaming pots of delicious sniffable soup. I greet them, "Good evening, ladies. We are sorry to disturb you at work. By the way, what is that yummy fragrance?"

I am afraid I startled them. They jump and swirl around to see us. David apologizes. "Please forgive us, ladies. We wanted to see who was cooking such wonderfully fragrant foods. Gosh, I wish we could be here when that bread comes out of the oven hot and heavenly with a bit of sweet butter."

They smile at David with that glazed look women get when he is around. David mesmerizes them. "Bones and I are here to help Dr. Wagner modernize the kitchen. I see you have two old Garland gas ranges. You can't find quality like that today. How long have the ranges been here?"

The lady with a severe gray bun at the nape of her neck says, "I am Agnes, sir. The Garlands have been here since 1957. You know, solid, sir. Them is better than anything they make today." She chuckles that the good-looking stranger knows his ranges.

David, looking his most sincere, tells the ladies that Dr. Wagner has given them the rest of the day off, and they are free to leave.

A gray-haired lady sporting a red apron and sensible shoes steps toward David, "I'm called Nina. Nice to know ya. As you can see, we ain't done all our work. I don't want to cause no problems for the Doc." I allay her concerns. "Dr. Wagner asked that we have the kitchen to ourselves so that we won't disturb you. You are free to go and enjoy your evening." Big Soph nods her head. Yep, what she said.

Nina and Agnes look a trifle worried, then grin, grab their sweaters from hooks on the wall, and throw off their aprons. They fly through the back door like children off to play in a babbling brook.

The only worker left is a lovely, slender, blonde girl with big blue eyes. She has been cutting vegetables and listening to our conversation with Agnes and Nina. Blue-eyes looks hesitantly at David and says, "Hello, I'm Bayleigh. I haven't worked here for long and don't want to lose my job. They pay very well, and the work isn't hard. Are you certain it is all right to leave? Look, we haven't baked the bread for breakfast, and a couple of loaves are still in the oven." She points at the bread dough on the counter and the oven. We suggest that she remove the loaves from the oven and join her friends. She quickly removes the baked loaves from the huge oven and puts them on the counter, filling the room with a heavenly fragrance.

David pats Bayleigh on the back, reassuring her that she can leave without any nasty repercussions. Big Soph goes over and licks her hand. That does it, and Bayleigh throws a brilliant smile our way and runs for the door. Our hostile takeover could turn dangerous, and we don't want innocents involved.

I am amazed by the old, divided in two-basin sink propped up on painted red legs and sporting a plaid skirt. For some reason, it reminds me of an 1890s pub dancer. No, I don't know why. You had to be there. This kitchen is a time capsule with lace curtains that sway in the breeze through the large open windows.

The kitchen is unlikely to yield anything we are hunting for, but just to be sure, we search the cabinets and pantry. Nada.

We shake hands, kiss, and walk toward a lab to help Red and Angus. I hear Red's booming voice before walking down the long, carpeted hall to the laboratory. Red is yelling at eleven scientists, three women, and eight men sitting on their lab stools doing whatever. Most are middle-aged scientists who are deadly serious about continuing their work. They are screaming back at Red, telling him to get out and leave them to their essential work. One man with steel-hued hair and a Hercule Poirot mustache is fighting mad. Poirot is off his stool, stamping his feet and excitedly waving his arms. Next to him, an attractive, petite woman with coppery hair and very red lipstick encourages mustache to fight the intruders.

The other scientists are simply watching the show. However, one bulked guy wearing red sneakers seems about to jump into the ring to show he is courageous, like Mustache. Slowly, Red Sneakers sits back down as we walk into the room. For reasons not apparent to me, David inspires fear in men. Angus is calm, while Red is furious and ready to knock heads together! David whistles to get their attention. "Good evening, gentlemen and ladies. We need your cooperation in our investigation. We are not arresting you, but you must accompany us to the library. We may change our minds about arrest if you do not cooperate." David's words seemed to have calmed or frightened the White Coats. They walk ahead of us down the hall.

When we get to the library, Dr. Einstein and Sir Winston are there with five White Coats of their own. Men make up their group, and they look terribly unhappy. Two tall men are of African descent, and one heavy, good-looking guy is probably Hispanic. They all have the requisite round glasses, which makes them look sincere and intellectual. They are younger than our prisoners. Sir Winston asks Abigor, "We are getting quite a large gathering of guests here. Would you oversee them while we look for others?" Dr. Einstein says he is going ahead to look for the journal. Red removes a dozen computers from each lab and transports them to the Savoy. Abigor nods to take on this challenge, but he doesn't look thrilled about jailor duty.

David and I go into the hall and stroll toward the next laboratory. I wear bullet protection under my T-shirt and jacket, so I am not particularly concerned about my wellness. We have cleared out two of the four laboratories. The White Coats are with Abigor in the Library, and we have searched for evidence. Red took care of the computers. It's not bad for the relatively short time we have been here.

Red ambles toward us and offers to help us search this lab. We push the door open and walk in to face our next annoyed group of people. We see about a dozen White Coats bent over their microscopes or peering at their Dell OptiPlex7080 XE computer screens. Doc Wagner has received some serious money from someone, probably NGA, because these computers cost about $15,000 per unit. We stand at the door, silently looking around until someone finally looks up. Then, of course, everyone is upset and wants to know why we are there, so they tell us to go away. We know the drill by now.

I could write the script for these people. Naturally, one person wants to yell at us. This time, a tall, blonde, stocky woman with oversized silver earrings and chic black high heels, an odd garb for a scientist. She yells at David after looking him over, "Who are you? You don't work here. I would remember you! The ditzy woman with the red high heels doesn't work here either, and neither does the pirate! Get out, or I shall call security!"

Red is losing patience with these people calling him a pirate. This group of scientists annoys him, and he yells at them to follow us and shut up! White Coats look at us with curiosity but are not particularly emotional. Most of the researchers are middle-aged men wearing thick glasses and drinking from heavy diner coffee cups. The other woman, a dark, striking woman possibly of Indian descent, sits at the end of the counter, watching us.

David calmly chats with them. "Please stay seated for the moment while we search the room. You are not under arrest, but we require your help with our investigation. The sooner we finish, the sooner you can go to Dr. Wagner's office." The stout blonde sits back on her stool since no one seems interested in helping her attack us. She is pouting in disappointment. We search the drawers under the lab countertops and examine documents lying in the open. Papers spill out of a small glass front cabinet—nothing there. David and I move to the closet and are rewarded with several research notebooks, which go into my sizeable purse. Red starts transporting the computers back to the Savoy. David and I walk with our reluctant, but nonaggressive prisoners to the library at the end of the hall. We hear loud noises and shouting coming from the library.

We herd our captives into a temporary holding cell and see the remaining White Coats are in full, vigorous rebellion. Abigor is getting that malevolent demon look again. Two men with very red faces have duct tape across their mouths. I can't imagine how that happened. Sigh. Their comrades are foolishly attempting to fight back. The library looks like a riot at Rikers Prison. When I thought things could not get worse, suddenly, out of thin air, Archangel Michael appeared. Those 15-foot wings make the library even more crowded. Oh hell, this will not be pretty! Naturally, he sympathizes with his fellow angel Abigor and starts lobbing a few lightning bolts—just little ones. Sir Winston and Dr. Einstein come in all big smiles, with a couple of canvas bags and ten more White Coats. They then stop dead!

The mayhem does not amuse Sir Winston. He chomps on his cigar, cutting it in half and spitting it out, and shouts, "Stop all the noise immediately! Who duct-taped these scientists? Michael, please cease the fireworks demonstration!" Then he turns his ire to the scientists, "Riots are inappropriate for men and women of science!" Michael is a great fan of the war hero Sir Winston Leonard Spencer Churchill. He lobs only one more bolt and sneers in silent protest.

Abigor faintly apologizes, "Sir Winston, I had two choices: kill these two wretches or tape their mouths shut! I chose the less violent of the two. Undoubtedly, thee and Dr. Einstein agree with my more conciliatory choice!" Dr. Einstein is trying not to laugh. He knows this is a pivotal moment, but he can't stop. Einstein clamps his hand over his mouth and turns away, and no one other than me notices his mirth.

Red runs into the room, accompanied by a middle-aged man wearing a white coat and glasses. I recognized him immediately! Dr. Suggs! The kidnapped scientist is with us again. We take a few minutes to welcome him back to freedom and assure him he is safe. Dr. Suggs looks well after his long confinement by the wicked Dr. Wagner. He is smiling and hugging the team, evidently thrilled to see friendly faces. Despite our first meeting, which was an OK Corral shootout in his lab in Austria, he is pleasant. I suppose he doesn't hold grudges.

Everyone is finally calming down. I think the lightning bolts did the job. Michael looks at Sir Winston. "I said I would be here to help you. I had to leave earlier. The John F. Kennedy's Team called me away. Verily, I returned here just in time. Where are the Neo-Nazis? I must have a word with them and Dr. Wagner. I made a promise. I expected to see men on their knees in repentance." His statement sounds calm if one could not see Michael's face. His jaw is set, and his eyes are hard, throwing off sparks.

The door is violently thrown open, and Dr. Wagner, Advik, and the 11 remaining armed Neo-Nazis surge into the room in a mass of animosity. My team forms a line between the armed men and the scientists. We cannot allow them to be killed, even if by accident. I am at the end of the line. Before David can reach me, Big Soph leaps into the air, pushes me to the side of the room, and stands in front of me, growling, snapping, and snarling. Everyone slides to the far side of the room. A tall, bulked Nazi decides to be stupid. He goes down on one knee, aims his rifle at Soph, and fires. Michael sees him and throws a deadly lightning bolt in his direction. Nazi falls to the floor, never to rise again in this life. Michael storms at the Nazis and Wagner, "I told you to repent, and yet one of you attempts to kill an innocent animal! Monstrous evil!" Yes, Michael knows Soph is not an innocent animal. Maybe he meant me?

He pulls the hearse to the door, an old Southern saying, "No more! Your time is up! Mortals, Nazis, Advik, and Wagner, go out those doors to the patio, kneel and repent. If you do not repent, you will die." He points to the doors, and there is a mad dash in the direction he points. Everyone, Neo-Nazis and scientists alike, shove each other out of the way to reach the doors before the giant changes his mind. Two scientists stumble and fall to the floor. Soph and I grab them out of the danger before their cohorts trample them.

Red is back from carting computers to our suite, and he brings in the last ten scientists he found hiding in a closet upstairs. They see the human stampede and go rushing after them out through the patio doors.

Michael yells to the newly arrived humans, "Mortals, I have never seen you before this moment. You are not included in my commandment. Please be calm." Looking at the Nazis, Wagner, and Advik, he reminds them, "I have already warned you. I told you I am willing to save your souls for all eternity. All I asked of you was to go to your knees and genuinely repent." He pulls out his sword and swings it around. They don't hear him in the terrible din. Everyone, including the scientists who are not in this conversation, run in abject terror. I think the sword was the last match to the gunpowder barrel.

Dr. Suggs dashes across the room, throws a mighty right to Wagner's jaw and left to his stomach, and Wagner falls to the floor, moaning. We did not have time to react and probably would have let Suggs take a swing. He deserved a little payback after being confined and forced to work for Dr. Wagner for several months. Wagner looks up at Suggs, stunned by his Rocky Balboa speed and fancy footwork. Suggs sneers and struts back to us.

Unknown to us, Miles and his twenty officers have been listening in and think we need help, so they are waiting at the patio's edge to snag everyone in their net. Several men and the stout blonde woman refuse to go with them. They insist they must kneel, and no one can dissuade them. I am confident there have been more chaotic takedowns in law enforcement history, but I have never heard about one.

Sir Winston asks Michael to address the distraught people. He agrees. He tries to calm them. "Mortals! The scientists and Nazis may go with the police, and Wagner shall come back inside. When I want you, I can find you. Your time is not now." Strangely enough, his words only increased their terror. Yes, David will have to create a story to explain Michael to Miles, wings and all. Theater should work. It worked for Wagner. Miles will deliver our bunch to the underground cells and his campus.

Wagner, who is unarmed, will stay with us until we transport him to the underground cells. We cannot afford to lose him. David, Abigor, Red, Angus, and I must pull three Neo-Nazis from their knees to leave with Miles. Even with Michael's permission, they were still highly resistant to leaving, but we ultimately managed. Who can blame them?

Fortunately, Miles brought several transportation buses for our large haul, and finally, Miles and his crew had almost all the detainees loaded up. We helped—but kept Michael incognito.

No one can remove the terrified blonde from the patio. We decide to leave Blondie kneeling on the stone terrace until she gets hungry and comes inside. We will transport her to MI5 HQ tomorrow. The underground cells cannot hold everyone. I admire tenacity. I threw a blanket over her so she wouldn't get cold tonight and gave her a plump pillow. Abigor brought a cup of coffee to her. Yeah, caffeine is just what she needs.

Dr. Suggs tries to remain strong, but his eyes are damp. He tells Dr. Einstein, "I want to go home and hug my wife. I was afraid I would never see her again." Angus returns him to his jubilant wife and children in Austria after using the angel "voodoo" thing so that he won't remember the, uh, unconventional trip. David had told Dr. Suggs we would debrief him in a few days. After his long sojourn from home, we will go to him for the interview. He has earned a relaxing rest with his family. I am amazed at how stable and controlled he is after what he has been through.

Sir Winston and Dr. Einstein are smiling again.

Chapter Twenty-Six

Triumph

Sir Winston is grinning ear to ear and more excited than I have ever seen him. He asks us to take a seat in the library. "We have excellent news for you! We searched #4 laboratory and found!" The Great Man stops for effect and then continues, "The journal and the viable cells!"

We go crazy! We are jumping up and down, uh, not Michael. David, Angus and I are dancing. We are yelling in triumph! This is our *Miracle of Dunkirk* moment!

Finally, we have our battered Mengele journal back and what we have never captured before: the viable cells of the three monsters! The evil Doc admitted they had only one cell from each fiend. From my research a few months ago, their bodies were destroyed or lost. Hitler committed suicide, and his body, Eva, and his dogs were buried in Rathenau, Germany. His body was burned to ashes in 1970. Himmler's body is not quite as tightly tied up. He committed suicide with prussic acid on May 23, 1945, in Luneburg, Germany. Captain Thomas Selvester was interrogating him when Himmler bit into a glass suicide capsule. Himmler is buried in an unmarked grave in an unknown location. Goebbels and his wife also committed suicide. The fanatics were buried near Berlin. Later, the KGB removed their bodies and threw their ashes into a river. Naturally, we cannot depend on these accounts to be perfectly accurate. It was a chaotic time in Europe, and primary source material varies. Is it possible for the Nazis to find other viable cells? Hedging my bets, I would surmise it is implausible. I cannot close that door entirely.

We are relatively confident that our next mission will involve tracking down Neo-Nazi nests and NGA members worldwide. We do not fool ourselves, it won't be easy, and anything could happen. It is an expansive mission that could take years to complete unless we let Michael handle it. Nah, we had better not do that.

Sir Winston hands out our 'smiley faces,' saying, "I am honored to acknowledge each of you for your impressive work under extreme circumstances. In my long life, I have never had the privilege of working with a more gallant, unshrinking, and lion-hearted group. The Powers have asked me to congratulate you on a job well done. The world and all humankind owe you a tremendous debt. Sadly, they will never know you even existed. If we can stand up to our enemies, all the world may move forward into broad, sunlit uplands. But if we fail, then the whole world, including all that we have known and care for, will sink into the abyss of a new Dark Age made more sinister and, perhaps, more protracted by the lights of perverted science. Let us therefore brace ourselves to our duties and so bear ourselves that if the British Empire and its Commonwealth last for a thousand years, men will say, 'This was their finest hour.'

"I said this many years ago in extreme times, but it also applies to this group sitting here in front of me." The Great Statesman wipes his eyes with his linen handkerchief.

I shed tears, too. My pride in my team is impossible to express in words. Big Soph puts her massive head in my lap, and I feel her tears dropping on my hand. David puts his arms around us and hugs us to him. No, he is not tearing up.

David stands and looks toward Sir Winston, "Thank you, Winston. Your generous words humble me. I agree with you completely. I have been fortunate to work with remarkable men and women during WWII and in my extended career with MI5. I work with some of them again, Red, Angus, and you, Sir. I could not ask for a better group of warriors to be in a foxhole with me than this team, especially when the foxhole is taking heavy fire. Abigor, you are new to the team but responsible for getting Aaii and Michael together when we needed them. Thank you!" He reaches out to shake Abigor's hand. Abigor looks embarrassed by the praise.

David says, "Sir Winston, you inspire us as a brilliant leader, a great and honorable man. Working beside you has been the highlight of my career." What can I possibly say that will do justice to the enormous contributions of our genius, Dr. Albert Einstein? It isn't enough, but we wholeheartedly thank you! David pauses, giving the rest of us a chance to cheer Churchill and Einstein, and we do so at the top of our lungs. David moves on, "Now, we get to our vulnerable mortal, Bones. She has suffered severely during our dangerous mission. I want to thank her for never weakening and being the consummate trooper. Sometimes, she was too foolhardy, like when she attacked a demon. What sane human attacks a demon?" I stare David down, and he stops. Yet, we all know he is right. Sigh.

David wisely changes direction, "Now, let's talk plans for the future. Sir Winston, Red, Angus, and I will take turns interrogating the Asylum group. We hope to learn more about the other medical and Neo-Nazi groups. We don't know if other researchers are doing monstrous medical research on innocents. I understand there are numerous Neo-Nazi groups worldwide. We have no idea how many or how well organized they are. Between our Team and Michael, we should be able to add to our knowledge base. We must keep them from uniting into one enormous octopus organization with tentacles stretching worldwide. That would be catastrophic. We must also stop the NGA from expanding its elite one-government influence. Using stealth, we shall weaken their work whenever the opportunity arises. We cannot allow them to enslave the world. When they learn they will not have Hitler to unite their potential followers, they will look for another antichrist figure. We shall be alert when they choose their next psychopath and will deal with him when that time comes. Also, we have viable cells, so it is unlikely anyone can clone the three Nazis. We believe we have all the notes, the Journal, and the computers for the cloning procedure and the Youth Formula. However, it is impossible to know if other notes exist. Again, we must be diligent and keep our ears to the ground. Michael will also be using his resources." He looks to Micheal, who is now Druid.

Michael is ready for business. He begins, "Let's discuss our immediate plans. I have an appointment with Fritz, the Director of HGA International. He is unaware of our meeting, but I shall visit him in his self-indulgent New York City apartment this afternoon. I intend to learn the names and addresses of other members of the top hierarchy. Seth will report later today on the local NGA Committee. It seems they have had some chilling experiences recently. Also, when you release them, I plan a serious discussion with Dr. Wagner, Advik, and his Neo-Nazis." Miles has possession now. We perk up when we hear the name Seth. Abigor said Michael could tell us about Seth. I ask Michael, "Who is the mysterious Seth? We understand he is a member of the Team. We didn't know about him until Abigor mentioned him. He said you could tell us more about Seth's role in our mission."

Michael glared at Abigor for a long time and then answered, "Bones, first, I want to say how pleased I am that you are well and safe. Keeping you alive was important to me for more reasons than you know. Seth is a very old friend who helps me on important missions. He is unique. Seth can easily infiltrate any group or organization and fit in well. He reports directly to me, just as in the NGA assignment. Seth will still work on that task until the Committee members are harmless or repentant. He will also help with the International Organization, and he was my link to Aaii so I could monitor him. I knew the day would come when I would have to rein in the Demon. I took him back to his boss in Hell last night. He is the one who started the rumor about the Dark World and the fantastic machine. I believe the Dark World is a gateway to Hell. If you had entered, you would have never returned. Aaii put a spell on the compass, and it is powerful. I do not know its potential power or how it can be used. That is why Abigor, as a demon, desired the compass, though he does not remember it now. Thank God you did not enter the gateway, Bones!"

David and Abigor gasp in horror. "Michael nods at them and says, "I sent her a dream about the horrors of that evil place." Now, it is my turn to gasp. I remember that dreadful dream. How could I forget? It was incredibly vivid. I told Red and the Padre about the nightmare when we were on the Jet to Poland, the jet that fell apart. Michael sees my reaction and continues, "Abigor could have returned unharmed, but he would have been devastated by Bone's death. Aaii would have disposed of two enemies. Also, he knows about the Hell Gate dream I sent to you and could use it against you. Be aware. He had been tracking your Team, and I was tracking him. I have warned him of the consequences if he tries to destroy you again. It would be painful for him. I will deal with him about the Fox's death. I have not forgotten." Fear scampers up my spine. Aaii is a hell-bent psycho.

Michael finishes, "I shall return to the demon chamber and permanently close the gateway." We are in our usual perpetual state of shock as we process Michael's information. There were so many dangerous secrets lying in wait behind the curtains. If David had not disappeared, would I have gone into the Hell Gateway? Michael didn't fully answer my question about Seth. He remains a question mark.

Dr. Einstein takes the floor, "My priority is to find the Time Machine. Alpha and Omega reached out to tell me it is in the basement at Humboldt University in Berlin, where it has been sitting abandoned since WWII. Dr. Otto Wolffe should be able to help us with that. I would also like to know more about those people who were intently interested when they learned Professor Wolffe had the Rosen and Goldmann Book. I shudder when I consider what could have happened if Abigor, Soph, and Bones had not scooped up Otto and kept him safe with us. If Rosen and Goldmann never completed the Time Machine, as Omega told me, wouldn't it be wonderful if we could make it functional? I had a long conversation with him recently. He said he had a special assignment for me and knew I would be rather interested. Omega chuckled when he said that." Peculiar, I did not realize they could chuckle.

Einstein shakes his head. "Naturally, I am thrilled about the opportunity to see and touch the Fantastic Machine! I never dreamed I would get to work on a Time Machine! We will transport it to my lab at the Savoy. Otto will be staying with us to help me." I am thrilled for Dr. Einstein and Otto. The machine is their ultimate dream challenge. I can't wait to see it myself!

Looking around the library, I realize Michael left without saying anything. He could say goodbye when he pops out. Manners are essential even for archangels. I would guess the unfortunate Fritz is about to have a visitor.

Abigor whispers something in Sir Winston's ear. Churchill grabs his silver-headed cane and tells us, "I have received a summons from Alpha. He asks that I go to Beyond immediately and bring Abigor and Albert. I don't know how long we will be gone. Please continue refining our plans to tackle our mission. As has been our fate much of the time, details often remain hidden. Keep in mind that no new mission has been assigned to us yet. Perhaps that is why Alpha summoned me." Abigor, Sir Winston, and Dr. Einstein are simply gone. Could the summons be for that unfortunate event between David and Axel? That frightening thought chills me to the bone.

They continue to discuss preparations for the expanded mission if the Powers assign more to us. I cannot keep my mind on what they are saying. Big Soph comes over to sit by me. She knows.

Chapter Twenty-Seven

David's Trial

Sir Winston, Abigor, and Dr. Einstein pop into the surreal waiting room in Beyond. Dr. Einstein hasn't been there as frequently as Churchill, and he is absolutely enthralled by all he sees. The doctor leans out of one of the arched windows and visually absorbs the nearly overwhelming scene of glorious colors and perfect harmony. He is mesmerized by the winding, gurgling rocky stream that flows lazily through the lush vegetation. Astonishingly vibrant tropical birds and delicate butterflies dart and glide for his amusement. Albert wants to dash outside, throw off his brown leather wingtip oxfords, and splash in the stream. Sighing deeply, he removes his often-furtive pipe and searches his rumpled jacket pockets for a match. Sir Winston sees Albert's predicament and offers him a match from his silver holder.

Abigor is pacing around the room, concerned about the reason for their sudden invitation to Beyond. He knows they will reexamine David's interaction with the thug Axel because they admitted they would do so once the Team completed its mission. There is no reason to speculate; the Powers will enlighten them when they arrive. Still, the tension weighs heavily on him while he waits. Being a narcissistic, psychopathic demon was less worrying. Caring and loving bring a substantial burden he is not accustomed to hefting.

Sir Winston is also afraid the conversation will turn to David. The Powers warned him that the trial was coming soon. If that is true, why not invite David to attend? Will they try him in absentia? Churchill is terribly uneasy with anything he perceives as unjust, and this possibility troubles him. Alpha appears in the room, jarring Churchill, Abigor, and Einstein from their reflections.

Alpha looks as flawless and awe-inspiring as always. He almost smiles and greets them, "Dearest Winston, Albert, and Abigor, how happy I am to see you today. What a treat! Please excuse Omega. He will join us soon. He is consumed with a moral issue concerning homelessness in San Francisco." He shakes his magnificent head to emphasize the complexity of the problem. Strangely, he adds, "Such a complicated problem in so many ways. It will require a comprehensive plan designed by an INTJ." How does he know the Myers-Briggs Personality Inventory?

He pulls his attention back to his guests. "Winston and Abigor, we recently chatted about David and his behavior when he shot Axel. I wish to revisit that conversation, and since Albert was there, he is aware of the likelihood that Bones would have or would not have died if David had not acted promptly. We have talked to Father Antonio, who was also a witness." He pauses, his brow furrows as if trying to remember something.

"Oh, on another issue, Father Antonio asked me to please tell David and Bones it really was him in St. Albans. They probably have watched too many Hollywood picture shows and become cynical. Father Antonio chuckled when he realized they thought he might have gone to the Dark Side. I had no idea he was so familiar with recent shows. Ah, but I digress. His manifestation was unique because the Godly man will likely be Sainted."

How sweet, Alpha thinks 1977 is recent. I am excited that my dear padre might become a Saint! Alpha looks down at his perfect hands and reflects, "Gentlemen, let us return to the reason for our meeting. Father Antonio was quite firm in his belief that David acted aptly under the circumstances. Yet, we know Father Antonio was not fully aware at the time. I have also consulted with The Admiral and Thelma Dove for their opinions about David. They, too, were exceedingly generous in their praise for David's character and decision-making ability. Naturally, his character was never questioned since he is on a Guardian Team. We question his ability to make a just decision about shooting Axel when Axel was choking his beloved Bones. Obviously, we are held to a much higher standard than mere mortals. David has often walked the line between the lowest level of force and more force than is necessary. This is not the first time we have wondered about his impulsivity."

He lets the statement hang for a beat and continues, "I wish to discuss what happened and hear Dr. Einstein's opinion firsthand. Shall we all sit comfortably while considering this critical issue?" Sir Winston is still uncomfortable about this 'trial' and asks Alpha, "I am a little confused. This meeting is about David and his decision to shoot when the thug Axel tried to choke the life out of our dear Bones. Yet, David is not here to defend himself. I am distraught. Would you please explain this process to me?" Dr. Einstein and Abigor silently agree with Churchill's rather subjective description of the behavior that led to the thug's demise.

Alpha is perfectly serene as he answers, "I understand your concerns, dear Winston. I value you all the more because of your love of justice. Yet, this is not a formal trial with lawyers, a judge, and a jury. We want to understand why Axel is dead. If the facts support his actions, David will remain on your team. He will be returned to Beyond if we conclude that he shot before it was necessary. I have heard from you, Winston, and Father Antonio. Dr. Einstein is here to give his professional opinion. Albert, Winston told me what you said concerning the confrontation. To clarify, would you explain the physical aspects of choking to me?"

Dr. Einstein shares his limited medical knowledge with Alpha. "As you know, I am a physicist and mathematician, not a physician. However, my career has taught me much, especially during the war. I will repeat what I told Winston. When Axel, a powerfully built man, was choking Bones, she could have been unconscious in 10 seconds and dead in 3 minutes. Axel could easily have crushed Bones' larynx, causing asphyxia, and compressed her carotid artery, resulting in cerebral ischemia. This is all that I can tell you. There was little time for David to decide whether to shoot or not, and it would have been impossible to guess accurately. David had to fire before Axel crushed her larynx. Hear me on this; she would have suffered a horribly painful death. Truthfully, I would rather Axel, a violent Nazi, die that day than Bones."

Omega strolls in as Einstein is speaking. He sits down quietly and listens. Then he responds to Dr. Einstein, "I have the greatest respect for you and your opinion, Albert. As you say, this is not your field, but you are kind to share this information with us. Is there anything else you can tell us about David that will assist us in deciding what to do in this matter?" Before answering, Dr. Einstein studies his pipe for a long time. "I have worked with David on a highly complex and dangerous mission for many months. David is one of the finest men I have ever met. He is responsible, intelligent, dedicated, honorable, and rock solid. I would bet my life on David's ability to make excellent, well-considered decisions without a moment's hesitation—if I had a life to bet." Omega contemplates Dr. Einstein's words and nods to Alpha.

Abigor considers his duty and speaks, "Alpha and Omega, I respect you and applaud your concern about Axel's death. I hast not known David for as long as Dr. Einstein and Sir Winston, yet I understand evil, having been a demon for eons. Axel wast evil. He battered frail Father Antonio, which probably led to his death. Axel and Weber attempted to kill Angus before I joined the Team. David is gallant and unbeatable because he won't stop when he is right. David had to make an impossible decision. Waiting too long to shoot would have doomed

Bones. If he did not wait to shoot, Axel might die. There was no feasible way to see the line separating the two options. I fully support Air Marshall Smythe. I must share some painfully personal information with you so you will understand my delicate position."

He looks off at the blooms and stream outside the window. Finally, he tightens his jaw and continues, "I love Bones with all my heart and soul. If David were sent back to Beyond, I might have an opportunity to express my eternal devotion to her. I have an excellent reason to speak against David, but my words would be false and self-serving. I cannot and shalt not do that." Alpha and Omega stiffly embrace Abigor. Sir Winston wipes away tears and sniffs. Dr. Einstein absently pats the former demon's shoulder. Abigor accepts the emotional outpouring with dignity and grace. He is at peace.

Alpha makes eye contact with Omega. "Gentlemen, we appreciate your time and assistance today. We shall consult with another individual and decide what to do in the next few days. We don't know his schedule. He has been rather busy saving Israel." Our team members say a hasty goodbye and pop back to the Savoy, unsure what to expect from the Heavenly Duo.

Otto and I are eating our delicious lunch from room service: roasted cod, confit fennel, mussels, a pot of tea, and a caramel latte with whipped cream. Abigor, Sir Winston, and Dr. Einstein pop back into the room. Their eyes are downcast, and their mouths are turned down. They don't look happy. I venture Alpha didn't invite them to Beyond for a lovely afternoon tea with Queen Elizabeth. Their long faces chill me like slivers of ice in my veins.

David, Angus, Red, Big Soph, and I are looking at them quizzically, waiting for information. Otto continues to enjoy his lunch, oblivious to the deadly tension in the room. He knows nothing about the shooting. Big Soph is concerned, and her sad eyes give her away.

Sir Winston sits down and suggests we do the same. He will not soft-pedal the news. "Alpha and Omega wished to discuss the Axel shooting. They asked for our opinions, and we were glad to share our well-considered thoughts with them. We were steadfast in supporting David and aggressive in pointing out that Axel caused his own death by his violent behavior against Bones and Father Antonio. They also talked with Father Antonio, Admiral Stallings, and Thelma. By the way, it was Father Antonio in St. Albans. He wanted Bones and David to know." He pauses and grins at me. I am thrilled that my loyalty was well-placed.

The former PM continues, "They, too, were unfaltering in their strenuous support of David as the honorable man he is and has always been. Our Team could not have been more supportive because David is dear to us, and we have been successful in part because of his exceptional leadership ability. Alpha said they would talk to someone else and contact us in the next few days with their recommendation. David, do you have questions for us?"

Before David can answer, Red jumps up and paces the room, yelling at the top of his lungs. "What the Hell are they talking about?! David is one of the finest men and professionals I have ever met, and they have the unmitigated gall to question him about shooting that gutter scum?! They have never left Beyond and have no idea what this evil world is about. They dared to tell me how to fight vicious evil men who killed brave women without a second thought?! Yes, I killed many of them, and I wish I had killed more. How dare they!" Red's face is bright scarlet with fury. I am afraid Red will have a heart attack! Wait, he can't have a heart attack. Whew! I am so accustomed to Nazis' dropping dead from heart disease that it is the first thing I think.

Angus stomps his feet and shouts, "Here, here!" I have never seen the dear, sturdy man this emotional.

David walks over to Red and gives him a masculine semi-hug. Of course, Red is also outraged with the Powers because they unfairly condemned his wartime ferocity. Red's spirited defense touches David deeply. I can see it in his handsome face. Red sits back down, exhausted from the emotional exertion. Yet he is still hitting the chair with his fist.

David runs his hand over his face. He looks directly at Sir Winston and manages to say, "I cannot tell you how much it means to me to have your unwavering support. I will never be able to repay your staunch belief in me, and I also mean Abigor, Dr. Einstein, Admiral Stallings, Father Antonio, and Thelma Dove."

I weep to hear how our friends vigorously supported David against Alpha and Omega's outrageous accusations. I pause for a moment while I consider the word—friends. I have seldom thought of them in that way. They were simply my team. Yes, they are dear friends. I owe our friends my most fervent gratitude. David kneels in front of the sofa and embraces me, but I can't stop weeping. God, I love this man!

At this moment, unbeknownst to me, Alpha, Omega, and Gabriel are having a life-altering conversation . . . about me.

At the Old Royal Naval College, two reverent souls pray for us.

Chapter Twenty-Eight

Fritz and the Giant

Fritz Helms is an important and influential man in International New Global Agenda circles. He knows all the national leaders, too. He is surprised that he has not heard from the American group. He counts the National Committee Members as close, uh, friends. He is genuinely worried about what this lack of communication means. He has reached out to Annette, Julian, Juan, Emerson, and Seth, but no one has responded. They are shockingly dismissive. The committee members know their survival in the group is at stake as their positions depend on his support. He has known Emerson and Annette for many years. Someone else in the INGA told him Emerson was supposed to be in a private hospital in France. Why would Emerson go into a hospital without telling him? Another associate told him Annette was recently in the ER in Manhattan. There is a rumor no one could chase down that Annette had been shot, but that sounds entirely too fantastic to be true. Fritz sent his skeletal butler to call at Annette's apartment and determine what has happened.

Fritz looks around his apartment as he considers these strange occurrences. He spends most of his days in his apartment, so he asked the most sought-after designer in Manhattan to update it for him. Seth has used him and recommended him in the most glowing terms. The designer worked for everyone who is anyone in New York City. He is well known for his trend-setting use of white and purple with a dash of red. The renowned artist spends weeks scouring stores and auctions for just the perfect artwork for his masterpiece interior designs. Fritz had to move into a hotel for a week while the master designer, Thornton, transformed his enormous living space. Fritz was shocked when he entered his apartment and went snow-blind. He was not amused yet still lived with the purple ceiling and chilling white floors and walls. According to all the right people, Fritz should have been thrilled Thornton accepted a commission from him.

The elderly resident had stopped dead when he saw the piano. Helms immediately ran his fingers over the smooth surface of the pricy Bluthner black with gold inlay grand piano. His mother had played when he was a small boy. Young Fritz loved listening to her play as he sat on the stool beside her. How could he have forgotten that for so many decades?

Fritz loves the piano that reminds him of his dear mother and ignores the rest of the apartment.

He sits comfortably in his leather Bozeman chair, sipping Petrus Pomerol 1972 from a St. Louis Botticelli wine glass. He had just begun to relax when the doorbell interrupted his musings. Fritz slowly and unsteadily maneuvers in the general direction of the door. He assumes his dinner from Le Bernardin has been delivered. He has a special arrangement with the restaurant because NGA spends thousands of dollars for their conferences dining at the unsurpassed Le Bernardin. Their food is exquisitely palatable and precisely what Fritz enjoys and cooked perfectly. And they never disappoint. Sadly, his stomach is delicate, and the chef must puree his food before he can eat it—such a pity. Fritz peers through the peek hole in his heavily carved mahogany door. A waiter in a white uniform with a name tag stands beside a rolling cart. The name tag reads Druid. Fritz thinks that is an odd name. If he only knew.

He opens the door to allow the waiter to enter. Druid rolls in the food cart. Fritz looks at the Giant, who now has on his dull black suit and bowler hat. No, I don't know how he changed clothes. Fritz is mesmerized by the giant in the old suit. He has never seen anyone like this in Manhattan. Druid speaks boomingly, "We have some things to discuss, Fritz Helms. Why don't you go back to your Boseman chair and relax? I shall sit across from you on the sofa." Fritz is shocked. "How do you know my chair is a Boseman? I don't know you." Druid smiles his most affable smile. If he is hoping for friendly, it falls a tad short.

He pats the elderly man's hand and says, "I know everything; remember that, and we will get along well. I will request information I can attain in other ways, but the quickest way is to ask you. Undoubtedly, you are eager to help me. Now, shall we chat?" Fritz sits in his chair, growing angrier by the moment.

Fritz, the old psychopath, trembles and says, "Who are you? What are you? I demand an answer! How dare you come in here under false pretenses! I will call the police and have you forcefully removed or shot! Get out! Get out!" Druid looks at him in disgust. He sees the man's numerous sins staining what is left of his blackened soul. Druid has no desire to bully a fragile old man. He replies, "Fritz, believe me, you don't want the answer to those questions. I have no intention of harming you. But I know you want Dr. Wagner's Youth Formula because you weaken more each day. Am I right? You can barely walk, you must eat baby food, and you can't catch your breath after a short trek from here to your bedroom. I can give you information on the Formula in exchange for your help." Druid points toward the bedroom, and Fritz remembers how painful the short journey is for him.

Fritz is losing some of his bravado. His voice lowers: "How do you know these things? Who are you? I see death written on your face. Am I dying? Are you death?" Fritz moves as far back in his chair as his size allows, futilely trying to get farther away from Druid. The warrior angel almost feels sorry for the old reprobate.

"I have questions for you, and if you answer my questions, I shall leave you to your miserable life and your embarrassment of riches. Who are the other senior members of INGA? I want the officers, and I shall walk out of that door as soon as you tell me."

His bravado has passed, and Fritz is utterly terrified. He wants Druid to leave and will tell him anything. He gazes at his bedroom door and wishes he were in there safe from this monster. He looks directly at Druid and immediately diverts his eyes. "I will tell you. In fact, I will write the names for you. We have ten senior officers who live in various countries around the world. You will leave? Why did you mention Dr. Wagner?" The giant ignores the last question. Druid has no desire to linger longer than necessary. He moves away as he scents evil emanating from this old sinner.

He looks around at the opulence and wonders if Fritz has ever felt genuine joy. He directs his startling eyes at the INGA director. "I will leave as soon as I get their names. There is something else I direct you to do: close down the organization immediately. It operates to enslave the people. I know your plan to use Hitler and his favorite fiends to create a worldwide dictatorship. That will not come to pass, Fritz. I want to leave you in peace for the time you have left on this plane. Verily, I say you can yet repent and save your battered old soul. You will not like the alternative, I assure you. I can help you attain eternal life. This is your last chance. If you wisely decide to take my generous offer, call out my name, and I shall return and guide you to Beyond. My name is Michael." Fritz has been scribbling the officers' names on a legal pad. He cares nothing for these people. Let them deal with Druid or Michael or whoever the hell he is. Fritz tears off the sheet and hands it to Druid.

Druid purposely moves toward the door. "Fritz, you won't hear from Julian, Annette, Seth, Emerson, or Juan. Shall we say they decided to take early retirements? Call the officers of INGA and warn them. I will be coming to visit them, and I don't think they want to see me. What do you think? Oh, call Dr. Wagner, too. I think he is taking a nice long holiday." Druid could have disappeared on his way to the door, but he didn't want to shock the man.

When Druid walks out, Fritz is left alone with his indifferent, chilling abundance. He notices a shadowy figure shrouded in black standing in a dark corner near his massive grand piano. Fritz wipes his glasses and looks again. Slowly, he distinguishes the shape of a woman in a long, funereal dress. He is captivated, staring in amazement as her face gradually becomes more distinct. Dear God, it is his beloved mother, Hannah! "Mother?" He feels her precious love surrounding him in warmth. He remembers the soft patchwork quilts she lovingly stitched when he was a young boy. He shakes his head in disbelief. What is happening? Fritz vigorously rubs his eyes. When he looks up again, Hannah is still there. She whispers softly after struggling to speak, "Follow me, my sweet boy. Follow me." He weeps with joy as he unsteadily stumbles toward her, his arms wide and open.

As Druid strides away, he hears his name—Michael. Fritz cries out to him. A brilliant smile lights up Michael's impassive face. He whirls around and walks back through the door.

Michael will have to close down INGA. Fritz is going home.

Chapter Twenty-Nine

Ghostbusters and Angels

David, Angus, and Sir Winston are below the teeming streets of London in the tunnels below Abbey Mills Pumping Station. The pumping station known as the Cathedral of Sewage was designed by Joseph Bazalgette and Edmond Cooper in 1860. It is considered a building of Special Architectural or Historic Interest. The vast machinery once pumped water through the London sewers. The interior of the building is dark. Their flashlights throw distorting lights on the brutish iron monsters rising two stories high. Strangely enough, Corinthian columns with acanthus leaf design are interspaced among the machines.

This scene is so startlingly incongruent that they must blink several times to assure themselves that it is real. The stately columns seem embarrassed to be here. The musty room is surreal in its absurd idiosyncrasies. They move forward in silence, each absorbed in his thoughts. Soon, they come to an opening in the floor. A ladder descends into the silent, lifeless sewer. Since the station is no longer active, this sewer system section is thankfully empty. Our three holding cells are down in the tunnels. We had only one cell when we imprisoned Dr. Mengele and Franz in our first adventure. Neo-Nazis broke them out, killing two men in the process.

One man was an MI5 agent, and the other was simply an 'oops' who worked with them. Hey, these things happen. When they removed Mengele and Franz, they planted a bomb that detonated while Spears Westbrook's Met Team was working on the scene. Several team members and the medical examiner died in the blast. It was a horrible blow to our Team and Spears' Elite Crime Scene team. Happily, the leaders of the prison break, Weber and Axel, are now dead. We don't have to worry about them again. The damp, musty cell has been used a few times since then, and MI5 recently added two more cells for the comfort and convenience of our mutual guests.

Sir Winston, Angus, and David are here to visit the Neo-Nazis who labored in Dr. Wagner's lab, a former insane asylum. They also imprisoned the good doctor himself. Everyone has been suspiciously quiet and cooperative. I think Archangel Michael traumatized them with his massive wings and glowing sword. A couple of the Nazis are still on their knees here in their cells. They plan to stay on their knees until Michael gives them permission to rise. David explains to them that it is safe to stand now. Michael would not be coming here, and they probably imagined the entire incident. I will admit David's version of the angel angle isn't exactly truthful.

Dr. Wagner taps on the cell bars to signal David to come to his cell door. He whispers while anxiously glancing around the room, "Who are you, and where is your big blonde brother? I don't like him. Tell him to stay home. My mother doesn't allow me to associate with kids who play with swords. You will keep him away, right?" Wagner's eyes are wide. His pupils are dilated for better vision. Adrenaline and his 'fight or flight' response bring this tool to him. David recognizes the signs and tries to calm him.

David is taken aback by his words. He pauses to process the extraordinary request and smiles at the doctor, "I am David Smythe, former MI5. Yes, I understand your mother's concern and have asked Michael not to come here. However, Sir Winston, Angus, and I must ask you some questions. I hope you don't mind. We need your assistance in our investigation. Will you help us?" Sir Winston and Angus listen to this bizarre conversation and slowly nod in agreement. They, too, smile encouragingly at Wagner.

Dr. Herman Wagner appears to calm down, and his shoulders fall as he sighs. He suspiciously inquires, "Are you certain Michael cannot get in here? Michael seems to be remarkably strong. I don't like him even if he is your brother. I like the hot woman with the red high heels. I will talk to her." David unlocks the cell Wagner is sharing with two Neo-Nazis. They are intently watching and listening to this peculiar exchange.

The underground area has been blessed with a table, a few old chairs, a workable coffee pot, and a few chipped cups. The Team feels like royalty with all their recent perks. Angus asks Wagner to have a seat, pours a cuppa, and places it in front of him. The doctor looks skeptically at the cup of steaming brew and asks, "Did Michael touch the coffee? Don't think I am paranoid! I am not paranoid! Michael may have poisoned it." Angus assures him that no one outside this room has touched the coffee. Sir Winston's eyebrows seek his sparse hairline, and he narrows his eyes. He looks for his snifter. Perhaps this conversation will require some refreshments. He reaches for a fresh cigar. Happily, he can handle both simultaneously.

The Team sits around the table with Herman Wagner. Sir Winston opens the conversation. "Dr. Wagner, we are interested in learning about your budget and who provides funds for your research. You have an extremely costly operation funded by someone, so please be honest and thorough in your answers. We also want to know if you have other research groups. If you and the others are forthcoming, we will add outside time for exercise to your schedule. We want you to be comfortable while you reside with us. Keep in mind, we know the answers to some of our questions, so be candid." Herman moves closer, squints his eyes at Churchill, and inquires, "Are you Winston Churchill, the WWII Prime Minister and hero?" Ah, this is a tricky question, and the former PM is unsure how to answer it. The doctor has already been exposed to a few shocks too many, and his mental wellness is shaky.

Finally, David answers the doctor, "Yes, this is Sir Winston Churchill. Would you please answer his question about the source of your research funding?" Bad choice.

Herman is not as happy with this answer as David had hoped he would be. He looks closely at Churchill again, squints, and starts screaming! Wagner jumps up on his chair and uses another chair to keep Sir Winston at bay as if he were a charging lion. Our Team is stunned by his sudden psychotic behavior as he yells, "Michael sent a ghost! Michael is the devil. Make the ghastly ghost go away! Go away! Go away! I command you to leave!" He is frantically making the sign of the cross as he screeches. The Cavalry arrives! Dr. Einstein walks in because David sent an SOS to him.

Dr. Einstein approaches the researcher and calmly starts a conversation. "Dr. Wagner, please come down from that chair. I must talk with you. Calm yourself. You are a scientist, and we do not climb on chairs and yell about ghosts. You are perfectly safe. I shall protect you from Michael. Please come down and drink your coffee before it gets cold." Dr. Wagner stares closely at Einstein. Still standing on the chair, he demands, "Wait one damn minute! Are you Dr. Albert Einstein, the E=MC2 guy? Oh, Hell, another ghost! Go away! HELP!" Here we go again. He should not have been able to recognize either spirit. Perhaps the psychosis sharpened his senses.

Well, we know what not to say this time. The team decides to huddle and consider what to do with Wagner. Dr. Einstein confirms what they were thinking. "He has had a psychotic break, and we cannot question him at present. We will call in a psychiatrist to evaluate him. He probably requires meds. I am sorry I was unable to help you. Psychosis is not in my field of study. Bones could probably help you more than

I." Dr. Wagner runs around the room singing, "Ghostbusters, something strange in the neighborhood. Who ya gonna call? Ghostbusters! I ain't afraid of no ghost." Great! Now, his cellmates begin singing along. Who knew the song was so popular? Angus and David put Dr. Wagner back in his cell. With their combined strength, it is a piece of cake.

The team returns to Mill Abbey Pumping Station tomorrow after the psychiatrist has talked with all the prisoners. Miles leaves an agent to guard the prisoners. Yeah, that worked just awesome last time when Mengele escaped. David and Angus will speak with Miles about his luck interviewing the scientists and Neo-Nazis. They have most of the prisoners. If Beyond drops a hammer on David, Sir Winston and Dr. Einstein will return to the Savoy and strategize David's defense. A decision may have been made that the team is not privy to.

David and Angus find Miles in his office, reading papers scattered about his big executive desk and talking on his cell. He motions them to sit in the padded gray chairs in front of him. Of course, Miles has worked with them before, but he does not realize David is a former Deputy Director-General because David died in 1965. Everyone at MI5 who was there in 1965 has retired, moved on, or died. Angus retired decades ago, but Miles wasn't working with MI5 then. Angus looks as young as when he was a new hire. Agents there now would not recognize his Clint Eastwood-ish face—a perk for being dead.

Miles puts down his phone and greets the two former MI5 agents. "David, Angus, how is life treating you today? Would you like a cup of coffee? It isn't too horrible. I survived it. I think you planned to interview Dr. Wagner today. What did you learn about his funding?"

They don't look as if they have just cracked a big case. In fact, David and Angus appear discouraged. Miles asks them, "What's wrong? You look like you have already tried our coffee. What is going on?"

David tries to decide what story to tell him and then says, "Miles, our prisoners are being resistant and uncooperative. They are not answering our questions as we had hoped they would. We know INGA was providing funding, but there may be others of which we are completely unaware. We must learn more to broaden our investigation. Now that I think about it, perhaps our expectations were too optimistic. I digress; Dr. Einstein and Sir Winston were also there. We plan to give the prisoners overnight to think about their options. It is cold and damp in those tunnels under the old sewage station. We will try tomorrow. How are you doing with the scientists and the others? Do they know anything helpful?"

Miles grins, and his eyes twinkle with mischief. "I don't know what is wrong with them. A few are all right and answering our questions, but one is especially troublesome, a robust blonde woman behaving quite strangely. She, Dr. Susan Duggens, insists she must kneel until 'an angel' tells her to rise, or he will smite her with his sword. I suggested that our Counseling Team might talk with them. No, we don't have any helpful information. They insist they were hired to do a job and know nothing about funding or who else might be involved in the operation of the lab. The security guys aren't the smartest criminals I have ever seen. I believe them when they say they have no information to share about funding or Herman Wagner's operation." Clearly, Miles did not see Michael in full archangel gear. We thought Miles or one of his officers had seen our showy angel on the patio at the asylum. Evidently not, since no one had mentioned it. If they had, Michael would have been a popular topic of conversation. I wonder if our archangel can block human memory if he chooses. I will ask him the next time he shows up.

Miles stops for a minute, sips his coffee, makes an awful face, and asks, "I am going to have to give this garbage up. But I am afraid it is the only thing clearing the muck from my arteries. You know how we eat." Angus and David grin at him. Yes, they know what MI5 agents eat unless they have joined the water-schlepping cult.

Miles looks up from his notes and asks, "Do you have any idea what these people are referring to? An angel with a sword is utterly crazy. Do you think they were using psychedelic drugs? I don't have their blood tests back yet. I see little to gain in questioning that bunch. A couple of the scientists were with Dr. Mengele when he was still on a bloody crime spree. We will probably let the other scientists go, except for the blonde and those two Mengele leftovers. We know the London Neo-Nazis have committed crimes. We will thoroughly investigate each one of them. Back to the blonde; if she is not on drugs, she needs professional assistance. We will arrange something."

We know why she is in shock and do not want her harassed by the system. A return to her loved ones and home will help her recover. She can find a counselor on her own. If she sticks to her Angel story, a psychiatrist will diagnose her as delusional or psychotic, or both. Delusions are idiosyncratic beliefs that are contradicted by reality. Psychotic means a person's thoughts and behaviors are disturbed, and they may have difficulty determining what is real. Patients who have chatted with an angel, in Dr. Duggins's experience, do not qualify for either diagnosis. An archangel threatened her with a wicked sword. As Joseph Keller wrote, 'Just because you're paranoid doesn't mean they aren't after you.'

David inquires about the homeless subjects. "Miles, what will we do about the homeless residents at the clinic? Thank God we got to them before Wagner started his dangerous experiments. Will social services take care of them when the food runs out? Also, will the three kitchen workers still have a job? To convince them to leave a dangerous situation, I had to tell them their jobs were not in jeopardy." I knew David's reassuring words to those ladies would trouble him.

Miles said, "I understand your concerns, David, local social services will provide food and medical care for homeless residents for at least the next couple of months. No one has told them they must move. The ladies in the kitchen will have jobs for at least that long. The funds for their salaries are available, and Wagner's executive assistant will pay them. Fortunately, they can continue cooking for residents, which works out nicely. I sniffed about the kitchen when I was there, and the fragrant stuff made my mouth water. I want to return when their freshly baked bread loaves come out of the oven. I asked them to let me know ahead of time."

We had discussed our trust issues with MI5, and David decided this was an excellent time to address them. He is keenly aware that the room could be bugged and probably is. He leans closer to Miles and says, "How are things going here in the organization? Are there any problems? Are you doing well?"

Miles appears surprised by the questions and sounds open when he responds, "We are doing great, David! He smiles widely to show his delight with his job and says, "As you know, there is always some intrigue or another going on. We had a challenge for a while, but we resolved it." Miles winks at David when he says that, then asks, "By the way, have you met our 'new' Deputy Director-General, Dame Cynthia Benson? She started last week and is bursting with ideas for revitalizing the organization. It is an exciting time to work at MI5. Have you thought about coming back? We could use both of you; talented people are always welcomed with open arms—and coffee. Salaries and benefits are not bad right now. You must think about your retirement. Am I right?" David blinks rapidly as he considers the likelihood that they will want an agent who has been dead for almost 60 years. At least Angus has been dead for only a few months—an excellent prospect.

David replies, "I will consider your offer. I would appreciate it if you would transfer Dr. Duggens to our cells. Dr. Einstein wants to question her." He winks at Miles and says, "So good to hear everything is going well here, Miles. Thank you and your guys for helping us with Wagner and crew." They are both aware of listening devices.

Angus shakes the Director-General's hand and agrees to consider his offer. Right.

David remembers hearing that a member of Agatha Christie's team was playing butler for Dr. Wagner. He will reach out to the 'butler" for information. He makes a note in his little notebook to look him up when he has time. They will save poor Dr. Duggens and send her home after Bones talks with her.

Chapter Thirty

The Darkest Nightmare

Otto and I take bus #188 to the Old Royal Naval College. I received an invitation from Abigor to visit with Admiral Stallings and Thelma. Otto wants to talk with Stallings about his youthful appearance again. The poor man has no idea why Stallings looks young and why Einstein and Churchill are still alive. As a serious scientist, he is curious about cause and effect. Most people don't recognize the former PM or the genius because of the marvelous makeovers Madame Dubois from the Royal Theatre created for us. I think there is a little cloaking going on, too, like Romulan Starships, courtesy of Beyond. Recreating the guys' appearance was theater at its very best. I don't think Otto will learn anything from the Admiral, but I could not dissuade him from trying. Perhaps he really wants to see Thelma. She fascinates him. I want to ask Stallings about the Doomsday Machine. That whole thing ended very oddly. Why was it necessary for me to be there? Absolutely freakish and unfathomable! Stallings seems to know something about everything connected to WWII and weapons.

We are enjoying an uneventful ride on my favorite bus, #188. The bus is empty except for the professor and me, which is Twilight Zone enough to make the hair on the back of my neck stand. I no longer look for the Lady in Black sitting and waiting to present me with ancient books on demons. The lovely Thelma and I have become friends, fellow combatants, or something. A thought occurred to me: This may be my last ride on bus #188! My heart starts pounding to a heavy metal beat.

What is going on? I look at Otto calmly sitting beside me, and I am terrified. Something supernatural surrounds us, and I must protect him from the dark side. When I gather my courage to peer around, shadowy, swaying figures fill every seat. Oh God, I am living my nightmare—the Dark World! I am in the absolute deepest darkness, a blackness I didn't know was possible. It is dreadfully disorienting and terrifying. I cannot see any trace of light or shapes. I assume I am standing; I cannot feel my body. Where am I? What has happened to me? As I stand here, trying not to freeze in terror, I sense the darkness enveloping me. I am using the powers of survival instinct, ingrained boldness, and blind faith to counter the darkness and fight against its assault. What is that? I strain to hear an almost imperceptible dragging, slithering sound. I am not alone in this damnable darkness and am excruciatingly aware of everything. Instinctively, I feel a malevolent presence moving toward me—close, closer. My body shivers as the entity tries to overwhelm me with an essence of undiluted evil. Its iciness is biting into my skin. I must battle the encroaching evil as I shield myself from the greedy darkness. My strength is slowly ebbing away.

I must fight against evil and darkness. Fight, Bones! Then, I hear voices moving toward me. Suddenly, the dark is gone, and I can see. Thundering down the aisle, a frighteningly furious face, Stallings is rushing toward me with an equally furious Thelma following behind him. He shouts, "Get away from her, you miserable, sniveling abomination! How dare you pit your pathetic powers against me and my forces! You will suffer my righteous anger!" Aaii is standing beside me, baring his teeth and snarling like a beast of prey! Thelma gives the demon a mighty shove, tossing him out of her way, and embraces me. I let out my breath and began to breathe again. I didn't realize that I had stopped breathing.

Stallings grabs the doomed demon by his jacket collar, throws him against a seat, and pummels him in righteous anger. He jerks the demon up and asks him, "What are you doing here, you hellish, unholy freak?

How dare you touch this girl! She is under my protection! All the demons in Hell cannot deter me from destroying you if you threaten her!" Aaii is literally dying to explain his transgressions. "The woman must suffer my revenge for torpedoing my Machine. I had the power to bring Armageddon to earth. Get away from me, Stallings! My fight is not with you! I used her nightmare to terrorize her. What if she died? She has done it before!" He is trying his best to pull away from the Admiral, without much success.

I am shocked that Aaii is not wearing his usual trademark clanking armor. He looks less threatening in jeans, a jean jacket, Lucchese boots, and a T-shirt. Then I realized that Otto is gone. I lunge for Aaii, shake him, and shriek, "Where is Otto? What did you do to him? God forgive you if you have harmed that man! I will not!"

Then I hear a shrill voice calling from the back of the bus, "Fraulein Bones, I am perfectly well. Do not trouble yourself, for I am here, my dear. Oh, good evening, Admiral, delighted to see you again."

I move back from Aaii, who is staring wide-eyed at me, no doubt thinking I am insane. He is certainly not the first to believe that. Aaii did not kill Otto, and I am so relieved that I reel, feeling giddy and lightheaded. Thelma pulls me away from the despicable devil, suggests I sit down, and gives me a sip of coffee. No, I don't understand how she had coffee on her. My kind of woman! I get up, go back, and kick Aaii in his ribs with a sharp, pointed, red high heel just for meanness— without spilling a drop of coffee!

The next thing I know, the Admiral, Thelma, Otto, and I are sitting in the Admiral's office enjoying the ghost movement of the rolling waves. The hanging ship's lantern sways back and forth, providing its meager light. I am stunned to be here and not on the bus! I think I live on adrenaline and cortisol. Hoping the Admiral could explain that to me, I stared at him and said, "I don't know what happened. How did we get here? What happened to the gutter scum, Aaii? Thank you so much for defending us from the demon. It looked very black for a while. I truly believed we were going to die."

The Admiral comes around his desk, warmly embraces me, and answers, "Abigor transported all of us from the bus to here. He and Michael are taking good care of Aaii for us." He shakes his handsome head and says, "No, you did not see them, Bones, but they were here. Abigor alerted me. He has been following you and Professor Otto just in case he was needed. He wanted to allow me to rescue you. Dearest Bones, Thelma and I have much to tell you. I think she would like to tell you the rest. Otto looks as confused as I feel. Good, it's not just me."

Thelma is sitting next to me. She leans toward me, smiles, and pats my hand. "Dearest Bones, it is a long story that weaves through many decades. You are our sweet girl, and our blood flows in your veins." I know how the asylum scientists felt when Michael lobbed lightning bolts around them. I don't know what to think.

Thelma sees my shock, pats my hand again, and explains. "I will keep the story as short as possible. After the horrid Nazis killed Jeffrey, I delivered our baby girl. Our daughter went to live with my sister when I went to Beyond. When Marilyn grew up, she moved to America, married a loving man, a physician, and had a bonnie little girl, Virginia. Sadly, Marilyn died in an automobile accident. Beautiful Virginia married your dad, a career military man. Jeffrey was proud of your dad, a courageous man. Virginia and Fred were delighted with each other and their life together. Then, in another tragedy, Virginia died in childbirth. We were heartbroken, but we had you, our raven-haired little girl."

"You know the rest of your story. When their time came, we welcomed Marilyn and Virginia to Beyond with joy and celebration. They are at peace. Virginia asked us to protect you since she could not and to tell you she loves you dearly. She is so proud of the woman you have become."

A message from my mother is precious to me. I can feel her arms around me. I am at peace, too. Thelma smooths my hair fondly and says, "The Powers in Beyond were kind enough to Bless Jeffrey and me for our work during the war. That Blessing flows in our bloodline. Because you are blessed, you were crucial when your team destroyed the Doomsday Machine. The scientists Rosen and Goldman told me about the horrid weapon before the Gestapo executed them. When I heard about the cursed weapon, I fell to my knees and prayed for humankind and our planet until I was soaked in sweat. I prayed for hours. Alpha and Omega heard me and granted my prayer to stop that weapon if it were ever found. They created a miracle. The miracle would be triggered if the time came when the world was in danger. The machine started ticking down to final destruction when Aaii triggered it with the phantom. You are our only blessed descendant. Aaii could never be allowed to be the answer to a prayer, in this case, my prayer. He is evil, and evil can never be our savior. Thus, Aaii could not destroy the machine without you. You became his mortal enemy." I shudder upon hearing her terrifying statement. Calm yourself, Bones. The danger has passed.

I have a maternal family, my own family! Of course, I have always had my dad's family, but he knew little about my mother other than he loved her dearly. I managed to choke out, "You are my great-grandparents? That is why you have done so much for me? The demon books saved us from Abigor when he was still on the dark side, helping us so many times when we were lost and struggling to complete our mission. Thank you so much! May I still call you Admiral and Thelma?" We hugged, laughed, and cried. Otto cries, too. I don't know why he weeps, but I love him for it.

Chapter Thirty-One

Sir Winston, for the Defense

The senior members of our team sit in the parlor at the Savoy. Sir Winston is poking his lit cigar at Dr. Einstein, trying to ram home his point. They are arguing about how they should plan their defense for David. Both are relatively certain they will have to battle with Alpha and Omega. Of course, they know they have no power over the two Beings except the power of persuasion. They liked the way Abigor handled himself at the last meeting with the Duo, so they shall ask him to join the defense. Their differences are around the path they should take. Should they be low-key as Dr. Einstein advocates or vigorously hammer their points home as Sir Winston advocates? He has always said, "If you have a point to make, don't try to be clever. Use the point once. Then come back and hit it again. Then hit it a third time-a tremendous whack." And he wants to apply the tremendous whack theory in David's defense.

Dr. Einstein pushes his wild hair from his face and rubs his chin. He doggedly asserts, "Winston, I understand what you are saying, my dear friend, but we must produce facts logically and rationally and let them speak for themselves. One thing worries me: we have already presented all the facts we have. I suppose we can try to organize them better. Perhaps that would help. Suppose we told them more about Axel. No, that won't work. They have a general sketch of his entire annoying existence in the Book of Life. We could add some meat to the bare bones. What do you think?"

Looking for the matchbox he dropped on the floor, Churchill is down on his hands and knees, crawling around. He looks up at Einstein and hotly argues, "Dear Albert, facts don't speak for themselves with a loud hammering voice unless we kick them in the arse. We need more witnesses to parade before them. I believe we made a dreadful mistake in not asking Bones to speak the last time we met with them. I know we did not want to alarm her, but if we return, Bones must come. She is the most dramatic witness. After all, she is the one the brutish monster was choking. You know what the brilliant American author Mark Twain said: 'Don't say the old lady screamed. Bring her on and let her scream.' That is what we should do. That lovely young woman talking about her pain and fear will make an impression. Then we hit them with what David felt as he saw Axel choking her."

Einstein, still fighting his hair, does not appear convinced. He reasons, "I think we may harm our case. We may harm both their cases if we are not cautious and fail to plan carefully. I am not in favor of asking old ladies to scream! Remember, dear Winston, they will also decide what to do with Bones. That task was so complicated that they brought in someone to help them deliberate. If we are too dramatic with our screaming, they may decide Bones has suffered too much and should return to her previous life. Truthfully, Winston, I wonder if they would be wrong. She has suffered greatly, and we don't know if her regular dying ordeals will end with this mission. We tried our best to protect her before, but we failed miserably. We may well fail again. I will not oppose Bones going home. I love her very much and want to know she will be happy and healthy. Not dead!"

Winston had been pacing back and forth while putting forth his argument. He sits now and peers over his round glasses at the genius. "I have worried about this very issue, Albert. She is a young woman and should have a life. I know what it would do to David and Sophie, not to mention the rest of us if she were to be killed. Abigor has admitted he adores her. Of course, that situation cannot have a happy ending. Red, Angus, Michael, and I love and respect her for her many qualities. God

Bless Bones, for she is a warrior of whom we are justly proud. Yet, you are right. I cannot deny the wisdom of your words. With profound regret and sadness, I admit that we cannot protect her. Our failures in the past haunt us. In addition, this is a deal killer. Alpha and Omega have been adamant they will not raise her from the dead again."

As they discuss what to do, they receive a summons from Alpha to report to him post-haste. Everyone else is gone except Abigor. They snatch him up and pop to Beyond. One does not toy with a summons from Beyond, even if one is a great man.

They stand in the room with unsurpassed beauty everywhere. Alpha and Omega do not keep them waiting. Gabriel is with them this time. The team met him briefly during other meetings. Gabriel sticks out his hand and shakes with Sir Winston, Dr. Einstein, and Abigor. He remarks to Abigor, "We are grateful to have you back on our side. We missed you while you were off walking on the wild side." He smiles at Abigor and pats him on the back. He has a delightful sense of humor and is much less severe than the deathly intense and highly dangerous Michael.

Alpha asks everyone to sit. "Gentlemen, we are delighted you are here with us today. You are acquainted with Gabriel. He has been a blessing to us in our deliberations. We have two decisions to make, and I am convinced the situations are intertwined. We have discussed David and the shooting in which he was involved. Well, he was the shooter. And we have discussed Bones and her excessive number of deaths since she joined thy Team. I understand Abigor saved her from death again. Aaii had her and the Professor trapped on a bus. He despises her because of her significant contribution to destroying the Doomsday Weapon. Thank thee, Abigor! Thank thee!" Sir Winston and Dr. Einstein were unaware of the almost fatal situation. They are distraught to learn that Bones came so close to disaster at the hands of the psychopathic demon. They embrace Abigor in gratitude. Omega continues for Alpha, "We have discussed the fatal situations that have plagued Bones and thine team since she was recruited. We all know why she was recruited. She was the answer to a prayer made many years ago. We needed a miracle, and because of her bloodline, Bones was a crucial part of the miracle. She is aware of that now and of her family history. Her devoted great-grandparents, Jeffrey and Thelma, have welcomed her with joyous love."

"Sadly, she is frequently killed and assaulted. We just heard about another attempt on her life foiled by Abigor. The other related issue is David. We did not anticipate their relationship, which is impossible under the circumstances. We will hear from Sir Winston, Abigor, and Dr. Einstein and then give you our recommendation. I think the American Civil War was the last time we had this many meetings." Alpha points at Sir Winston.

Sir Winston stands to speak. He likes to pace. "Thank you for this opportunity to speak, Alpha and Omega. You have been quite generous with your time. Albert and I were debating the issues when we were summoned. I don't want to lose Bones. She is our heart. However, we both admitted we had done a horrible job protecting her. There is no reason to believe this will change drastically as we proceed with other missions. As Omega indicated, Bones was chosen for this mission because she had to be there when the demon machine was destroyed. That danger has passed. It breaks my heart to say this: she must go home and have a life. We cannot selfishly take that away from her." Churchill paces the room, mopping away his tears.

Dr. Einstein is next to speak. "We were torn in our deliberation by our love for Bones and our responsibility to her. As Winston said, she deserves an opportunity to have a normal life." He rubs his eyes and continues, "I cannot allow her to be killed, which could happen at any moment. It could have happened when Aaii trapped her and Otto on the bus. The monster Aaii could have killed them both. I say, with regret and sorrow, she must go home." He sits down and looks out of an open window. The mild breeze flowing through soothes him.

Abigor remains seated, gathering his thoughts. "Thou all knoweth mine feelings about Bones. The next time she needs protection, I may not be there. Mine guilt would be unbearable. I vote to wipe her memory and send her home. We can drop by her new life to stay in touch. She just won't know who we are or how much we hast loved her." He joins Sir Winston in mopping up raining tears.

Gabriel is deeply moved by what he has heard and the apparent love. "Gentlemen, I have spent much time in thought and prayer since Alpha and Omega requested my support. You, who love her the most, other than David and Sophie, have voted to send her home and let her live a normal human life. Alpha and Omega have assured me they can seamlessly pop her back into the life she had before the Team recruited her. No one will ever know she was gone from her new office in South Carolina. It saddens me that she will not remember the heroes who loved her dearly. She will never know she was a warrior and a hero. She has been worthy of her great-grandparents. Too worthy for her good. Make it so and send her home." He bows to Sir Winston, Dr. Einstein, and Abigor.

Alpha is saddened to be the one who must 'make it so,' "Gentleman, the plan is to wipe her memory and take her back to her home in South Carolina. She will continue to counsel clients, and I think I will get a teaching job for her at the University of South Carolina. Yes, I like that idea. Maybe I shall make her President of that fine institution. No, then she couldn't counsel. Bones has much to share with new counselors. I have researched her life, and her good friends will be there for her. Naturally, they will not realize she was gone for all these months. She has a wonderful life there and will be happy and healthy. Her Dodge with the 5.7 Hemi is waiting in the driveway. We shall also give her a 1951 MG as a gift from her friends in England. We even put insurance on it. We will do everything within our power to get Bones off to a lovely start. She will be successful and loved." He looks around, smiling, thinking he will see happy faces. Not this time.

Sir Winston asks, "What about David? What are your plans? He is a valuable part of our team. We will still have our memories. It will be a melancholy group as we adjust. David requires our support to get through this great disaster in his life. Don't you agree, Albert and Abigor? However, I have also given his future great thought." Both nod energetically. No one says it, but this will also be a terribly painful adjustment for Abigor.

Alpha and Omega make eye contact. Omega stands by Sir Winston, pats his shoulder, and says, "We do not have a plan for David. Though we are aware, we must plan. We wanted to decide about Bones first since continuing threats to her made it urgent. Does anyone have a suggestion they wish to make? Now is the time to speak." Sir Winston lights his Havana cigar and whispers to Omega, "I have a plan." His eyes twinkle.

The former demon, the Great Statesman, and the genius agree they will not mention their trip when they return from Beyond. They won't mention their trip or the decisions made.

Angus and David return from MI5 with new information. Otto and I came in at about the same time. We will not be sharing our adventures with the hideous Aaii. There is no reason to alarm the guys, and I need to think and emotionally process what I learned about my new family before sharing. After we visited the Old Royal Naval College, I took the professor to the library to look for a rare book he and Einstein needed for their Time Machine work.

David told us that Red and Abigor went to fetch the Time Machine from Humboldt University. The professor drew a diagram to make finding it less troublesome. They left late at night, and we expect no problems a former MI5 agent and a former demon couldn't handle.

Abruptly, they are back, startling all of us except Big Soph. Red shouts, "We plopped something in the genius's laboratory. Guess what we found at Humboldt College in Berlin? It is bigger than a breadbox and red. Yes, it was quite the find, and it is sitting in your lab, Dr. Einstein." I don't know who ran faster to the lab, the good doctor or the octogenarian. Red is laughing as he sees them so excited about their new toy. We all gather in the lab or at the door. I will be damned. There, the Time Machine sits in all its glory by the window. It does look like a traditional English phone booth! The diagram we saw in the Rosen and Goldmann book is remarkably accurate. A time traveler can sit on the seat and play with the various knobs in front of them. At least we don't have to worry about it detonating and wiping out the planet. I hope not. How exciting is a Time Machine? Everyone is talking at once except Dr. Einstein and Otto. They are struck dumb in awe by the shiny red contraption. Otto runs to get his Rosen and Goldmann book to compare it to the original.

Miles calls David to tell him the MI5 psychiatrist, Dr. Flynn, examined and assessed the Neo-Nazis and Dr. Wagner. Miles suggests they meet at the cells to discuss his recommendations. David kisses me, and he and Angus pop over to the cells.

Miles and his agent are waiting for the guys and drinking some of our new coffee. Miles greets the former MI5 agents with a cheery, "Hey, David, how did you get this tasty coffee? Who do you know? Get some for me?"

David grins and says, "I know people in extremely high places. So, what did Dr. Flynn say about our patients? What should we do?" Dr.

Wagner had been quiet until now. He sees David, and he is beating on his bars, yelling, "Where is your brother? Did you tell Michael and the ghosts to stay away? Wait a minute, what is your date of birth? And you with the nice suit, when were you born?" Miles says to no one in particular, "A brother, huh? I didn't know anything about a brother."

Angus and David ignore Wagner and request a rundown on the psychiatrist's recommendations. Miles pulls some forms out of his briefcase, "Dr. Flynn is a good man, and he was very thorough. He said most of them are a little odd but fine. I didn't know 'a little odd' was a diagnosis. However, Wagner and the two men, who are still on their knees, are quite likely experiencing a break from reality. At the very least, they share a delusion. He said that is hugely rare, and he may be able to get a journal article out of it. Those three will be transferred to the psych unit at Bethlem Royal Hospital. After he runs some tests and confers with his colleagues, he can tell us more then. Flynn is sending an ambulance for the prisoners now."

Wagner is still screaming that he wants to know their birthdates. They continue to ignore him. He is an evil thug with a few graduate degrees.

The Admiral and Thelma had agreed they would not tell Bones she was the only Blessed human. Thelma's special beatification was the reason for the Blessing, and the Powers had not awarded that honor to anyone still living. Thelma's Blessing will end with Bones.

Chapter Thirty-Two

Welcome to Yorkville

It is a beautiful spring morning in Yorkville. I rise early for a short hike with Sophie, my Harlequin Great Dane before I prepare for my day of seeing patients. We will spend the remainder of our day sitting and chatting with patients after we visit the new bookstore, so we need some exercise. My counseling room is a screened-in porch in my 1941-era house. It is like having an office outside surrounded by giant old pecan trees, magnolias, azaleas, and hydrangeas.

My old brick house is downtown in the historic district, so restaurants, shops, and hair care salons are just a short trek away. While I am counseling, the birds and squirrels keep us company with their friendly chirps and squeaks, but they never repeat a word they hear. I have a couple of roomy swivel high-back wicker chairs so we can rock and twirl if the mood strikes us. Lots of plants in pots make the porch feel tropical and lush. My therapy dog, Soph, lies out there and gives hugs when needed.

After our hike, we run into Father Brown, the priest at Little Flower Catholic Church. Father Brown is a legend at the church, having served there for several decades. He is talking with another elderly priest. He waves me over and says, "Bones, I want to introduce you to our new associate priest, Father Antonio. He came all the way from St. Albans Cathedral in England to work with me. Father Antonio, this is Bones, our local therapist. I look at Father Antonio, feel dizzy, and almost fall. Father Antonio gently grips my arm and steadies me. "Are you all right, dear Bones? You look pale. Do you need to sit down?" The kindly priest peers at me with warm concern. Oddly, I felt better when he touched my arm. I assure him that I am fine.

Soph stares intently as I welcome the padre. "Father Antonio, I am delighted to meet you and to welcome you to Yorkville. Please allow me to treat you to coffee and pie soon. The Garden Café has absolutely scrumptious buttermilk pie. If that works for you, I will call you next week to arrange it. I can't wait to introduce you to all the nice folks at the cafe. Father Brown has a huge congregation, with so little leisure time. He must be thrilled you will be lending a hand. Maybe he will have time to drop by, sit on the porch, and sip tea with Soph and me now. Please feel free to drop by, too. We have plenty of tea." Father Antonio smiles and pats my hand, and I give them each a big hug and continue with my tasks. I am surprised at how comfortable I feel with Father Antonio. Yes, I think the kindly Padre and I will be great friends. As I move away, I hear the Padre say, "Maybe the Garden Café has our special Earl Grey tea." I jerk my head around and stumble but catch myself with Soph's help. What? How does he know I favor Earl Grey?

Still dazed, I walk unsteadily down the sidewalk—focus, Bones. I have heard the bookstore is extraordinary. The owners specialize in WWII books and audio, including Churchill's speeches. I am surprised that a bookstore dedicated to WWII could survive financially in a small town. But selfishly, I am thrilled they are here because Churchill is my hero, and I have read almost everything written by or about him. Now, I can find new books by just walking around the corner. Sweet! Soph will go with me because storekeepers are buds with her and sometimes have little treats for my giant Dane.

I ask Soph, "What do you think? Should we grab a coffee and two frosted oat muffins at the Cup of Joe to munch on?" Soph is all for the idea, so we do just that. I am starting to feel more relaxed after my dizzy spell. We sit outside the Cup of Joe on their park bench, basking in this sunny South Carolina day. Soph sits up on the bench next to me like a human and eats her muffin. We get a lot of curious stares.

After our indulgence, we strolled to The World War Books. When I opened the door, I heard a jingling bell and felt transported back to 1945. It is exquisitely decorated with old posters, radios, typewriters, and hundreds of books. I am enthralled with this magnificent time capsule. At first, I didn't see anyone in the store, but then I noticed a man bending down behind the counter.

Soph and I mosey over to introduce ourselves to our new neighbor. He straightens up, and I am pleasantly surprised to see a Clark Gable look-alike in a navy uniform. His smile is pleasant and warm. He reaches out to shake my hand and, in a beautiful English accent, says, "Good morning. I am so happy to meet you, young lady, on this bright, sunny day. I am Jeffrey Stallings. My wife and I own this shop. As you can see, we are trapped in the 1940s. Who is your large friend here?" He reaches over the counter to scratch Soph's ears. For the second time today, I feel light-headed, and I must reach for the counter to steady myself.

The door to the shop opens, I hear the jingle again, and a blonde giant in a black suit and hat walks in. He looks as if he belongs in an old Sherlock Holmes movie. I stare impolitely because he is enormous and, well, extraordinary. He smiles benignly at me, turns around, and walks back outside. I look at Jeffrey for his reaction, but there is none. I want to ask him if he had just seen what I saw. I don't because I am terrified that his answer will be no. Could this be what a psychotic episode feels like?

I break out of my daze and stammer, "I am so, yes, so pleased to meet your, uh, Jeffrey. This is Big Soph, and I am Bones Wyndot, the local shrink. I absolutely adore your store. It is magnificent. Someone is an extremely talented creative genius!" I feel as if I have seen Jeffrey before, and I can't shake the disquieting déjà vu. A door opens in the back of the store, and a striking blonde woman in her mid-thirties, wearing a long black dress, glides in. Her pale curls surround her head like a glowing ring of fire, and her big blue eyes are the color of the sky reflected in a cool mountain stream. When she smiles, her eyes flicker with humor.

What is wrong with me today? I have met interesting, attractive, and even highly unusual people before, but I am never tongue-tied and muddled. Yet, I can't shake the feeling that neither person is new or that this isn't the first time I have met them. That is precisely the problem. It is as if they are old and treasured friends, just like the Padre. How can that be? And who the hell is the giant? He seems familiar, too, but certainly, I would remember a colossus in an 1890s suit. This is crazy, and I know crazy!

Striking woman glides over to me, pats Soph, and winks at her. She hugs me and welcomes us to their store. I can finally, with effort, speak again, "Hello, I am Bones. I met your husband a few minutes ago. Welcome to, uh, Yorkville, yes, Yorkville. I know you will enjoy our little, uh, town and the friendly people who live here. If you need anything as you settle in, please let me know. Yes, let me know. I would be happy to help you get to know the area." She must think I am a friggin idiot, but I don't care.

She smiles again and responds, "I am pleased to meet you, Bones. What a cute name! I am Thelma, and we are delighted to be here. I hope you will come by often to visit us. We love company. Thank you for offering your help, too. So, you are a psychotherapist? That must be fascinating work." Wait! How does she know what I do? I told Jeffrey before she came out. This whole encounter takes on a total Twilight Zone weirdness. My head is starting to pound.

I look at Thelma and then Jeffrey, "Yes, I need counseling. No, I mean, I enjoy being a counselor. It has been such a pleasure to meet you, Thelma and Jeffrey. Absolutely, Soph and I will be back soon.

Yes, of course, we will. We live close, a stone's throw away." Looking forward to those new books and feeling better on solid ground, I say, "I adore Winston Churchill, so this is my kind of shop!" Jeffrey puts his hand on my shoulder and says, "Bones, I would be willing to bet the ship that Churchill loves you too." He chuckles and walks behind the counter. Ok, that does it. I have a delusional disorder. Overwhelmed, I stumbled toward my house.

Walking behind Bones out the door, Soph turns around and winks at them. They wink back.

After the bizarre and disturbing encounters in town, Soph and I have a lovely day with patients, birds, and squirrels. I am at peace again. My imagination was in overdrive. It happens.

Inside the spacious sunlight-yellow parlor, hidden in an old, white-washed oak rolltop desk drawer, an antique gold compass pulses and glows. One word, Solarsteinn, is etched on the back. It is waiting.

We stroll downtown to pick up dinner at the Greek Café. I am addicted to their delicious moussaka. After this morning, I think I have earned cheesecake too. Maybe two pieces. OK, I will share one piece with Soph. After dinner, we plan to have a quiet evening and listen to some great Jurassic Rock on the radio. I can pick up a station coming from another small town close to Yorkville. They play the music that makes my heart and soul sing with a rock beat. One minor problem: a couple of times a day, they announce obituaries, which is way too intense and daunting for me. Yet, as I tell my patients, it is what it is. I keep listening to the station, obits, and all.

After dinner, Soph and I decide to sit outside on the screened porch and enjoy the small-town country ambiance, complete with frogs and crickets who sound like they are celebrating tonight. Oddly, I also hear enormous wings flapping. Hmmm . . . that is unusual. Perhaps a hefty

Great Horned owl is feeling lonely and decides to join in on the multi-creature celebration.

Soph barks, and I look to see what is disturbing her. There is a strange car in my driveway. What? I haunt car shows, so I love old cars. Why would a stunning green 1951 MG-TD, with a 1250 cc, be parked behind my Dodge Durango with the 5.7 Hemi? Something in me stirs. A fond memory now forgotten peeks through the fog in my brain. I shake my head to clear it of the madness that haunts me today. Shaking doesn't help.

Soph barks when a tall, broad-shouldered man disengages from the sexy sports car and strides down our sidewalk. Her bark is a cheerful welcome, not a serious "I will tear out your throat" warning. I walk to the screen door just as he moves to the top step. Cool, he is wearing a weathered black WWII bomber jacket. Why is my heart booming wildly with my every breath? What is wrong with me today? I open the screen door, and there stands a gorgeous dark-haired man with fathomless, dark blue eyes.

His brilliant smile knocks me back, and I reach out to steady myself against the door frame.

I struggle to breathe—he steps closer, stopping inches from my face, lays his hand gently on my shoulder, and gazes into my eyes.

My knees buckle.

Gradually, he leans in until his full, sensual lips touch mine. My blood ignites into intense waves that flood my body.

My quiet, small-town life just exploded into brilliant bolts of lightning.

Behind the magnolia tree in the front yard, unseen, stand dear, loving friends: Churchill, Einstein, Abigor, Angus, Michael, Otto, and Red.

Sir Winston says to the southern night, "My idea for David worked quite well, eh?"

Alpha and Omega are watching from above. They do a high five!

THE END

**What will happen to the Mysterious Secret Guardian Team?
We shall see.**

About the Author

Dorothy McCoy has authored several books, all of which have been published. She worked in law enforcement as a South Carolina State Constable, taught in the South Carolina Justice Academy, created their Master Instructor Program, and worked briefly in the Richland County Sheriff's Department's Cold Case Squad. McCoy is an expert in counseling and psychology, having been licensed for almost 20 years. She has spoken at numerous international conferences on psychopaths and narcissists, and written books related to counseling.

The material for *The Mysterious Secret Guardians Mysteries,* were pulled from McCoy's wealth of knowledge and experience. She also is a proficient researcher, a skill she heavily relies on in crafting her books. The history is accurate. The locations and science described are accurate. Before embarking on this project, McCoy read every book she could find on Churchill, as well as many of the 72 books he wrote. She also has read hundreds of mysteries. She has it down pat!